A THREAD
UNBROKEN

A THREAD
UNBROKEN

KAY BRATT

amazonpublishing

Text copyright © 2012 Kay Bratt
All rights reserved.
Printed in the United States of America.

Published by Amazon Publishing
P.O. Box 400818
Las Vegas, NV 89140

ISBN-13: 9781612184463
ISBN-10: 1612184464

Cover Design by Streetlight Graphics
www.streetlightgraphics.com

Dedicated to my mom, Vikki, with love.

As I developed my main character, she began to remind me of you—

Strong, courageous, and with the heart of a protector.

If I had known you at her age, I imagine you would have been just like Chai.

Being deeply loved by someone gives you strength,
while loving someone deeply gives you courage.
—Lao Tzu

CHAPTER ONE

Jun flung another shovel load of debris over his shoulder and hoped it landed in the wheelbarrow behind him, then he glanced back to see that it did. Even as hot and exhausting as the work was, he knew he should be thankful to have it. China was booming and new businesses were cropping up every day, even in this midsize city. Some of the contractors were so desperate for laborers that they were hiring men of any age—even older ones like him from neighboring villages as long as they could prove they still had the energy for a full day's work.

While he shoveled, he thought about what he would do when the construction for the new bank was done and it was time to move on to the next job. He wished for an easier task the next time. Only in his late thirties, he was afraid that his body already carried the look of a much older man.

Life had not been easy for him, but he had never let his humble beginnings stop his dreams to be something more. He had worked hard all his life. Maybe too hard—for if he had only known what the ending of this long workday would bring, he would have taken more time to drink in the sight of his daughter; he would have held her close and never let her go. Instead, like most impatient parents, he lived in the moment, not thinking of the sudden detours fate could throw into a father's life.

"Chai, what are you doing here?" Jun asked when he saw his daughter racing toward him. Her best friend, Josi, limped along next to her almost as fast as Chai ran. He set the heavy wheelbarrow to rest and put his hands on his hips. "I told you to stay at Josi's house until I get home from work."

Though the sight of Chai always brightened his day, Jun was embarrassed for his daughter to see him carrying bricks—to be reminded that her father was only a laborer. He wanted her to be proud of him, not see him sweaty and dusty, standing amid a pile of rubble. He would much rather she stay put in their small village, where the harsh reality of city life and fierce competition to get ahead was less evident.

The girls stopped in front of him, out of breath from their long run to his construction site. "I know, Baba. But Josi's parents are away, and her father said we could stay behind and go swimming. You told me never to get into the water without permission, so I came here first. Can we please swim today? *Qing... qing...*" Chai stood on tiptoe, grabbing her father's arm and smiling up at him. At only thirteen years old, she knew her father was unable to deny her requests most of the time. However, she was an obedient girl and would never go swimming without permission.

"One please is enough, but I don't know, girls. Have you done anything worthy of the reward of spending time playing in the water? Have you studied today? Read a book? Finished your chores? And where is your *mei mei*, Chai?" His stern voice stopped the girls in their tracks, and they looked at each other with raised eyebrows and blank faces. His eldest daughter knew her main responsibility was her little sister, and she'd better have a good answer as to why she had left her behind.

Josi bravely answered. "Lao Jun, we have not studied; it's summer break, and we don't have any schoolwork. Most of my chores were already done last night—I only have to feed the pigs after dinner. And if we must, we can take a book with us to the swimming spot and read while we are resting there." She bit her lip and looked up at Chai's father hopefully.

"Baba, Luci is with Josi's family. They took her with them to town."

Jun let out a long sigh. He dropped the tough act and smiled, tugging playfully on his daughter's braids. Though she was growing into a young lady right before his very eyes, the braids comforted him that she wasn't quite grown yet. "You girls can go swimming, but stay together, and go home before dark. When you return to Josi's house, be sure you help her with her chores to thank her for letting you stay. I'll come by to pick you up on my way home, but today it might be well after dark—especially since you've interrupted my work."

"Sorry, Baba." Chai looked appropriately chastised.

"I can't believe you girls came so far to ask me to go swimming. Now you go straight back, and do not dawdle or talk to strangers. And don't go into deep water at the canal!" He sighed and scratched his head. "You two together can get into too much trouble." He looked up toward the makeshift office, hoping his foreman had not noticed the girls and his break from work.

The girls jumped up and down, excited to be on their way. Chai threw her arms around her father and kissed him on his cheek. Her deep dimples shone as delight transformed her face. "Thank you, Baba. *Wo ai ni!*"

"I love you, too, Chai." His cheeks reddened but he still said it loud enough for his daughter to hear. He had decided long ago that he wouldn't let ancient superstitions get in the way of showing affection for his children.

Josi called out her thanks, "*Xie xie*, Lao Jun."

Jun shook his head at their young antics as he watched them race each other down the footpath and back toward their village. *Maybe I still have a few years to go before Chai realizes I'm not much*, he thought. He couldn't believe his genes had produced such a pretty and intelligent girl. But considering his wife was known through the village for her beauty, he was lucky Chai had taken after her with her looks. He had struggled hard to learn to read when she was born. He was determined his child would not be ashamed of her father, and he had met his goal of being literate by the time she was old enough to want stories read to her.

Next to his daughter, Josi did her best to keep up. The girl's father was a farmer and couldn't read, but she didn't seem to mind their status in life. Wearily, Jun returned to his job of clearing debris from the work site.

CHAPTER TWO

Soon the girls were winded from their rushed trip to the construction site, and they slowed to a fast walk. Chai grabbed the jade pendant around her neck to stop its steady thumping against her chest. She tucked it back under her shirt.

"We've plenty of time, Josi. We don't have to run." She didn't want to point out that Josi was limping more than usual, and she felt bad that she had rushed her friend on the way to her father's work site. She always took care to make sure she was sensitive without bringing attention to the disability Josi had been born with and was ashamed of.

"*Wo zhi dao.* I'm just very excited to get there. I haven't been swimming yet this summer, and the weather's perfect to play in the water. And I'm so happy to get away from my brothers and sisters for a while."

"*Dui,* I'm lucky your parents took my *mei mei* with them. I'm free!" Chai threw her hands in the air and twirled around on the sidewalk in front of her friend.

Josi laughed. "Chai, this summer we really need to learn to swim. My cousin teases me that we don't know how and only splash about like babies."

"I agree. When we say we're going swimming, I want to really *mean* swimming. So today we'll begin our first lesson! I know how to float, so the next step can't be too difficult."

As they walked, the girls chatted about trivial things, like what teacher they might get the next school term and who would be in their class. Chai told Josi that her baba planned to replace their old stools they carried to school each day. She described what he had told her: that they could fold up the new ones and carry them like backpacks.

"I can't wait until we can go to a better school that already has desks and seats," Chai said as she sidestepped a newspaper someone had spread on the sidewalk to catch a toddler's waste. She grimaced as the smell wafted up, and she wondered why they didn't at least roll it up and throw it in the bin that stood nearby.

Josi laughed at her expression. "Well, I'll just be glad to be done with school and have summers that never end. I don't care if I go to university or not."

"But Josi! You have to go with me if I get to go! Don't worry, I'm going to help you with the end-of-year exams. You'll be promoted." Chai knew Josi wasn't as thrilled about school as she was. The truth was that she could barely get through her homework most evenings. But Chai was determined to help Josi start to like it more.

They took turns pointing to things they passed. It was noisy but exciting—taxis and cars competing to get ahead while blaring their horns, bicycles flying by with passengers balancing sideways on the back racks, and even street-side vendors loudly hawking their items.

Unlike Josi, Chai loved coming to town—the flurry of energy was so much more exciting than that of their quiet village where she was known to everyone and couldn't take a step without being noticed. In town, Chai felt like she could be anyone or anything she wanted, and no one would know the difference. Even with the heavy traffic her baba complained about and the smog that coated everything, if Chai had her choice, they'd move to an apartment right in the middle of all the chaos.

Soon, the girls noticed someone walking very close behind them. The woman was struggling to carry a bag of groceries over one arm and a small boy on her hip, as he fidgeted and whined to be let down.

"Girls, *keyi bang wo*?" She let the boy slide down her body to the sidewalk as she asked the girls for their help.

The girls stopped and turned around. Chai answered first; she had been taught to be very respectful of her elders. "*Hao de*, okay. What do you need?"

"I'm walking the same way as you, it appears. If you could hold my son's hand while we walk, I can carry these groceries. I'm afraid he'll walk into the street and be run over if no one holds on to him."

Traffic was dangerous around them and the little boy did appear to be very rambunctious, though Chai thought he was cute. He seemed enamored with them as well. He smiled at them shyly as he fidgeted from one foot to the other, his energy pent up and ready to go.

"I'm not sure if we'll be going the same way. We're going back to our village, just outside of town," Chai answered.

"Oh? Which one is that?" the woman asked.

"The village on this side of the pearl farms," Josi answered quickly, despite Chai's elbow to her ribs.

The woman smiled happily. "That's exactly where I'm going! I'm going to visit my parents. We can walk together, and you can hold my boy's hand." She instructed her son to take Josi's hand, and the group moved along together.

Chai leaned over to whisper to Josi, "You shouldn't have told her where we live, and I don't think we should walk with her. If we do, it's going to take much longer to get back." Chai thought she knew everyone from the village, and she didn't remember seeing this woman, but it wasn't unusual for people to live in the city and visit their family homes in the village on weekends or holidays.

"But Chai, she seems nice, and she needs our help. We'll hurry," Josi whispered back.

The woman overheard their conversation. "If you're in a hurry, I know a shortcut to the village. Follow me." She turned the next corner and quickly led the girls down an unfamiliar side street. A few blocks later, she turned again, then again. Soon, both girls were completely confused about which way to go.

Chai stopped and called to the woman, who walked quickly ahead of them. "*Qing wen*, excuse me, but this is taking much longer than we thought. Can you lead us back to the main road so we can go the way we know?"

The little boy was also getting impatient; he had tired of walking and wanted one of the girls to carry him. The woman did not offer to hold her own son, just let them continue caring for him.

She finally turned around. "*Mei guan xi!* Don't worry. Because you've both been so nice to help me, I want to buy you each a new dress."

The girls looked at each other, hesitant to accept such an offer but also interested in the prospect of having something new to wear. Their families were very poor, and new clothes didn't come along often.

Chai looked at Josi, who answered her unspoken question in a whisper. "I think we should let her buy us a dress."

"But Josi, I don't know what Baba would say. And he told us to go straight back home; he might be angry if he finds out we've been shopping." She leaned in closer to Josi's ear. "Don't you think it's weird that she wants to buy us a dress just for helping her with her son?"

Josi sighed. "Please, Chai. Some people are just nice like that. Don't be so suspicious. You know I'll never get another dress any other way—and you might not, either."

The woman watched the girls debating her offer. "It will only take a few extra minutes, and then we'll be on our way, girls. Please let me do this. I only have a son and I've always wanted to shop for girls."

Josi squeezed Chai's hand, looking at her pleadingly.

"Fine. We'll let her buy us a dress. But then we have to hurry, and we aren't going to have time to swim today. We need to be back at home before Baba." Chai readjusted the boy on her hip, impatient to get moving again. The entire situation was bordering on surreal, but she didn't want to disappoint Josi, and maybe she was too suspicious after all.

By the big smile on her face, Josi obviously thought a dress was a great trade for swimming; Chai wasn't so sure. But they did have the rest of the summer to get into the canal—and an opportunity to make Josi so happy might not come along again. Chai knew the truth was she was much more likely to get new things than Josi, so she decided to hold her tongue and just let go and have fun for the day.

The woman smiled and led the girls down another alley, farther from the main road and even farther from their path home.

CHAPTER THREE

J osi and Chai sat across from the woman in the noodle shop, holding their bowls to their mouths while they slurped what remained of the broth from the bottom. It was late afternoon, and the restaurant was almost empty. Other than them, only one other customer sat at another table pointed in the opposite direction, sipping a milky yogurt drink. Despite the rusty fans creaking and whirring over their heads, the blades only caused a slight breeze to stir the oppressive heat filling the tiny shop.

Chai hadn't even balked at the suggestion to stop and eat, as the woman had been nothing less than friendly during their short shopping trip. She couldn't believe their good luck—a new dress and a meal. Eating in restaurants was a very rare treat for them, and they were both shy about ordering. The woman laughed at their reluctance and then told the waiter to bring out his best recipe of local noodles.

He brought bowls of long noodles floating in a beef broth, set them on the table, then returned to his counter and laid his head down to resume his interrupted nap. The broth was delicious—the first taste spicy enough to bring tears to Chai's eyes, but just the way she liked it. They quickly emptied their bowls and leaned back in their seats. Chai was anxious to start moving again and waited for the polite few minutes to pass before standing up to leave.

"Did you girls enjoy your lunch?" the woman asked, shifting to give her son more room on her lap. The little boy was exhausted and had only eaten a small bit before his eyes became too heavy to hold open any longer. Now a low snore was the only thing they heard from his previously relentless chattering mouth.

"*Shi, xie xie.*" They both murmured their thanks in unison.

"What about your new dresses? I think you both look very beautiful."

The girls looked down at their dresses. The woman had insisted they put them on over their swim clothes and shorts. Chai had chosen a red dress, and Josi had gotten the same style but in a bright blue. They were the nicest dresses either of the girls had ever owned.

"Yes, the dresses are really nice, *xie xie,*" Chai answered for them both, raising her eyebrows at Josi. They had already thanked the woman numerous times.

Josi didn't get her meaning. Instead she leaned over and whispered to Chai, "You look prettier than me, as usual. I should have gotten *hong se* like you."

"Oh, Josi, you look just as pretty. Don't be silly." Chai looked up to see if the woman was listening and saw she was.

"It's okay, Chai. I'm happy to be your shadow." She hung her head, looking embarrassed that the woman may have heard their whispered conversation from across the table. Josi had often lamented they would grow up and no one would ever want to marry her because of her disability. Chai got angry every time Josi insisted it was true.

"Stop it, Josi. That's silly talk." Chai smiled at the woman, a bit uneasily. "We love our dresses, and you're too kind. You've bought us clothing and now a nice lunch. We have no appropriate way to thank you enough."

The woman put her finger to her lips, thinking. "You can thank me properly if you'll help carry my things to my home. I don't live far from here at all. We've been gone much longer than I expected, so I'm going to reschedule my visit to my parents' home. And I'll have my brother give you a ride to the village in his car, so you'll be able to return much quicker than walking. I apologize for taking you so far off of your path, but I knew we'd find much better dresses at that shop."

Chai looked at Josi. They were both tired and only wanted to go home. However, her father would have been disappointed in her if she didn't mind her manners and properly thank the woman for her kindness. And if it would be quicker to get home by going to the woman's house and riding with her brother, then that was probably the best solution.

"Okay. We'll go with you to your home. We can take turns carrying your bags." The woman had bought a few things for herself at the shop, too. Juggling the bags and her son would be difficult, Chai thought.

The woman paid their bill and struggled to pick her son up and prop him over her shoulder. He didn't wake, only stirred a bit and went slack. The girls picked up the woman's bags and followed her out of the shop.

* * *

After a short walk following behind the woman, they arrived in front of an apartment complex. The buildings—at least six of them in a row—looked like new construction, judging by the fresh paint and absence of layers of dirt found on most buildings. The parking lot only held a few hundred cars, bikes, and electric scooters—a light collection compared to most residential areas, where it was difficult to find a few spare inches to park anything.

Chai looked up and noticed that only one of the buildings was decorated with the usual rainbow of clothes hanging outside of windows to dry, a sure sign that the other buildings had yet to be finished. *The woman must be rich to afford to get a brand-new apartment*, she thought to herself. She couldn't wait to tell Luci that she had finally gotten to see into one of the towering buildings. On their trips into town they had both wondered what it would be like inside and many times had taken turns creating stories about people who lived there.

The woman led them past a grandmotherly woman busily sweeping the sidewalk. She beckoned for them to follow, and they climbed several flights of stairs to a small apartment. Josi was moving slower by the minute, causing Chai to slow down for her. Chai quietly held Josi's arm and propelled her forward, helping her to keep up.

As they walked into the woman's home, Chai looked at Josi, her eyebrows raised. The apartment was almost bare; all they could see were a table and chairs and a few boxes scattered about. Chai noticed the thick layer of dust along the kitchen countertop and wrinkled her nose at the musty smell all around her. *Perhaps she just moved in.*

The woman stopped and put her son in the chair at the table. He fought to wrap his arms around his mother again, but the woman pulled away. "*Deng yi xia*," she scolded him to wait a minute.

She turned to the girls and pointed to an open door along the other wall. "You can put the bags in that room."

Chai and Josi walked into the room and bent to set the bags on the floor. Suddenly the door slammed behind them, and they heard a lock turn from the outside.

They both turned in confusion, and Chai ran to the door. She began beating on it and screaming at the woman, "*Kai men!* Let us out! What are you doing?" Josi joined her, and they both beat on the door as Chai continued trying to turn the knob.

After a few minutes she stopped and put her finger to her lips to shush Josi. They listened, their ears to the door.

There was not a sound from outside the room. Josi dropped to her knees and peered under the door. She couldn't see anything. She stood and tried the door again, then dropped to sit on the floor.

Chai tried the knob one more time. Then she sat down next to Josi. She looked at her friend, her eyes big with fear.

"We should have gone straight home," Chai whispered.

CHAPTER FOUR

Chai woke first, sitting up to rub her eyes and look around. For a moment she forgot where she was, but as soon as her eyes focused on the ceramic pot in the corner, she remembered and jumped to her feet.

"Wake up, Josi! It's dark outside now, and Baba will have gone to your house to pick me up. Maybe he'll find us." Chai grabbed her throat, surprised at how hoarse she sounded.

Josi rolled over and sat up. She moved her head around, rotating it to get a cramp out. The floor was hard, but that hadn't kept the girls from falling asleep. They had yelled and beat at the door until they were both exhausted. Then they had moved over to the window. They finally decided it must've been nailed shut, because despite using all their strength, they couldn't open it. They had beat on the glass each time they had seen someone below, but they were too far up. No one had paid them any attention.

Their efforts had brought them nothing but confusion. The girls didn't know why the woman had locked them up, but they knew it couldn't be good. Exhausted and hot, they had huddled together until they had fallen asleep.

"Chai. *Wo yao hui jia.*" Her lip quivered as she looked around at the barren room.

"I want to go home, too, Josi. I told you we shouldn't have ever helped that woman. Now look at us—we're prisoners."

Josi began to cry, her tears rolling down her sweaty face.

"*Dui bu qi,* Josi. Please don't cry. We'll think of something. Do you have to go to the bathroom? I think that's what that pot's for." She apologized and pointed to the chipped ceramic bowl in the corner.

"I'm not using that thing. I can wait until we get out of here."

Chai looked around and saw the bags sitting in the floor.

"Let's see what all those bags she had us carrying have in them."

The girls went over and sat in front of the bags. Chai took the first one and dumped it out. She picked through the things, calling out each one. "Rice cakes. Bottled water. Toilet paper. Towel."

Josi sat back, uninterested. Chai dumped the next bag. "Flashlight. Batteries. Why would she buy a flashlight? Fan. A hairbrush." She opened the paper fan, admiring the dancing girl painted on the back of it.

Josi sat up, fear clouding her eyes. "Chai, I know why she has those things. It's for us—she plans on leaving us here for a long time. Oh, I want out!" Josi started to sob and pull her own hair.

"Calm down, Josi. If she left us these things, she means for us to have food and water. And look—it's getting dark, but she thought of giving us a flashlight." Chai stood and went over to the light switch. She flipped it, and her suspicions were confirmed: there was no power in the room.

"But what do you think she wants with us?" Josi asked the question aloud that Chai had asked herself over and over in her own head.

"I don't know, Josi. Whatever it is, when she comes back I'm going to talk our way out of here." She had her suspicions but she didn't want to scare Josi any more than she was already. It was common conversation between her parents that girls all over China were snatched every day and sold into prostitution or other terrible things. That was one reason her father had never wanted to move the family to the city; he said it was safer in the villages where everyone could look out for one another.

She went back over to the window, and Josi joined her. Together they peered out over the parking lot, looking for anyone who could help. Chai saw the same old woman who they had passed in the stairwell, this time using her broom on the trash littering the sidewalk.

She pointed her out to Josi, and they both beat on the window. The woman looked up at them, then shook her head from side to side, seeming to tell them no. The woman turned her back and resumed her sweeping, her face hidden by the colorful scarf wrapped around her head.

"She saw us! Did you see that, Josi? She saw us and turned around the other way. She knows we're here, yet she won't help us."

"Maybe she thinks we live here."

"Josi, think. I didn't see another person in this building on the way up. Except for her. I don't think anyone else lives here. That's why no one has heard us beating on the door."

Chai knew that when apartment complexes were built, it was common for some of the buildings to sit empty until they each filled up with new residents, one a time. Chai feared that no one would ever hear them, for it sounded as if they had the entire building to themselves. Now, she knew, they were at the mercy of the woman. They could only hope she would come back and allow them to leave. She settled herself on the floor again and reached for a rice cake. She was hungry, but she didn't want to be too greedy—she didn't know how long they would have to remain in the room with the small amount of supplies they had.

"Josi, here. Share this rice cake with me. We must ration our food in case the woman doesn't return for a while." She tore the dry, round cake in half and handed a piece to Josi.

"I don't like rice cakes, Chai."

"Well, you'd better learn to like it, Josi. Unless you want to go hungry."

They sat quietly, taking small bites of their cakes and sharing one of the three bottles of water. Chai thought about her father and how disappointed he was going to be with her. She usually obeyed him, but this one time she hadn't, and now she was paying for it. She wanted to cry, but she knew that if she cried, Josi would be even more scared. She needed to be strong for Josi.

CHAPTER FIVE

Jun signed his time card and put it in the metal slot. Using the bottom of his work shirt, he reached up and wiped the thick dust from his face. He grabbed his empty lunch pail and left the foreman's office. Weary from his long day of hauling debris and bricks, he slowly made his way down the path that led to the street. At the sidewalk, he stepped around a half dozen young men guiding an enormous tree ball into a freshly dug hole. The landscaping had begun, which meant only a few more weeks and the building would be finished and ready for the new business owners to move in. He marveled at how only three months before, the same piece of land had held smaller buildings that had been home to many families for generations.

He shook his head in disgust. So many memories wiped away so quickly. But when the government said to get out, people reluctantly listened. He was glad he lived in the relative safety of a nondescript village. He doubted the suits would ever come knocking on his door with the dreaded eviction papers and their measly consolation money, all in the name of "a bigger and better China."

He wondered how long Chai and Josi had stayed at the canal, and he hoped his daughter was tired out and ready to go when he arrived. Tonight he had promised her a new adventure in their ongoing stories of famous—and sometimes fallen—emperors. Jun formed the plot in his head as he walked, knowing Chai would expect a tale of mystery, danger, and drama.

If all went well, Wei would be at home waiting for them with a hot meal, but he wasn't sure that was going to happen because sometimes his wife worked even longer hours than he. It could be hard on the family, but they were lucky—Wei had gotten a job as a housekeeping *ayi* in the home of a foreign family.

When Wei landed the maid job they were excited to be working in the same town, but then they found out that she would be located at least an hour from his work site, in the fancy expatriate community that had sprouted up when the city started booming.

It took Wei much longer to get home, making it his responsibility to look after their daughters while she was away during the week. He hated when she had to stay late to cook at her boss's house, because he knew she felt guilty that her own family was waiting at home hungry, too. But like others in the village, they did what they had to do to make a living.

Twenty minutes after leaving work, he had walked through town and was only a few minutes from Josi's house. Unlike most other villages that had succumbed to the frenzy of becoming bigger-better-faster, his village still had not allowed any of their paths to be widened to accommodate vehicles. If it wasn't on legs or less than four wheels, it wasn't coming into the village. Though Jun was always striving to better their lives, he wished to keep his family away from all that came with the onslaught of construction. He was glad not to have his home life soiled by the constant noise of motors, horns, and the dangers that vehicles presented. In the village he could shake off the stress of the city and relax.

Jun suddenly felt something in his stomach—a nervous flutter. He climbed the hill and saw both his house and Josi's sitting side by side. Everything seemed to be in place, though quiet. The first of about a hundred or so houses, the two on his property were centered on the hill and surrounded by a low stone wall that created a protective courtyard for the children. The wall also enclosed chickens and other wayward animals that always found their way into his youngest daughter's path. A source of irritation for him, his Luci was always begging him to let her keep the latest village stray. Other men in the village poked fun at him for what they considered weak behavior when he allowed his daughters to get their way with the requests, but he considered it good character that they cared about other living things.

Jun looked up at the houses. Josi's place was lit up, making his own look even more sinister with the dark windows. *Wei must not be home yet*, he thought, and picked up speed to get to the neighbors and pick up his girls. He didn't want to take advantage of their kindness, and he knew they had already minded his daughters for most of the day.

He didn't mind another family living in the house that had been a part of his family compound for generations. In the old days, and still in many places, multiple generations lived together on property such as his—rows of houses hemmed in by courtyards, many adorned with smaller outbuildings that were makeshift kitchens and outhouses.

When his parents had died and the house stood empty, Shen had come around looking for a place to bring his wife and children and raise pigs. He told Jun he was tired of pursuing migrant work around China and wanted a place to settle. Jun was a bit leery when Shen explained he had been shunned by their families and had nowhere else to go. He didn't elaborate but it only made sense to let them rent the empty house and use the old outbuilding to make a pigpen. He told them if they could somehow get the proper living permits for the village, they were welcome to it.

It wasn't much, just one of two simple adobe houses that had surprisingly withstood the ravages of time. Their roofs, once made of grass but now tarred over, were strong and never leaked. Jun was also proud that they had a gas stove to cook on inside their home instead of only a separate, small building like most in the village. They even had beds to sleep in, whereas some of their neighbors, in houses identical to those on his property, still slept on bamboo mats.

They could have had even more comforts if they chose, but most of their monthly income was put aside to save for the future of their daughters. They lived a meager life so that they could continue to pay for the girls to have at least primary educations and, hopefully, worthy weddings, one day.

He called out and then entered his neighbors' home, only to find Josi's family sitting around the table eating steamed rice and vegetables. His youngest daughter, Luci, sat eating with them, but he didn't see Chai or Josi.

"Where's Chai?" He didn't bother slipping off his shoes—he wasn't staying long and wouldn't come farther than the entryway.

Josi's mother looked up, her brow creased with worry. "We thought they were with you. They weren't here when we returned from town, so we thought you came home early and took them somewhere."

"No. They came to see me to ask permission to go swimming. I said yes, and then they left. Have you been down to the canal?"

Josi's father, Shen, stood up and looked out the window. "They wouldn't be down there now; it's too dark. Maybe they're with Wei? Has she come home from work?"

"No. She'd have a light on for me if she'd returned. Since she's not home yet, I don't expect her until much later. She must have had to make dinner for the town people."

Silence filled the room as the parents contemplated where the girls could be.

"I didn't see them return, but I'll go check and see if their swimming clothes are hanging on the line. Then we'll know if they were here after they swam." Josi's mother rose from the table.

Jun followed the short, round woman out the door and around to the side of the house where she hung clothes. The line was bare. Only a lone owl sat atop it, blinking his displeasure at their intrusion into his hunting time.

"They weren't here; I'll go to the canal." The woman turned to go.

Shen had followed behind them, and he held his hand up to his wife to stop her. "They'll be along soon, don't worry. It's not too late, after all."

"Shen, it's well after dark. You know Josi would never purposely stay out after sunset. I'm going."

Jun cleared his throat to stop the bickering. "*Bushi*. I'll go. You both stay with your family. First let me check my home. I don't see any lights, but maybe they are there. If not, I'll go to the canal. When I find them, Chai is going to be in serious trouble."

"Yes, Josi, too." She retreated back into her home to finish her supper, mumbling about disobedient girls, with her husband straggling along behind her.

* * *

Jun crossed through the gap in the hedges and entered his home. It was dark, but the moonlight flooding in through the windows and open door lit the area. He walked over to the lamp and switched it on. He could see no one was there, but he walked through the house anyway. He stopped at the bed Chai and her sister slept in. He looked behind their mound of pillows, hoping they were playing a joke on him, but he only found the stack of books Chai had received for the last Chinese New Year.

"Chai? Josi? Are you in here? *Ni zai nali?*" He called to them, but no one answered.

Jun set his lunch pail on the table. He walked past the bed, moving through the tiny living area. He pushed aside the curtain that provided privacy and peeked into his own bedroom. The bed was neatly made and everything in place. His eyes wandered to the antique side table given to them by Wei's father, a wedding present that held the only formal family photo they owned. He glanced around the tiny space—everything was just as it should be, but no Chai. He had really hoped she'd be there, as sometimes she used their room for a quiet place to read. She never complained that their house only had one bedroom, she just figured out a way to make it work when she wanted to be alone.

Jun walked back out into the night. Even though it was totally out of character for Chai to be so irresponsible, he was irritated at her. Tired, he didn't need to go chasing around after her, and he planned to let her know how disappointed he was in her. He doubted she'd get a spanking, as he'd never been able to follow through with physical punishment, but she'd suffer enough just knowing he was upset with her.

As he went around back to follow the trail down to the canal, he tripped over a stone and cursed at his throbbing toe. Ahead, a weeping willow cast an eerie shadow in front of him, knotting his stomach even more than it already was. A sense of foreboding took over his entire body, and he felt dizzy. Walking more carefully, he continued down the worn dirt path to the canal.

CHAPTER SIX

Chai and Josi sat huddled together in the corner. In the last bag, they had found a large shirt, and they used it as a blanket to share. They weren't cold—unfortunately, the stale room was swelteringly hot. But to them, the blanket felt like a tiny bit of security in the dark. They had the flashlight, but Chai was worried about how long the batteries would need to last, so she only allowed Josi to turn it on occasionally. While they waited for the sun to come up, Chai told Josi stories. So far she had told her almost every story she knew, but as long as she kept talking, Josi stayed calm.

It came as no surprise that Josi was afraid of the dark. Chai didn't like it either, but she didn't fear it as much as her best friend. She tried to tell Josi that the dark held nothing that wasn't already there in the light, but those words floated away unheeded as night fell.

"Chai, when will the woman come back?"

"Maybe in the morning. Don't worry. Why don't you try to sleep?"

"I can't sleep, Chai. What does she want with us?"

"I don't know, Josi. Maybe she has kidnapped us for ransom." Chai had so far kept all her dark thoughts to herself, but she was starting to feel very nervous, and it just slipped out before she could guard her tongue.

"What's ransom, and how can we get it?"

"Josi, ransom is money. That means they'll tell our parents if they can pay a certain amount, they can have us back."

"But our families don't have any money! How will they pay?"

"I don't *know*, Josi! Will you please go to sleep? I'll stay awake; you close your eyes." She wished she had not talked about her fears in front of Josi. They were the same age, but Josi was easier to frighten. She wasn't even allowed to watch the scary movies on television, a treat that Baba often let Chai take advantage of if her little sister was out of the room.

"Talk to me some more, Chai, and I'll try to sleep." She laid her head on Chai's lap and pulled her legs up close to her belly.

"Okay, but close your eyes. Hmm...tonight my *mei mei* has our bed all to herself. She has always said she wanted it, and now she gets to see how it is to have room to stretch."

"Do you think she'll like having the bed to herself? I wish I had the bed to myself. Instead I have two brothers to share with."

Chai laughed softly. "I think she *thinks* she'll like it, but I believe she'll be lonely. She likes to snuggle against my back, and I have to tell her stories to get her to sleep, like you. I guess I should be glad I have Luci and you have your brothers to share things with—if we lived in the city, we'd be the only children in our houses; at least in the villages, people can have bigger families."

"Sometimes being an only child sounds like a good deal." Josi smiled. "How long have we been best friends, Chai?"

Chai thought for a moment. "Forever. Remember, Mama always said we learned how to walk and talk together."

"I hope you'll always be my best friend, Chai." Josi's voice was getting softer. Chai knew Josi was almost asleep, but she continued to stroke her friend's hair, giving her the comfort that she needed to relax. Her own eyes felt heavy, and she thought that if she had to be kidnapped, she was glad that she at least had her best friend with her. She finally drifted off to sleep, her hand still tangled in Josi's long hair.

CHAPTER SEVEN

Josi and Chai both were woken from their restless sleep by the sound of a key in the knob. They jumped to their feet and stared at the door, holding tightly to each other.

The door swung open, revealing the woman from the day before.

Alone.

Chai spoke first. "What are you doing? Why have you locked us in here? We have to go home!"

The woman entered the room and shut the door behind her. She leaned against the door and examined the girls from head to toe. Her smile was sarcastic—gone was the friendliness she had fooled them with to get them to do her bidding. In the light of their new predicament, the woman looked uglier than she had the day before.

"I see you figured out that the supplies you carried were for you."

Josi started to cry and pointed her finger at the woman. "You locked us in! When I get home, I'm telling my father what you did!"

Chai threw her arm around Josi's neck and put her hand over her mouth.

"No, she doesn't mean it—she's just angry. We won't tell our parents anything about you. Please. Just let us go, and we'll tell them that we stayed out all night at the canal. They'll believe us, and they never need to know we even met you."

The woman narrowed her eyes at Chai. "We'll see about that. You didn't realize it, but we're a long way from your village. I'm going to take you by bus to a stop near your road. If you cooperate, I'll send you back. Gather your supplies."

She still hadn't explained why she had locked them up, but the girls were so relieved to hear they'd be free that they didn't ask. They frantically picked up the rice cakes, water bottles, and other things they had used and stuffed them into two bags. They each carried one and obediently waited for the woman to let them out through the door.

The woman stared down at them to speak eye to eye. "Let me tell you something, girls. If you try to run, you'll get lost. Then you'll be picked up by very evil men who will do bad things to you. If you stay with me, I'll make sure you are protected until you get home. Do you understand?"

Chai squeezed Josi's hand to signal her to stay quiet.

"Yes. We understand, and we won't run." The thought had crossed her mind, but even if she found the opportunity, she knew Josi wouldn't be able to keep up.

"Then follow me, and keep your mouths shut."

The girls obediently followed behind the woman. Chai still had hope that the woman would keep her word, take them to a safe place and leave them to find their way back home.

Chai looked down at her dress with disgust. As soon as she got home, she planned to take it off and burn it.

* * *

An hour later the girls were still on the hot bus, sitting together and watching the scenery fly by through the window. The woman had made them sit on the inside, and she sat on the outer edge of the seat. *Probably to keep us from talking to anyone*, Chai thought.

Through the window Chai watched a woman with her sleeping toddler tied to her back pull sweet potatoes from the field and drop them in a basket at her feet. The wide-brimmed hat she wore couldn't hide her skin, darkened by long hours in the blistering heat. Chai squinted but couldn't tell if the woman was young or old; the sun had leathered her face so much she could have been the child's mother or grandmother. She pointed out the sleeping child to Josi, knowing her fascination with babies.

At the next farm they spotted a teenage boy on the porch, a ball cap pulled low over his eyes as he kicked back in a chair, tapping on his mobile phone.

It was amazing to Chai how different things were in only the blink of a moment. The farm woman had looked like she was painted from the pages of one of Chai's books of an era gone by, and the boy only a mile or so from her could have been dropped in from the set of the latest Chinese reality show. *This is what Baba meant by China's changing too fast*, she thought.

When Chai saw even more of the next few miles were made up of manicured squares of wheat crops, she realized they had driven quite a way out of town and must have already passed the small road leading to their village.

"*Qing wen.*" She tried to get the woman's attention but was ignored. "*Excuse me!*" she said again, a bit louder this time.

The woman whipped her head around, her eyes angry. "What do you want? I told you no talking!"

"We've already gone a really long way. Are you sure this bus is taking us to our village? I think we should've been there by now."

"You are what? Twelve? Thirteen? What could you know of distance? You have no idea how far we've gone or where your village is. Be quiet, and when we get there, I'll tell you."

Chai sighed. She wasn't going to tell the woman anything about their ages. She also knew they were going too far, but she didn't know what to do about it. She had thought about running when they were let off the bus, but the woman wasn't that old— maybe not even as old as Chai's mother. She could probably catch Josi, and Chai wouldn't leave her alone with the woman.

The bus went around a curve and began to slow. The girls sat up straighter and looked out the window, stretching to see if anything looked familiar.

It didn't.

They both sat back against the seat, disappointed. Chai lifted one leg up off the sticky seat, put it down, and then lifted the other. She was uncomfortable and felt she might just faint if she didn't get some fresh air soon. The window only came down a few inches, not nearly enough to feel a breeze. Chai looked over at Josi and could tell she was feeling the same, if not worse.

The bus stopped, and the woman told them they were getting off. Relieved to finally get outside where they could get some air, the girls gathered the two bags and followed her off the bus. The crowd outside broke up as they disembarked, some going inside the small building to buy transfer tickets or refreshments, and others immediately climbing aboard the next waiting bus. Chai looked around. She badly wanted to tell someone that she was kidnapped, but the woman was so close that she would hear, and Chai feared what she'd do.

Outside the bus, the woman went to a bench and sat down. She beckoned for the girls to do the same. As they sat and looked around to get their bearings, the woman took out her cell phone and made a call.

"*Dao le.*" The woman confirmed they had arrived and nodded as she listened to the person on the other end of the phone.

"Two of them. As he said, only one is acceptable." The woman eyed Josi as she spoke, looking down at her bad foot and then looking away. Her voice grew impatient. "I brought them both—they're more willing to cooperate when they're together. You can consider the other one a bonus."

Chai grew more worried as she tried to piece together what the woman was saying. Finally the woman hung up the phone and threw it in her bag.

"Now we wait. Our ride will come."

"But you said you were going to let us go!" Chai exclaimed, standing up quickly. The bus station was one of those small stops between towns. As far as she could see there were no other businesses or houses, only fields. She looked to her left at a few beat-up taxis parked behind the bus, but even if she and Josi could get away from the woman, they didn't have any money with them and she'd never met a taxi driver who would give a ride out of kindness. Chai felt helpless.

"*Zuo xia!*" the woman yelled at them to sit down. "Now. The bus has taken us the wrong way. We must get a ride back the way we came—unless you want to walk yourself about forty kilometers?" She looked at the girls, raising her eyebrows.

Chai considered it, but she knew that Josi could not walk that far. She looked around for someone—anyone—who might help, but other than a few straggling passengers who were distracted with their own issues, they were alone.

"Do you promise you're going to take us to our village?" She put her hands on her hips, glaring at the woman.

"Not that you are in a position to negotiate, but yes—I promise. Now sit before I slap you down." She looked irritated enough to do it, too.

Chai sat down next to Josi, who was even quieter than usual.

"Josi, what's wrong?" She looked at her best friend and was alarmed by her scarlet cheeks.

"I don't feel so good. Can I have some water?" Josi answered faintly.

Chai pulled the water bottle from the bag beside her and handed it to Josi. Josi couldn't get sick now. If they were going to get dropped off soon, as the woman claimed, she needed to be strong for the walk home.

"You must get us some food. Josi needs more than a few nibbles of rice cakes," she told the woman, but she got no reply.

Josi drank from the bottle and wiped the sweat from her face. She handed the water back to Chai just as an old blue work truck came to a screeching stop in front of them, causing both girls to cough at the dust he stirred up. One of the bus drivers looked up from unloading bags to shake his finger and scold the truck driver for his recklessness.

"Come on, girls. Jump in the back. Hurry." The woman gestured toward the bed of the truck.

"What? I'm not getting in there. That's too dangerous, and it's nasty in there." Chai refused to get off the bench, and she kept her hand on Josi's knee to keep her down.

The woman grabbed one of Chai's braids and yanked her from the bench.

"Ouch! Let go of my hair!" Chai twisted, trying to get away from the woman.

"I'm getting tired of your mouth. Get into the truck. Now." She pulled Chai toward the truck. Josi picked up the two bags and followed. The girls climbed in and settled down behind the rear window, ignoring the creepy stares of the shaggy-haired driver, who had turned around to watch them. The woman went to the front of the truck, opened the door, and climbed in. The truck pulled away from the bus stop, leaving a brown cloud of dust in its wake.

CHAPTER EIGHT

Chai finished braiding Josi's hair and twisted the tie around the bottom. The driver's crazy weaving had made the task more difficult than it should have been, but she hoped it would help Josi cool down a bit if she didn't have the heavy hair whipping around her face. She had taken down one of her own braids to use the tie for Josi's hair, and now they looked like sisters—each with a simple single braid down her back. So far it hadn't helped much, and they were both hot and parched.

After what felt like hours, the truck finally stopped in front of a dilapidated gas station. The woman opened her door and came around to the bed of the truck. The man got out and waved away the attendant, then began pumping his own gas. He stared at them with one hand on the pump as he used the other hand to pick the wax from his ear with a tiny metal pick. Chai shivered in revulsion and turned away from his piercing eyes.

"If you want to use the bathroom, come with me now," the woman said.

The girls climbed out of the truck on shaky legs. Their ride had so far been unbelievably bumpy, hot, and even painful with all the jarring. Neither of them wanted to use the bathroom in front of the woman, but they couldn't wait any longer. She escorted them around to the back of the building, and they squatted to relieve themselves. The woman took them back to the truck and told them to climb in.

Chai climbed in obediently then turned to the woman. "Please, can we have some food? We've had nothing but those rice cakes for so long now. We're hungry." Being angry hadn't worked in getting her way before, so Chai decided to act as pitiful as she could to see if that would help.

The woman rolled her eyes then told the man to watch them while she went inside. Chai and Josi sat huddled together, as far from the man as they could get. He watched them silently, his arms folded across the metal side of the truck, his eyes narrowed.

The woman returned with a bag. She told them to wait a minute and went to the front of the truck. She huddled over something and returned with a cup.

"I have a box of steamed rice, but if you want it, you must first drink this."

"What is it?" Chai asked suspiciously.

"*Yu-jin.* It is only an herb mixed in water to help you sleep. We have a long way to go."

"No. We won't drink it." Chai gave Josi a warning look.

"I can make you drink it." The woman looked over at the man watching them with a sly smile on his face. The insinuation that he would help force them to cooperate brought a wicked gleam to his eye. "But if you drink it willingly, I'll give you the rice. It won't hurt you, I promise."

Chai hesitated. "Yeah—and we know you keep your promises, right?" she retorted.

The woman turned to go back to the front of the truck. "Fine. We'll do it the hard way."

37

The man came around to their side, about to reach for Josi. The creepy smile he wore sent a chill up Chai's spine.

"Okay! We'll drink it. Don't touch her," Chai yelled at the two. "Josi, you need to rest anyway, and it's too bumpy back here. I've heard of this stuff. Sometimes they give it to colicky babies. Just drink it, and when we get where we're going, we'll be stronger." She gave Josi a look that Chai thought only she would understand.

The woman came back around and handed her the cup. "Only drink half, and then give the other half to your friend."

Chai looked at the black liquid and wrinkled her nose. She wanted to appear brave for Josi, so she put it to her lips and quickly drank half of it. Then she passed it to Josi.

"Chai, I don't want it," Josi whined, turning her head. Her cheeks were still flaming, and Chai was alarmed by how weak she sounded.

"Please, Josi. You need to eat, and this is the only way she'll give us the rice. We might not have another chance to eat for hours."

Josi took the cup from her and, with shaking hands, drank the rest of the sour liquid and handed the empty cup to the woman. She began to heave as if she was going to vomit, but with one scathing look from the woman, she continued to swallow until it stayed down.

The woman scowled at Chai, went back to the cab of the truck, and got the bag. She handed it over the side of the truck and walked away. The two adults climbed in and slammed the doors, and they were on their way again, the quick acceleration slamming the girls back against the glass in their rush to take off.

Chai opened the bag and took out the small square container of rice. She searched the bag but didn't find chopsticks. "We'll have to use our fingers." She scooped out a bite and then passed it to Josi. The rice was bland, but it would at least fill their empty stomachs, and she hoped it would make Josi feel better.

Josi took a bite and tried to pass it back to Chai.

"No, Josi, eat some more. I can wait."

Josi took a few more bites and then laid her head back against the glass. She handed the box back to Chai.

"I'll eat another bite, but then you finish it, Josi. I'm not that hungry." She hoped she sounded believable.

Josi waved her away. "I feel dizzy. I want to lie down."

When Chai realized Josi wasn't going to be forced to eat any more rice, she beckoned for her friend to use her lap as a pillow. Josi obliged, curling up in a ball as close to Chai as she could get. Chai finished the rice and set the box to the side. She pulled the big shirt from the bag and used it as a cover for Josi, shielding her face from the dust flying around everywhere.

"Chai?"

"What, Josi?"

"I'm sorry." Josi's voice was so weak that she could barely be heard over the loud motor of the truck.

"Sorry for what?"

"That I got us into this. That I was greedy and wanted a new dress."

"Don't even say that, Josi. We decided together, so we're in this together."

As they moved farther down the road, Chai wondered what her parents and Josi's parents were doing to find them. She tried to think if there were any clues left behind that would point to where they'd gone, but she couldn't think of one.

The driver hit a huge bump in the road, causing both Chai and Josi to fly up in the air and come crashing back down again on the hard metal bottom. Josi didn't stir; she was already snoring loudly. Chai wondered how far away they were, and if the woman was really taking them closer to home. *I should stay awake and try to remember the way we're going.*

It was hopeless. She sighed and closed her heavy eyes.

CHAPTER NINE

Jun shook his head and muttered under his breath. His third trip to the police station in three days, and they still could not tell him anything new about Chai's case. He was frantic about his daughter and Josi. They had just disappeared off the face of the earth—at least that was what it seemed like to him. They had been missing for almost a week, with not a single lead as to their whereabouts.

During the last visit the policeman had wasted his time with a long lecture on statistics of kidnappings and runaways. Because Jun was from a village and not the city, the man seemed to think Jun didn't know of China's widespread practice of trafficking women and the rare leads that resulted from investigations. Jun tried, but he feared the official still didn't get it that Chai and Josi weren't just numbers—they were cherished daughters of parents who wanted them returned.

This time the head policeman had urged him to forget about his daughter and move on with life. Jun would never do that—his Chai brought him too much joy to forget about her. Who would sit and count the stars with him? Who would tell him about the adventures she would take one day? Who would make him laugh

with her stories and lofty ambitions? Chai made his boring existence more bearable, and that was the truth.

His younger daughter was not close to him like Chai—she
would rather hang on her mother's clothes all day. Chai was his
confidant and his little buddy. With her unnatural intelligence for
a girl, she often made him forget he was a lowly laborer, and he
marveled at creating such an exceptional human being. He would
find her; he just had to get someone to help him.

"Have you spoken with the shopkeepers on the main road?
The girls would have had to pass through town to get back to our
village," he respectfully asked the officer. The official treated
him as if he were nothing more than a cockroach—and Jun had
to struggle to keep his temper in check. As he waited for the
man's response, he silently repeated his now-frequent mantra: *If
you are patient in one moment of anger, you will escape a hundred days of sorrow...*

"*Dui*—we've asked everyone. Shopkeepers, taxi drivers, and
even the street sweepers. They say they see many girls, but they
cannot determine if they saw *your* girls. This is a lost cause, but
we've put their pictures out, and our force will remain on alert."

"What about the children who played at the water that day?
I talked to them, but perhaps they're lying to me. I know that is
where the girls were going. Were you able to get anything out of
them?"

"*Bushi*, Lao Jun. They did not see your girls that day."

Jun sighed. "Well, I've gotten a mobile phone now, so you
can call me if you hear anything."

The official pushed a pad and pencil across the desk to Jun,
and he scribbled his number on it, wishing again that he had gotten the phone long ago so that perhaps Chai would have a way to
contact him. So far, his own investigation had resulted in dead

ends. He had spoken to many of the shopkeepers along the walk through town himself, but they all said they had seen nothing. The posters he hung along the main street had cost him a week's pay but so far had brought no calls, either. He didn't know what else to do, but he wasn't willing to give up.

After writing his name under the number, he pushed the pad back across the desk. He stood to go, looking at the clock on the wall. He only had thirty minutes to return to work before his lunch break was over. If he was late again, he'd lose his job, and then they'd all be in trouble. He still had to feed his family—even if it was down to only three of them. Keeping his job was more than a choice, it was a necessity. Jun had been born in poverty and only allowed to go to school for five years, so he knew he was lucky that he had even learned to read. Even so, each year it got harder and harder to beat out competition for work—his body just wasn't as young or strong as it had once been.

Jun reached in his satchel and pulled out a carton of cigarettes.

"Here's a gift of my gratitude. If you could please get your men to do another search and investigation, I would appreciate it." He laid the cigarettes on the grimy desk—another week's pay gone and one more thing to hide from Wei. She had scolded him to stop spending their money on things that the police were paid to do.

The police official sat up in his chair, taking his propped feet off the desk and setting them on the floor. He reached for the cigarettes and pushed them into a drawer, then reclined back and returned his feet to their resting place.

"*Hao de.* Tomorrow another search."

Jun said good-bye and hurried out the door and toward the construction site. He didn't really believe they would make much effort toward finding his daughter, but he still had to try.

CHAPTER TEN

Chai awoke drenched in sweat with a throbbing head and a bitter taste in her mouth. She twisted until she was sitting upright, relief filling her when she saw Josi curled up beside her. She looked down at her hands, puzzled to see that they were bound together with a strong piece of rough twine, knotted tightly and impossible for her to untie. She looked over at Josi, who lay asleep in the opposite corner, her hands also knotted. Chai felt a slight sway beneath her and struggled to clear her foggy mind. She wasn't sure how long they'd been gone from home, but she was sure it had been at least several days, maybe even a week. Wherever they were, it was hot. She looked around for a window, some way to get some air.

The room was windowless; the only light was a small sliver of white from the large crack underneath the door. The walls were some sort of metal or tin, and the floor beneath was made up of scarred wooden planks. Confused, Chai tried to remember how they had gotten there.

She remembered waking up a few times, but it felt dream-like, and she had closed her eyes to go back to sleep. Now that she was fully awake, Chai realized that the pieces of memory coming to her were not dreams; they were real events obscured by the strong concoction the woman had given them. Her last partial memory was of being carried onto a train or a bus; she wasn't sure exactly which. She had seen the dark face of a man she didn't recognize and then felt the cushion beneath her when he had thrown her on a bunk, before she'd gone back to sleep. Now Chai had no idea where she was.

"Josi! Josi! Wake up." She scooted on her butt to the corner where Josi lay sleeping. Chai used her foot to push against her leg, trying to nudge Josi awake.

Josi didn't move.

"Josi! Wake up! I mean it!" Chai began to panic, and then saw a slight flutter of Josi's eyelashes. "There you go; you can do it! Open your eyes, Josi."

Josi opened one eye and then the other. She stared quietly at Chai.

"Are you okay? Josi? Say something."

"*Ni hao*, Chai. *Women zai nali?*" Josi's voice was so soft it was barely audible.

"I don't know where we are. Please get up, Josi."

Josi closed her eyes again. "*Wo yao shui jiao.*"

"No, Josi, you can't sleep any longer. You have to wake up! That woman didn't take us home. We're in big trouble."

The door flew open and light poured in, blinding Chai and making Josi sit up. They both held their bound hands in front of their faces to block the sun that pained their eyes. Two men stood shadowed in the doorway, their faces obscured by the light behind them.

The girls were scared into complete silence.

"The one in the red dress is the one we're keeping." One man pointed at Chai.

"What's wrong with the other girl?" the smaller one asked, his cracking voice giving away that he was more of a boy than a man.

"She's a cripple."

Chai brought her hands down from her face. She hadn't caught most of what they said—their dialect was hard to pick up—but she *had* understood them calling Josi a cripple, and that made her angry.

The boy lashed out and kicked Josi. "We should just throw this one in the bay, then. What good is she for?"

"Who are you, and where are we? We want to go home." Chai scooted closer and wedged herself between Josi and the boy to block any more blows. She was afraid, but not so much that she wouldn't attempt to sway them to let them go.

A small woman made her way around the men and knelt down beside the girls. She examined their ropes and turned back to the men.

"Take these ropes off of these girls right now. You've caused them to bleed! They're not animals!" Though the woman's accent was strong, Chai was able to understand her words.

The man in front dug in his pocket and pulled out a small knife. He threw it at the woman, almost hitting her with it. She caught it with one hand while blocking her face with the other.

"You can cut the binds yourself. Start with the red dress— that's the one we'll keep. We will call her Jiayi—a name that means *fitting of the household*." He turned and stomped away, the other one following close behind. Chai heard them talking to a third person, and then their voices faded away.

The woman used the knife to cut the cord on Chai's wrists. Once it fell away, she rubbed them quickly, trying to return the blood flow to them. Chai didn't want to be touched by her and involuntarily pulled back from the woman's attempts. She stretched her numb fingers and looked at the woman.

"Where are we? Please, cut the rope from Josi's hands, too."

The woman began freeing Josi. "This is a fishing village. It's your new home. You can call me Mother."

Mother? New home? Chai was so confused. She wasn't sure what was going on, but as soon as Josi was unbound she planned on finding out.

As the woman worked at the cords binding Josi, Chai stood up. Once on her feet, she felt the floor beneath her sway, and she quickly sat back down.

The woman laughed at her expression. "We're not on solid ground. This is our home—the sway you feel under your feet is the water."

"But...what? Water? Home? I already have a home. Please, please take me back. My parents are worried. And Josi's parents, too. They must be frantic."

Josi had yet to say a single word—she sat silently with her eyes as big as the moon, staring at the woman.

"Do not call her that name again. You can never go back. You will be a part of this family, and you are new girls now. Your friend—until we find a place for her—we will call her Niu. And you heard my husband: your name is now Jiayi."

"No! You will not call me Jiayi—my name is Chai. And that is Josi—not *girl*. I demand you to take us home." Chai had never heard of a fishing village before. *And living on a boat? What kind of people are these? They can't just keep us here, can they?*

The woman stood and helped first Chai, then Josi to her feet. For such a small woman, she was unbelievably strong. Despite her ruddy cheeks and shortened hair, she was still attractive. However, the clothes she wore did nothing to flatter her—dark trousers, a dark blouse, and sandals that needed to be replaced told Chai that the woman didn't have the time or money for frivolous things. At first glance Chai had thought she was much older than she appeared upon a closer look.

"Come. I'll show you around, and then I'll tell you what you will do to earn your keep. These are your sleeping quarters." She turned and walked out of the metal room, leading them into the bright sunlight. Not knowing what else to do, and anxious to get out of their sweltering prison, the girls followed behind her.

CHAPTER ELEVEN

Out in the light, Chai held on to Josi, putting her arm around her friend's shoulders to keep her steady on her feet. The ground beneath them wasn't soil, but instead they were on some sort of floating house, with plenty of room to walk on the rough panels used for flooring. In front of them sat a large wood building with a crude piece of metal for a rooftop. On the door, a large red knotted tassel hung from a nail, the only sign of welcome the girls could see. To their left, a long clothesline drooped from the weight of men's long underwear and fishing waders in a variety of sizes. They stood in a large area, similar to a deck of a ship, filled with different piles of clutter, ropes, netting, and boxes.

Chai turned around to examine the room they had just come out of. It was nothing more than a small metal shack, no bigger than an outhouse or tool shed.

"*That* is our sleeping quarters?" She wrinkled her nose in disgust.

The woman—Mother, as she called herself—nodded her head. "Yes, and you're lucky to have shelter. The winds from the ocean storms get up at night, and at least you'll have protection over your heads."

The girls looked out over the edge of the deck. All around them were water, other boats, and walkways of bamboo or boards tied to plastic barrels and white piping. It was an entire village of floating houses, as far as they could see.

Chai turned the other direction to see land way off in the distance. Other than the small canals, she had never seen this much water at one time, and she was relieved that land was at least visible, an even more comforting notion as she felt the swell of a small wave under her feet.

"But what are we doing here?" Chai asked, her eyes glimmering with unshed tears.

"I have four sons. You were brought here to wed one of them. You'll be my foster daughter-in-law," the woman answered matter-of-factly.

"Daughter-in-law? I'm only thirteen! I can't marry anyone." Chai stomped her foot in defiance, momentarily forgetting that she was a captive in a dangerous situation. She didn't even like boys yet, and marrying one was not even a remote possibility.

The woman smacked her lightly across the top of her head. It didn't really hurt, but it angered Chai. Even so, she refused to show it and instead held her tongue.

"I don't mean *today*, stupid. You'll work in our household until you are of marrying age, and then you will wed our son. During that time, you'll learn the life of a woman in a fishing family, and you'll be molded to fit our expectations of a wife for our son." She looked over at Josi, giving her a pitying glance. "And your friend, she'll go to another place to live. Tomorrow we will find her a new home."

At that announcement Chai grabbed Josi in a tight embrace. Josi started to wail, and Chai held her tightly, pushing back her own tears.

"*No!* If Josi goes to another place, I go to another place. Or I swear, I will jump in that water and drown myself." Her eyes narrowed as she stared the woman down.

The woman muttered, "*Aiyo*, and we spent so much money on this one, only to have bought a stubborn girl attached to a useless, crippled one."

Chai continued to hold Josi, stroking her hair and hushing her softly.

"Oh, forget it. She can stay for now. But when Zhongfu, my husband, returns, he'll be angry at this decision. She'd better be good for something. What can she do? Cook? Sew? Keep children?"

Chai got her first clue of how traditional a family it was when she heard the woman use the word *Zhongfu*, the formal title for husband. Her own mother called her baba by his name. She thought for a moment. "She's very good with children, and she can cook. She takes care of her brothers all the time."

"You might have just said the magic words. If she isn't too much trouble and she doesn't eat much, my two smallest sons need a nanny; they drive me crazy all day and night. Come—I will introduce you."

* * *

They entered the larger structure and found themselves in a living area, simple yet complete with a table, mismatched chairs, and small sofa. An array of toy cars and action figurines covered a colorful braided rug. In the corner, four rolled-up bamboo mats were bundled together. Against the far wall was a kitchen area. A countertop held a small sink with crude piping run through a hole carved in the wall. Chai was disgusted that it appeared they used the salty bay water for washing and probably even cooking.

Next to the sink was the largest rice cooker Chai had ever seen, with eight small bowls stacked beside it. A hook above it held a wire basket of onions and various peppers. The room was surprisingly bright, considering the only light came from the one tiny window over the sink.

Another door led to a room that was obviously a bedroom, complete with a small bed piled high with pillows. A metal rack in the corner held hangers fitted with clothing of many sizes, a few pairs of shoes lined up underneath. Both rooms smelled strongly of fish, making Chai wrinkle her nose in distaste.

Two boys sat at a scarred wooden table, loudly slurping from the bowls of noodles they cupped in their chubby hands. At the interruption, they set their bowls down and stared at the girls, their eyes twinkling with mischief.

"The taller one is Ying, and his brother is Yifeng; they are three and two." The mother pointed at her sons, her smile wide and proud. "They are already much bigger than others their age. They will make fine, strong fishermen like their father and brothers."

The boys continued to peek at the girls curiously from under their shaggy dark hair, which needed trimming.

Chai didn't reply; she had nothing to say. She didn't want to take care of someone else's children, and she didn't want or need a new mother and father. She only wanted to go home. Josi stood silently beside her.

"You'll begin to care for them tomorrow."

The woman led them back to their room and beckoned for them to enter.

"Stay here and be quiet. The men have left to go fish for the day. If you're good, you'll help to prepare the family dinner for their return. If you're very quiet and do a fair job at your chores, I will give you food and blankets to sleep with. If you're loud and refuse to cooperate, you will not eat, and I won't return until morning. You must learn your place here. It's simple. If you are obedient, you will be treated well. If you bring shame to me, then you'll suffer the consequences."

She slammed the door and locked it behind her. Chai immediately tried to push it open, but it wouldn't budge. She kicked it, then went back to where Josi stood, shaking silently in the corner.

"It's okay, Josi. Don't worry, I'll figure out something." She put her arms around her best friend and coaxed her to the floor. They sat together, staring at the door, willing it to open again.

CHAPTER TWELVE

As evening began to fall and the light slowly disappeared from underneath the door of their small prison, the girls waited for the woman to return. Chai knew that soon Josi would be very afraid. She crossed her fingers that the woman would let them out before it got too dark.

Finally, they heard a door slam and the woman's soft footsteps. She unlocked the door and opened it, beckoning the girls to come out.

"The boys will be here in an hour. You girls can go in and prepare the fish for dinner. Remember, do a good job and you will eat, too. Do a bad job and I'll rename you Crippled and Useless."

Chai followed the woman, not saying anything. She wasn't sure how to prepare fish, but she hadn't been lying when she had said that Josi could cook. She just hoped that Josi knew how to make a meal from fish.

In the big house, the woman pointed at the counter. Four fresh croakers were laid out on a slab, their eyes staring, unseeing, at the girls.

Josi immediately went to the fish, with Chai close behind. She picked up the first one and turned on the spigot, then washed it under the water.

"Chai, watch what I do. Then you can do the next one," she whispered. After drying the fish by shaking it over the sink, Josi picked up a small knife and began using it to remove the scales. Chai watched carefully as Josi expertly used an upward motion from tail to head, scraping the scales off little by little as she let them drop into the tiny wastebasket at her feet.

Chai picked up a fish and began washing it under the stream of water.

"Now you have to get the guts out." Josi turned the fish over, cutting it from the gills on down. She pulled the insides out and dropped them in a pail sitting on the counter.

The woman stood behind them, hands on her hips, and her eyes burning holes in their backs as she watched their every move.

Josi motioned Chai to move over and then showed her how to wash out the empty fish cavity. When Josi felt it was clean, she made one more swipe with the knife to remove the dorsal fin, and then she dropped the clean fish into an empty pot.

The woman clapped her hands together. "Very good. You know how to clean a fish; now let's hope you can cook it."

Chai muttered so that only Josi could hear her, "How's that for crippled and useless, you old bat!"

The girls worked together to clean the rest of the fish, then moved aside as the woman lectured them on proper cooking techniques. Though the woman had said they would cook dinner, she decided to cook the fish herself and gave the girls a bowl of vegetables to clean and cook as they listened to her instructions. The three of them soon had a complete meal cooked.

They had just placed the meal on the table when they heard the loud voices of men outside.

"Now you will officially meet my older sons."

Before Chai could form a response, the door flew open, and the man they had seen earlier came striding in, trailed by two older boys and the strong stench of fish. The three of them stopped when they saw the girls standing in the kitchen area.

"So, you have put them to work already," the woman's husband said, his eyes narrowing at the girls.

"Yes, they know how to clean fish—at least the one does, and she has taught Jiayi. The crippled girl is quite handy in the kitchen, it seems."

"Don't get any ideas. We're not keeping two," the man scolded his wife.

"Can I talk to you outside, Zhongfu?" The woman beckoned her husband out the door. With one final glare at the girls, he followed his wife.

The two older boys stood still as statues, staring at the girls, their thumbs tucked under the suspenders that held up their green plastic coveralls. Chai recognized the tallest chubby brother as the one who had kicked Josi earlier that day. She shot him a disgusted look and he glared back at her.

His brother was slimmer with a kinder face—much less intimidating than the older boy. As they all stood around awkwardly, the little boys chattered and played with their toy cars in the floor, oblivious to the tension in the air around them.

Chai defiantly stared back at the boys as Josi stood behind her, hiding her face from the scrutiny.

"You're just a *girl*," the bigger boy stated, disdain on his pudgy face.

"Yes, you were expecting what? A monkey?" Chai didn't care if they were only a step above servants; she didn't like to be insulted. "And you stink like fish."

The big boy threw his head back and laughed. "A smart one, too! You will have to learn that you must show respect to me in my house." His smile turned ugly as he moved toward her, and Chai stepped back, tripping over Josi in her desire to put more distance between her and the bully.

"Oh, Bo, leave them alone. They just got here, and you can see they're afraid," the younger boy said, glancing at Chai with apologetic eyes. He looked about fourteen, at least a couple of years younger than his older—and uglier—brother.

For his interference, the younger brother earned a hefty punch to the arm that made him stagger back and fall against the wall. As he rubbed the spot, his older brother laughed and called him a baby.

The parents returned to the room, and the father gave Chai a scathing look, stomping past her to go into the bedroom to change out of his work clothes. The woman beckoned the boys to sit at the table. They didn't need to be told twice—they sat down quickly and piled their bowls high with the fish and vegetables.

Chai felt her stomach rumble and realized that she couldn't remember when she had last eaten. She inhaled deeply and caught the whiff of the fish the woman had deep-fried. She had never been very fond of fish, but then again she'd never been so hungry before, either. It smelled delicious. Even the teasing spicy aroma of the cabbage they'd cooked with garlic and red peppers was making her dizzy with hunger, and she knew that Josi must be feeling the same way, though it was hard to tell because she wouldn't raise her head up to look anyone in the face.

"You girls sit down over there and wait for the family to finish supper. If there is anything left, you'll eat," the woman told them as she pointed to the floor in the living room.

Chai leaned toward Josi and whispered, "With that fat toad at the table, there probably won't be anything left but a few grains of rice." She nodded toward the older brother. He must have felt their eyes on him, because he looked over and glared at Chai. Josi softly giggled, her eyes still downcast.

The father returned to the room, and they all sat down as a family to eat the evening meal. Chai and Josi sat cross-legged on the floor, waiting until they were summoned again. After what felt like hours, the boys all got up to go their separate ways.

"Don't forget to throw the scraps to the dogs, Mama," the oldest brother said. He cast them a sarcastic smile and patted his belly as he and his father left to go outside and smoke.

The other three boys sprawled around the living room, ready to rest after the meal.

The mother stood up and turned to the girls. "Clean up this mess, and then you may eat."

Josi and Chai jumped to their feet and began clearing dishes from the table. Chai looked up to see Josi wiping tears from her cheek.

"Josi, what is it? You're crying."

"They sat around their table just like I did with my family. I miss them, Chai."

"I know. Just be patient; we'll get home," Chai whispered across the table as she balanced the empty bowls in her hands. "Our families will find us, Josi. Baba always told me that people are connected to those who are supposed to be in their lives by an invisible red thread. We might be a little off track right now, but

I promise we'll find our way back to where we are meant to be." Chai struggled to sound more confident than she felt.

To their disappointment, the fish was completely gone. They wouldn't get to taste the woman's fish recipe, but at least there was a small amount of rice and vegetables remaining. As they washed the pots, the mother scraped the leftovers into two bowls, filling them unevenly first with rice, and then adding the remaining vegetables to only one of them.

"After you finish scrubbing the pans and the rice cooker, wipe the counter down, and then sit down to eat. You can hurry up, too. It shouldn't take all night."

Chai and Josi soon came to the table and sat down, anxious to fill their empty bellies. The woman grabbed the two bowls and set the fuller one in front of Chai, and the almost empty one of only rice in front of Josi.

"Josi—I mean, Niu—needs more food than that. I can share mine."

"No! You will not share. You must become strong, and she is a mouth we did not plan to feed. She is lucky to eat at all." The woman turned her attention to the smaller boys, telling them to get ready for bed.

When the woman turned away, Chai quietly scraped half of her food into Josi's bowl, and they began eating. It took a few bites, but soon her dizziness began to fade as her body greedily processed the food. Josi sat beside her, cheeks flaming red with shame as she ate her share of the dinner.

CHAPTER THIRTEEN

Chai and Josi sat on the scarred wooden floor in their new bedroom, staring at the crack of light under the door.

"Chai, it's so dark in here. Why can't we have a light?"

"Because this isn't really a room. They just threw it together as a place to keep me. They don't have electricity running to it." Chai had noticed the straggly power lines crisscrossing most of the floating homes in what appeared to be a homemade job.

"Do you think she'll come back soon?" Josi whispered, her voice shaking with fear.

"Maybe. I don't know." Chai reached across and felt for Josi's hand, then held it. "Don't worry; pretend we're in a fancy movie theater and the movie is about to start. Remember when Baba took us for our tenth birthdays?" She tried to think of anything that could help her ease Josi's fear of the dark, though she was still thinking about their evening and wondering if their future days were going to be a repeat of constant drudgery.

They had been escorted back to the metal room after they'd finished eating and cleaning up the last of the dishes. The woman hadn't said a word, just gestured for them to go in and locked the door behind them. At least an hour had passed, maybe more, and

Chai worried that they would be stuck in there all night with no mat, blankets, or light.

They talked about the movie they had seen for a few more minutes until they heard a door open and a shuffling of footsteps. The lock clicked, and the woman swung open the door. She held a few supplies in her arms, which she dumped on the floor in front of the girls.

"Here's your mat—you can share. I only expected one girl. Here's a blanket, a few clothes, and a light."

Josi snatched the lantern from the pile and hugged it to her chest.

"*Xie xie.*" Chai looked up at the woman to see if she accepted her robotic expression of thanks. On one hand she was glad for Josi that they'd have light, but she still couldn't squelch the fire within her that refused to be thankful to someone who was definitely a part of their abduction.

The woman sighed. Then she squatted down before the girls and looked at Chai.

"I am not a cruel woman. I want you to know that. I've been told not to coddle you, and if I do, it will only mean trouble for me and you both. We paid a lot of money for you so that we could ensure at least one of our sons will marry and carry on our name. Girls are scarce around here, especially for the fishing families. If you follow the rules, your life here will be simple but fair."

Chai stuck her lip out defiantly. She would never agree to live there, and she planned to find her way home as soon as she could figure out how.

"I can see the thoughts in your head, girl. Don't you even think about running away. You won't get far, and when Zhongfu finds you—and I promise he will—he'll beat you worse than you've ever been beaten."

"But why us? How did you even know about us? There are other girls out there; why can't we just go home?"

The woman pointed her finger at Chai and smiled. "*You* were chosen because of your beauty and lighter skin. There are people who scout the villages for girls like you and bring them to families with many sons. Your family is as poor as ours, so we're not really taking you away from anything. Actually, it may not look it, but we may be richer, because we'll always be able to bring in fish. You need to get used to the fact that you can't go home, and now your friend can't either. If we sent her back, she might lead your family to find you, and we won't take that chance. We'll find her a home to go to after you two are settled a bit."

Josi moaned and began to cry softly. Chai put her arm around her and pulled her closer.

"I will not let you take Josi from me. And you can't keep us here. Our fathers will find us." Chai remained defiant, though she was losing steam and becoming very tired now that she had food in her belly.

"No. They won't. You are many, many miles from your home. If you try to escape, you might run into very bad people who will sell you for worse things than you can even imagine. Tell me, do you even know the name of your village?"

Chai looked at Josi, alarmed that she didn't know the name— she had always just called it *the village*. But she did know it was close to Qinyu, for they had gone to that city when they saw the movie for their birthdays. She decided it was best to pretend to know nothing.

Josi shook her head from side to side, her eyes big with fear.

"That's what I suspected. And it was the same for me when I came as a little girl."

"You? What do you mean?" Chai narrowed her eyes at the woman. She had heard of girls being sold to families to raise as child brides, but this was her first time ever matching a rumored child bride to a real live person.

"I was also stolen from my village and brought to live in my husband's home as a child bride. Lucky for you, I won't beat you. My mother-in-law treated me very badly until I learned to obey her demands and do things the way she wanted them done. She dictated until I lost my will to refuse her whims. I soon forgot about my old life, and now this is who I am. I can't remember my first family or even my birth name. And I'm sure they no longer think of me."

Chai stuck her lip out again, and she crossed her arms.

"My family will never forget; they will remember me."

CHAPTER FOURTEEN

Chai was awakened by the rattling of the metal door. She listened—not moving an inch, just keeping her arms tightly wrapped around Josi's warm body. It was surprising how cold it was; they'd both guessed they had been taken farther north because the warm temperatures of the day gave way to a slight chill as soon as the sun went down. The woman had given them a blanket to share, and they had dressed in the clothes she'd left them, but still they were cold enough to want to huddle together for warmth.

"Psst. *Kai men.*"

Chai heard the voice of one of the brothers, the nice one, asking them to open the door.

"Josi! Wake up!" She shook Josi's shoulder until she sat up, rubbing her eyes.

"What, Chai? I'm tired. Go to sleep."

"Someone's at the door." Chai stood up and went to the door, pressing her ear to it.

She heard a hushed voice. *"Kai men!"*

"Bu keyi. I can't. It's locked."

"I unlocked it, but I do not want to enter uninvited."

Chai turned around and looked at Josi, her eyebrows raised. She pushed open the door and one of the brothers walked in. He stood framed in the doorway against the moonlight, only his profile visible, his hands in his pockets.

"What do you want? You're going to get us in trouble!" Chai looked around at Josi, who sat huddled in the corner, the blanket pulled up to her chin.

"I'm sorry my older brother was rude. The fruit peddler came by in his boat, and Baba bought a bushel. I want to give you some." He took his hands out of his pockets, holding a piece of fruit in each.

"*Huo long guo!*" Chai came forward and took the dragon fruit from his hands, then threw one to Josi.

"*Xie xie,*" Josi murmured, putting her fruit under the blanket.

"Does your mother know you're here?" Chai narrowed her eyes at the boy.

"No."

"Hmm. Okay. You want to sit down?"

The boy squatted down, and Chai sat across from him. Josi stayed in the corner, watching from behind the protection of the blanket.

"I'm glad you don't smell all fishy now, or I wouldn't let you stay."

The boy laughed. "You *are* a feisty one, just like Mama said. I took a bath. I hate the smell of fish on my skin and in my hair, unlike my brother, who thinks it makes him more of a man."

"So, what's your name? How old are you?" Chai began to peel her fruit, stacking the peelings in a neat pile in front of her.

"I'm Tao, and I'm fourteen. How old are you?" He looked at Chai and then toward Josi in the corner.

"We're thirteen years old, almost fourteen."

"Do you go to school?"

"We're on summer break, but yes, we go to school."

"Baba won't allow you to go to school here." He sat all the way down on the floor, making himself more comfortable.

"If we're going to stay here—which I have no plans of doing—we *must* go to school."

"Nope, there are other girls like you here, and they don't go to school. They stay and take care of the houses and the children."

"But how will we learn? How will I get to read?" Even knowing she had no plans to stay, the thought that until she escaped she would not get to read filled her with anxiety.

"You can read?"

"Yes, I can read! And I told you, I'm almost fourteen! Josi can, too, though she doesn't like it as much as I do." Chai put her fruit down in front of her and sighed.

"I'm not a good reader. I only go to school two days a week; the other days, I help my father bring in the load from the nets. But I can get you a book."

"You can? When? What book?" Chai sat up straight; he had gotten her attention with that statement. If she could get books, she would be able to read to Josi and help pass the time. "I have some in my room. I'll bring one tomorrow night, after Mother goes to sleep. You can hide it."

Chai smiled and picked up her fruit again. She remembered what her father had told her when he had given her a new book recently. "A book holds a house of gold." He was right, because Chai was happiest when her nose was buried in a good story.

"What about her? Is there something I can bring her?" Tao pointed at Josi.

"Josi? Is there something you want?"

Josi shook her head side to side.

"Can't she talk?"

"Of course she can talk, dummy. She's just shy—as you can imagine, your family paid for someone to *steal* us! Then we were thrown in this hole and had to sit in the dark, and Josi's afraid of the dark. It's a miracle either one of us can talk at this point."

"Calm down. Be quiet before someone hears us. I'm sorry. I didn't ask them to bring any girls."

"Well, which one of you is the one looking for a wife?" Chai narrowed her eyes at the boy.

"Not me! It's Bo." He held his arms out in front of him, palms up in a peace stance.

"That fat toad? Do they really think I would marry *him*?"

Behind her Josi let out a quiet giggle.

"I don't know; don't be mad at me." He lowered his voice even more. "I'll give you a piece of advice. When my brother gets mouthy with you, don't respond. Just ignore it. Trying to spar with him is like poking a caged tiger. He's mean. And he'll find a way every time to make you regret messing with him."

Chai crossed her arms, shaking her head. "I'm not afraid of your brother. He'd better stay away from me and Josi."

"Please just trust me—don't push him too far. But listen," he looked over toward Josi. "If she's afraid of the dark and you don't want to waste the kerosene in your lantern, I can fix the roof so you can see the moon." His voice was hopeful, and he waited for her to respond.

"How are you going to do that? And without waking your parents?"

"I helped put this room together. Some of the metal didn't match up, so we tied a tarp on top to keep the rain out. I can flip the corner of the tarp up where the hole is. Wait here." He got up and went outside.

The girls heard a few creaks and shuffles, then a beam of moonlight shone down from a place in the roof. They looked up to see Tao peeking in, smiling down at them, his face eerie in the dim light.

"See. I told you." Then he disappeared from view and in a second appeared in their doorway again.

Josi looked up at the small piece of sky and smiled at the moon and stars surrounding it.

"*Aiyo.* Wow," Tao said, letting out a low whistle.

"What?"

"She sure is pretty when she smiles." He blushed and turned around, going out the door. He closed it behind him, and they heard the lock click into place.

CHAPTER FIFTEEN

The woman dumped another bucket of cold water over Josi's head.

"I told you *I* can wash her hair." Chai stood behind her, hands on her hips, furious at the woman's callous treatment of her best friend.

"And I told you that I'm going to make sure you girls don't bring anything into my home. My boys have never had head bugs or any other filthy disease, and I have no idea where you came from or what either of you are carrying."

Josi stayed still, bent over the side of the deck, with her hair dripping into the water. Chai could see by the way Josi was standing that she was embarrassed and just wanted it to be over.

"Well, I'm going to wash my own hair. You can stand over there and watch me." As soon as the woman released Josi, Chai reached for the bucket and went to the hose and filled it up. She first dunked her head down into the bucket to wet it and then lathered it up using the shampoo the woman had brought out with her.

Josi stood beside her, picking through her hair with her fingers, trying to pull out the tangles without the benefit of a comb or brush. She wasn't given a towel to soak up the water, so she used her hands to wring it out over and over until it stopped dripping.

"Get closer to your neckline." The woman stood over Chai.

"I will! Give me a minute," Chai challenged back, her voice muffled as she bent over the side and scrubbed her head. "And if you want us to be presentable, give us back our brush."

Their bags of supplies that had been with them during the first part of their unwanted trip had disappeared, and the girls weren't sure who had taken them.

The woman stomped into the house and returned with a small plastic comb. "I don't have your brush, but here's a comb. Don't lose it, because you won't get another one." She handed the comb to Josi.

"That's so nice of you," Chai said.

"Don't get sassy with me, girl. Next is bath time. Do I need to watch over you as you bathe?"

Chai turned her head to the side, peeking out at the woman through her long, wet hair to see if she was serious.

The woman chuckled at her expression then winked at her. "I'm going to give you the chance to do it yourself. Wait here and I'll heat a pan of water to add to the bucket and bring you some soap. You can take it in your room and undress and wash. When you're through, if I think you didn't do a good enough job, you'll have to do it again in front of me. And throw those dresses out the door when you get them off—I'm getting rid of them. You won't need those kinds of clothes here." She picked up the empty bucket and headed for the house.

That was fine with the girls, since the dresses were the beginning of their troubles, anyway. The woman had given them boys' clothes the night before, and both Chai and Josi didn't care either way. They were a bit upset about their shoes being taken, but the woman had said they couldn't be trusted with shoes and had replaced them with cheap plastic slippers.

Chai shivered. "You could have heated water for our hair, too, you know," she called out to the woman's disappearing figure.

"Chai, *shhh*! You're going to make her angry. Who knows what she'll do?"

Chai stood up, wringing her hair out with both hands, and winked at Josi. "Oh, she won't do a thing. Her husband's the tyrant, not her. Don't be so afraid, Josi."

CHAPTER SIXTEEN

W*hat a long, exhausting day.* In only three months of living with the family, Chai had learned how to clean fish,
cook it, and complement it with many different side dishes of
spicy vegetables.

She dried her hands on the ragged towel and arched her back
to work out the kinks. She had come a long way and was no
longer the carefree child she had been before their fateful day of
abduction. She had learned to carry her part of the load because
Josi was a good teacher. Each night they worked side by side
to feed the family of six, and they had even learned to sneak in
extra portions to ensure there'd be enough left to have a fair share
for themselves. Chai had never imagined that she'd miss eating
pork, but in her new household, meals were fish, fish, fish, and
the memories of her mother's stir-fried pork dishes were constant
daydreams in her head.

During the day, Josi took care of the toddlers most of the
time, leaving Chai to clean the dwelling and mend clothing and
fishnets—and that was just the mornings. In the afternoons,
they scrubbed the decks and did all the other menial jobs around
the floating house. Josi joked that other than missing her little

brothers, her life wasn't much different than it had been at home. There, she had been the oldest child and had always done the most housework and caring for the little ones, which was obvious from the way the new little boys gravitated to her. She said that at least here she didn't have to care for the family pigs—a chore she had always hated.

Chai liked the little boys, too, and helped out when she could, but they had quickly attached themselves to the quiet, calm ways of Josi and followed her around everywhere she went. They even seemed to prefer her over their own mother, a fact that didn't appear to bother the woman. A half dozen times a day, they could find Josi holding one of boys over the water to urinate or worse, making Chai wrinkle her nose in disgust. On the cleaner side of being their nanny, it was touching to see them snuggled up on Josi's lap at every chance they could find. They loved for her to tell them stories, and it wasn't unusual to see them listening raptly while tangling their fingers through her long hair.

Chai wasn't sure, but she thought her birthday had possibly been a day or so ago. If the crude marks she carved into the floor of their room were correct, she was now fourteen. She didn't mention it to Josi; instead she silently wondered what her parents did to celebrate her day, and if Luci even remembered her *jie jie*.

She was surprised that despite their meager meals, she was growing. Mother had fussed about it but given her a few more of Tao's outgrown clothes to wear, with a rope to tie around her waist to keep them held up. Josi teased her about her new thicker body, but the truth was that neither of them had ever worked so hard, and it was inevitable that they'd gain muscle. Chai was also mortified that now she was getting curves in some places, and she didn't want to ask Mother for the bra she badly needed. Josi was, too, but at a slower pace than Chai. They joked that the first one to ask for a bra would get the other's share of meat for a week.

Looking out the window over the water, she was lost in thought until her belly growled in protest to awaken her senses.

She turned around and called out toward the bedroom, "Josi, are you ready to eat?"

"Just a minute; let me finish dressing Yifeng." Josi had even taken over the nightly bathing routine with the boys, and she usually did it while Chai cleaned the cooking pots. Then they sat down together to eat their evening meal while everyone else in the family went their separate ways until it was time to prepare for bed. When they were finished eating, Josi would wash the last dishes while Chai dumped the boys' bathwater over the side of the boat.

Chai was impatient to get done with her duties. She and Josi had started a good story, and she couldn't wait to dig back in. Thank goodness Tao had kept his promise about sneaking her books. Life was hard but they were both learning to make the best of it. The familiar feel of a book in her hand with a tale of adventure to occupy their thoughts proved to be the best deterrent to feeling hopeless on the nights they were both exhausted.

While she waited for her friend, she wiped down the last of the crumbs and hung the towel neatly on the wooden peg. She turned to the woman sitting in the living area chair. "Mother, can I get you a cup of tea?"

"Yes, Chai, that would be nice."

Chai poured Mother a steaming cup of green tea and brought it to her. Chai and Josi had decided that Mother wasn't so bad—they felt that before they had come along, the woman had also been treated as a slave in a way, working to fulfill the whims of her husband and sons. And they had struck a deal a few weeks after their arrival. Chai and Josi could keep their real names if they called the woman *Mother* and promised not to try to escape. Since they couldn't swim, escaping was out of the question anyway for the time being, but as soon as they became trusted, Lao Chan would once again leave the small sampan tied to the deck of their floating house.

Right now he tied it elsewhere because he didn't want to chance losing his investment in Chai. With the way the fishing village was constructed, their only chance at escape was if they jumped into the water and swam to the nearest floating walkway of piping, then crossed to a small shop or restaurant and begged for help. The fishing families protected each other, so finding someone to assist them and go against the old man was really not a possibility.

"*Xie xie*, Chai." The woman wrapped her hands around the teacup and brought it to her lips.

"*Bu ke qi*. No thanks needed." Chai turned to go back to the kitchen area.

"Chai, can you come sit for a moment?" Mother patted the stool in front of her chair. Chai returned and perched on top of it, ever wary.

"You and Josi have been here for a few months now. I want to know if you are happy."

Happy? How can I be happy when I'm being held against my will? Chai hesitated and then answered, "Yes, Mother. We're happy enough. You treat us well, and we have a roof over our heads." *Even if it does leak when it rains, and the wind rattles through it.*

"Do you think you can make this a home in your heart? Can you see yourself as the wife of a fisherman?"

"Honestly, Mother, I can see this becoming a home in my heart one day. But I cannot see myself marrying one of your sons. I'm sorry to say this—I wish it weren't true." Chai also couldn't truly see this becoming her home, but she knew how much truth to speak and how much to keep to herself.

Mother laughed softly. "You're still a young girl. We have plenty of time to change your mind. When you're sixteen, you will marry. By then you will see what I see in my sons—strong, smart men who will always be able to support a family by reaping the benefits of the sea."

Chai lowered her head to show quiet—but fake—submission. She also feared Mother might see the fire in her eyes. She would rather die than marry Bo and bear his children. Even though she was only a girl, she knew her heart would never accept him as a husband. She found him unattractive, sarcastic, and downright disgusting. Only yesterday he had once again shown his mean side when he followed Josi outside. She had lifted the tub of bathwater and swung it back to dump it over the side when Bo grabbed the edge of it from behind and caused her to dump it over her own head. Chai had heard her crying and ran out to find Josi soaked through and Bo laughing hysterically. He had her cornered and refused to move, instead continuing to laugh as he leered at her trying to cover her wet shirt. It was simple—he was a bully through and through.

Chai also would have liked to educate the woman on the true compass of her other son's ambitions. Tao hated being a fisherman and wanted to move far away from the sea. However, he had sworn her and Josi to secrecy about his hatred of the trade, in fear of how his father would react if he found out.

"I'm so tired." Mother mumbled and set the steaming tea on the table beside her. She leaned her head back and closed her eyes.

Chai got up and began sweeping the floor to hide her smirk, knowing the woman had done nothing to be tired about, but also knowing when to hold her tongue. She'd learned a lot over the past few months.

Chai opened the cabinet under the sink and pulled out the dustpan. She swept the dirt up into a little pile as she thought about the bitter man who was Mother's husband. To them, he was still Lao Chan, and they would never call him Baba. He was too cranky and continued to glare at them most of the time when he came in from his workday. Usually Bo followed suit, even stomping and spitting the same way as his father. The difference in the two was that Lao Chan treated the girls like pesky flies, mostly ignoring them, while his eldest son looked for reasons to yell at them or criticize their work. Only the day before he had made a scene before breakfast because he said his laundry wasn't done the way he liked it. He'd brought the freshly washed laundry into the kitchen and dumped it on the floor, demanding that they wash, dry, and fold it again. Mother had just turned away and let him have his tantrum. It wasn't going to affect her—she wasn't the one who had to spend hours doing it. When he had left for the day Chai had simply refolded it and put it away. There hadn't been a thing wrong with it, and she refused to give in to his ridiculous demands.

Josi was terrified of Bo, and when he was around, she didn't speak a word and tried to make herself as invisible as possible. Chai wasn't afraid—or at least she would never show it if she was. A few times she had even almost gotten caught making faces behind his back to entertain Josi.

Chai finished scooping up the debris and put the broom and dustpan back. She went to the basket of clean clothes that had been brought in earlier and began folding them. Her thoughts lingered on Tao and how lucky they were that he was a part of this family. So far he had proved that he was the only one in the pack to think with his own brain, and he was even kind to them. He frequently snuck treats of fruit and nuts to them, in addition to keeping their book supply current. Chai wondered what his teacher thought about some of the girlie books he had recently borrowed from the schoolroom collection. She and Josi had begun to look forward to Tao's visits after bedtime and were disappointed on the nights he didn't come. Josi didn't say much, but it was obvious when they heard the rattling of the door that she was happy for his arrival each time.

Sometimes Chai read aloud as Tao sketched in his leather-bound book, a treat given to him by his teacher. Josi would sit and watch his creations come alive under the tip of his pencil, her fascination at his talent evident on her face. It frustrated Chai that he had to keep his artistic abilities a secret from his family. She encouraged him to show his mother his sketches of the water village, but he insisted she wouldn't approve.

Other times Tao talked, and the girls snuggled together and listened to him tell stories of his adventures on the sea with his father, the constant bullying of his older brother, and his distaste for the fishing life.

During their long, quiet talks, they found out a lot from him, even some facts that Chai was cataloging in the back of her mind to use one day. Tao didn't know it, but she memorized every word he spoke and every detail he unknowingly gave about the area during their visits. Chai almost felt bad for the facts she was gathering from Tao—she knew he and Bo had been warned not to mention any details of the village or the towns surrounding it to the girls. Sometimes he got so engrossed in his tales that he let things slip that they could use to plan for the future.

One day, he told them about losing his balance and falling off one of the walking planks and into the bay. Upon more questioning, he told her that he was on his way to the post office when he took his unexpected bath. Chai and Josi laughed at the mental picture he painted of him floundering in the water, trying to climb back onto the narrow beam. It was especially funny because he had admitted his fear of sharks. Though the bay was almost completely landlocked, it still felt like they were on the ocean and brought about fears of all sorts of strange creatures lurking under the murky surface.

Ironic for people living on the water, but he told them that hardly anyone in the village could swim, either. It was an intriguing way of life—an entire village floating on water. At first Chai had thought that only the floating houses were a part of the small water town, but Tao explained that they had their own post office, police station, and even a few small shops and restaurants on the water. They only needed to go to the mainland to get the freshest fruits and vegetables and the kerosene for their heaters. So far they hadn't been allowed off the floating house, but with all the stories from Tao, Chai was starting to feel as if she would easily know her way around.

She held up a tattered pair of women's underwear and glanced over at Mother. The woman was still dozing, oblivious to the racket her sons made in the next room while Josi bathed them. She wondered if the two little boys would follow in the footsteps of their big brother and be bullies, or if Tao's quiet ways would rub off on them.

Tao might be kind but he wasn't stupid. He had seen the gleam in Chai's eyes when he had mentioned the police station. He told her then that going to them would not help her a bit, that buying brides was common and overlooked by officials in this part of China—that sometimes the officials even participated in the black-market trafficking and became richer for it.

Chai wasn't dumb, either. She knew the best way to get what she wanted—freedom—was to begin to make Mother trust her. Then she would have more opportunities to find a way back home. She missed her family and couldn't imagine what they thought had happened to her. Josi had stopped mentioning hers, and Chai didn't press her to talk about it; she knew that it was too emotional for her friend.

Their evenings locked in were spent reading, usually with Chai telling the stories aloud by the light of their lantern. Sometimes, if they were still too alert to sleep hours later, they read from the light of the moon shining through their so-called window. They were both always careful to conserve as much of the kerosene in their lantern as possible, knowing it was only replaced once a week.

Chai finished matching the last of the socks and tucked everything neatly back in the basket just in time to hear Mother clatter her cup against the saucer.

"Chai, come back over here. I have something—"

Josi interrupted Mother, returning with the two wet-headed boys and leading them to their mother, who looked disappointed at the interruption. By the expression on her face, she appeared to have something important to say to Chai.

"Yifeng cried because Ying poured water over his face. I told them if they couldn't behave in the bath, I wouldn't be able to play with them anymore." Josi winked at Chai, who already knew that she was only faking disappointment in the troublesome two.

The boys quietly sat at their mother's feet, looking petulantly at Josi.

"Come on, Josi. Let's eat. I'm so hungry." Chai nudged her toward the table.

The girls sat down and dug into their bowls of rice. Between them, one plate held a single small fish, cleaned and fried. They took turns stabbing at it to spear pieces of the tender white meat. Several times, they both snagged the same piece, making them smile at each other over their chopsticks.

Behind them Mother cleared her throat. "Girls, I have some news."

Chai and Josi turned around to give her their attention.

"We've found a home for Josi. Tomorrow, she leaves."

CHAPTER SEVENTEEN

Chai jumped up from the table, her elbow hitting her bowl and sending it to the floor. Rice scattered everywhere. Josi sat still as a statue, the color draining from her face.

"What are you saying, you crazy woman?" Chai could not stop her tongue—her anger was out of control.

"Chai, before you get into trouble, clean up that food and sit down," Mother whispered, looking behind her at the door to see if her husband had heard from outside. "Lao Chan is the master of this home, and he has sold Josi to another family. She will not be far away, only across the bay in another floating house. If you behave, you two can still see each other." Mother crossed her arms across her chest, not moving from her comfortable seat.

"But you promised! You said she could stay!"

"*Aiyo*, I promised no such thing. I did my best. You have had her for three months now. How do you think I feel? Now there will be more work for me. You can't possibly do everything."

Josi looked up and softly asked, "What about the boys? What will they think? They'll miss me."

"That is what I'm saying! Now I'll have to go back to caring for them most of the time; Chai can't do everything. But they will adjust. We all will."

Chai sat back down, ignoring the command to clean up the scattered rice. She didn't care what they did to her. Her worst nightmare was coming true: she and Josi were going to be separated. Josi came to sit beside her and put her arms around her shoulders. Both girls wiped at the tears rolling down their faces.

Lao Chan heard the commotion from outside on the smoking deck and barged through the door, with both boys following behind him. Tao looked alarmed, but Bo only sneered at the girls, peeking around his father to try to see what was happening.

"*Zenme le?*" Lao Chan bellowed at his wife, asking her what was wrong as his cigarette smoke wafted to the ceiling of the small room. The stench of fish came in with him, causing Chai even more misery. She was beginning to hate fish and all that it represented.

"I told them, and they're upset. It is to be expected, Zhongfu. These girls are very close, and they're barely more than children, after all." She got up and went to the table, bending down to help gather up the food on the floor before Lao Chan got even angrier.

"I will not have disrespect in my house! You'll both do what you are told, or I'll take you out to the sea and feed you to the sharks. Don't think I won't. You are nothing but maggots in the rice bag, and if I can't get peace around here, I'll be rid of you both."

Chai and Josi were afraid—so far the man had kept his anger from erupting directly at them, though they always felt it was simmering. This was the first time he looked like he really wanted to do them harm.

"Told them what, Mother?" Tao asked, his cheeks flaming red. Bo stood beside him, a self-righteous smile pasted on his face as he rocked on his heels, his thumbs hooked through his suspenders like an old man.

"Tomorrow Josi will go to live with a new family. Your father has found her a place."

"What? Why? I thought it was working out fine? She does everything for you, Mother! How could you?"

Lao Chan turned around and struck his son across the face. Tao fell backward against the small sofa. Bo smothered a guffaw, obviously delighted with the turn of events.

"In the house of Chan, you cannot talk to your mother like that."

"Zhongfu! No! Do not hit my son." Mother stood up and ran to Tao. She sat down beside him and held his head to her breast while he struggled to free himself from her.

"And you need to stop coddling that boy. He thinks I don't see him whining and carrying on about being a fisherman. He better find his pride for this life, for it will be all he ever knows, and I'm not raising any land-loving wimps."

"Zhongfu. Do not talk about family matters in front of these girls. Please."

"Be gone with you, then!" Lao Chan waved his hand at Chai and Josi, causing them to both jump up and run out the door and into their room. They were terrified of Lao Chan and had no doubts that he would follow through on his threats of disposing of them if he was pushed enough.

Behind them, they heard the sarcastic voice of Bo. "I think they'd make good shark bait."

In their metal room they closed the door and dropped to their pallet.

"House of Chan! Who does he think he is—the leader of China? He can't do this." Chai's chest heaved up and down as she fumed and searched her mind for a solution.

"Chai, it's decided. There's nothing we can do."

"No. Don't say that. Let me think."

Josi sat next to Chai, tears still staining her face. They didn't bother to light the lantern; they were both shell-shocked at the news of their impending separation.

"She said I'd be on a floating home not far from here. Maybe we really can see each other."

"No, Josi. What if you're in a dark room? What if you don't have a light? What if they make you do work too heavy for you to handle? I won't be there to help you."

"Chai, I can do it. I don't want to leave you, but I don't want us to get in more trouble with Lao Chan. You know Tao said he can be very mean."

"There has to be a way to stay together."

"Maybe I should go willingly and then we try to find a way to plan our escape, and we won't be far away from each other. If you know where I am, you can come get me when the time is right."

"Josi, I can't do this without you. We're nothing but slaves here. I have tried to be strong, but it was only because of you. I can't do it anymore. I will explode from the frustration without you here."

"Yes, you can do this, Chai. If you struggle against Lao Chan, he'll hurt you. We can do this. We'll both be strong. We'll work, and at night we'll stare at the same moon, and it'll be like we are still together. Now, come on, let's lie down. You know Mother will have us up at the crack of dawn to care for the boys."

They lay on their pallet, and Josi wrapped her arms around Chai, comforting her as she cried. They both went to sleep thinking of home—a place that was unfortunately becoming dimmer in their memories as they fought to survive the new life they had been thrown into.

CHAPTER EIGHTEEN

Jun pedaled as fast as he could to the police station, ignoring the pain in his calves from the long ride. At the building, he jumped off the bike and let it fall to the ground unheeded. He ran through the door to find the captain lounged back in his chair snoring, his feet crossed and propped on the top of his dusty desk. On the other side of the small room, another uniformed man sat in a small metal chair, staring up at a tiny television mounted on the wall. He took one look at Jun, then turned back to the loud black box.

"Captain! Wake up!" Jun let the door slam behind him.

The captain startled awake and just about fell out of the chair. When he saw Jun standing there, he straightened himself up and sighed. "Jun. What do you want?"

"I've just heard a girl was found yesterday wandering in another village and was brought here. Is it my daughter? Is it Chai?"

"*Ni feng le*. I have no idea what you are talking about, Jun. You have to stop coming here and bothering us. It's been months; your girl is gone."

"I am not crazy. And it's been three months, one week, and two days." Jun walked over to the desk and picked up the heavy rotary phone. He slammed it down in front of the captain in a rare show of courage.

"Call someone. Your boss. The district office—anyone who will know. This is not a rumor. Find out the details, or I will not leave."

The captain narrowed his eyes at Jun as he tapped his pen against his scarred desk. "You do know I could have you thrown in jail, right? I can either make you leave, or I can make you wish you had. Which is it you want me to do?" Dropping the pen, he pulled a cigarette from the pack in his pocket and lit one, inhaling deeply and then releasing the smoke into Jun's face.

Jun dropped to his knees. "Please. I beg you. *Make* the call. What else can I do to convince you this is not a rumor?" Inside, Jun cringed at the power one small, stinking man could hold over so many because of the tarnished badge pinned to his shirt.

The captain sighed again. The uniformed officer in the corner let out a grunt, a fart, and then rolled his eyes.

"You. *Qu wai mian.*" He pointed at the officer. The man got up and shuffled out. "Now, Jun. I don't want to arrest you, but I will if you continue to make such a nuisance of yourself. I'll tell you what—if I make this call, will you agree to stay away for a while? At least for one month?"

"*Dui.* I will not come back for a month." Jun got up and moved over to the desk, picked up the phone again, and, gently this time, set it closer to the captain.

"Sit down over there; give me some space. I don't like you breathing down my neck." He pointed at the shabby yellow plastic chairs across from his desk.

Jun backed up until his legs met the edge of the chair. He lowered himself into it, never taking his eyes from the captain. The captain dialed the phone and put it to his ear. He leaned back in his chair again and put his shoes on the desk, the dusty soles pointed directly at Jun in an outright insult to his face.

"*Wei ni hao*. This is the captain, and I need to know if a girl was found yesterday and brought into the city? Maybe someone who was lost or kidnapped?"

The captain listened at the phone, nodding his head up and down. "*Hao de, hao de.* You are sure?" A pile of ashes dropped from the end of his cigarette onto his desk as he talked.

He kept nodding as he looked up and locked eyes with Jun. He said good-bye and hung up the phone. "You are right. A girl was found walking along Old Shu Road."

Jun jumped to his feet. "Where is she? Do they know who she is? Was she wearing a jade necklace?" He clasped his hands together to stop them from trembling.

The captain smiled slyly. "They don't know who she is, but they do know she is only about five years old, maybe less. She has already been taken to the welfare institute."

Jun dropped back into the chair and put his head in his hands. He didn't want to show his emotions in front of the captain. He cleared his throat before looking up again.

"My supervisor—he told me it was a girl about the same age with the same looks as Chai. He said he knew for a fact. Are you sure? Can you call someone else?"

"Lao Jun, I'm sure. Now go before I really do have to throw you in jail."

Jun stood and slowly walked out the door, his shoulders bent. He still had a full day of work to decide if he would tell Wei of the false alarm or not. Lately she had begun to refuse to talk about Chai—going as far as turning her back and leaving the room when he'd try. He knew she was devastated, and he didn't know if she could take any more bad news. Adding to the misery of today's outcome, he wondered if she realized Chai had already turned fourteen while she was gone. He hoped his daughter was able to acknowledge her step into her teen years, wherever she was.

"Oh, Jun?" the captain called from behind him.

He turned around, hope filling his face. The captain was smiling menacingly, his tobacco-stained teeth lined up like crooked headstones in a haunted graveyard.

"You owe me a carton of cigarettes for making the call. Bring them on your next trip in."

CHAPTER NINETEEN

Chai sat cross-legged on her floor, using a flashlight to read her latest book from Tao. He had also given her the light, because he knew that she had pushed their lantern into Josi's hands to take with her to her new home. Six long months had gone by since Josi was taken away, and they hadn't seen or spoken to each other.

Luckily, Tao managed to pass short messages back and forth between them. Those messages were few and far between, but she was indebted to him for finding excuses to take the sampan around the water village so that he could stop by and check on Josi for her. He was able to answer a lot of her questions about how they were treating her friend. Chai had insisted Tao also make her likeness on paper, and he delivered it to Josi with the message that she should pretend Chai was still reading her stories before bed.

Chai turned the page and sighed. She was tired from finishing all the laundry and cleaning for the day, as well as helping with the little boys, but she still couldn't sleep alone until she literally couldn't hold her eyes open any longer. Only then could she fall back and finally nod off.

The day they took Josi away had been the worst day of Chai's life so far. At least during the kidnapping they had relied on each other for support. Now Chai felt so alone, and she was getting headaches from worrying about Josi every day.

When Lao Chan had come for her, Josi had slipped into a still silence, obviously terrified to be separated from her lifelong friend. Chai had wailed and begged and tried to hold on to Josi, but Lao Chan had pushed her aside and shoved Josi into the boat, then used the oars to glide through the water until Chai could no longer see her friend staring over the side of the sampan at her. If Chai had known how to swim, she would have jumped in after her, but instead she had helplessly watched her go, sobbing loudly at the injustice of it all.

That night Chai had refused to come out of her room, not even to cook for the family or eat her own meal. Even when Lao Chan had come and kicked her she hadn't flinched. She didn't care if he beat her or even drowned her—she was at her lowest point and couldn't move. Mother came in for just a moment and clucked her tongue in sympathy and left again. Without Josi, she felt defeated and found herself agonizing about whether her mother and father had moved on with life or if they still even remembered her. She had allowed herself to sink deeper and deeper into a rare moment of self-pity.

Tao had come late that night and found her lying curled on her side, her knees pulled up in a fetal position, her face soaked with tears. Though she was mortified that she had let everyone see her in her weakest moments, she also knew that if it weren't for Tao, she would have just closed her eyes and died quietly.

He brought her a bowl of hot soup and talked sense into her foggy head. He reminded her that she was the stronger one and Josi was depending on her. Without saying it outright, he implied that he knew of their eventual plan to escape and that Chai had better shape up or Josi would be lost to her forever. At that, Chai had sat up and begun sipping the broth.

Since then, Tao had made her see the positive parts of their latest ordeal. And she *was* relieved that at least Josi was close and that, unlike her, she was allowed to sleep on the floor of the family rooms. It was nearing the coldest part of the year now, and at least she didn't have to worry about Josi being left all alone in a darkened metal building. Still, the lantern had come in handy after all, because each night after dinner duties, the girls found a way to send signals to each other with the light of the lantern and flashlight. Tao also made sure Josi didn't run out of propane, even chancing his father's wrath if caught stealing from his own family's barrel to give to the girl. Surprisingly enough, his family had provided Chai with a small heater, and Chai skimped on using it at times so she could be sure Tao had enough kerosene to take to Josi for the lantern.

According to Tao, Josi had gone through a bad few weeks, but she didn't seem as hopeless now. Using code words, Chai gave Tao messages that would affirm to her best friend that she was still working on a plan to escape. So far she hadn't thought of much, but Josi needed to believe that Chai would eventually get them home. They knew that to try to leave to travel in the coldest part of the year would be suicide—especially without money.

Tao told her that Josi was being used as nothing more than a slave. With her leg disability and the superstitions the local people had about passing on bad luck through the generations, the people had no intentions of letting her marry into their family. But she was cheap labor and took care of the laundry and cooking, and she helped to care for the one small child in the home.

Chai put down her book and reached for her extra pair of socks from their basket. She was pulling them on over the other socks she wore when she heard a soft knock on her door.

"Come in, Tao." She didn't even look up when the boy came in. With Josi gone, the talks with Tao weren't as anticipated; life was fairly mundane without being able to share it with her friend.

"Chai. I have to talk to you. It's important." He sat down across from her.

She sighed heavily. "Tao, you know you shouldn't come without Josi here. If your father finds out, he'll have your hide. Especially since your brother thinks he owns me."

Bo had been making more inappropriate comments and gestures to her. She felt sick remembering how just that evening he had brought his empty glass to her as she stood at the sink. He had stood so close behind her that she could feel his hardness in the small of her back before she jerked away. Now that she was growing taller and filling out quickly, she caught his attention more often. It not only sickened her, but the possessive way he acted could mean danger if he thought Tao was spending time alone with her.

"Something good has happened. Mother is pregnant again. Six months already."

"I thought she was getting fatter! Eeww...how many children does she want, for goodness' sake?" She slapped the book shut and rolled her eyes.

"I don't know, Chai. But you're missing the point."

"What point? That I'm going to be working even harder now because your mother will refuse to do housework, and soon I'll have a baby to take care of along with all my other duties?"

"I heard her talking to Baba, and she said she wishes they had not sold Josi—that she was so good with the boys, and she needs help with the new son coming."

Chai sat straight up. She felt tingles start at her wrists and travel up to the hairs on the back of her neck.

"Tao, what else did they say? Are they going to get her back?"

"No. They can't. Baba told her he already spent the money they got for her on the new cages and netting for the winter. Obviously, it wasn't much because of her leg." He sat back and ran his fingers distractedly through his hair.

"Well, can't you get the money, Tao?"

"Me? From where? I only work for Baba, and he doesn't pay us. I work from sunup until sundown; when can I work for someone else?"

They both sat in silence, staring at the floor. Chai unconsciously flicked the flashlight on then off then on again.

"Tao! I have an idea." She reached up and pulled her necklace from underneath the heavy work shirt she wore. The oval-shaped green gemstone sparkled in the moonlight. She turned it over and studied her initials her father had carved on the back.

"Where did you get that?" His eyes widened with surprise and awe.

"From my father. It belonged to my grandmother and was passed down to me. He made me wear it for luck, though so far, it has proved useless or I wouldn't be sitting here now. Maybe now is the time it was waiting for. Can you sell it?"

"I don't know. I can take it to the mainland and see what I find. But what about Mother? If she finds out you were hiding this, she'll be angry."

"We'll have to come up with a plan. You can tell her you've been asked to help chop wood or something. Then a few days later you can present her with the money and tell her you want her to get Josi back so she can get off her feet and rest for the coming of the baby. In the meantime, I'll start doing less and being slower at it so she gets frustrated and wants Josi back even more."

"Hmm. It might work—if I can find someone to buy it. I'll need to see if I can also find out how much they paid for Josi so I know what I need to get for it. I'll go by tomorrow and see if their son is there. He's my age, and if he knows, he'll tell me."

Chai jumped up and threw her arms around Tao's neck, making his cheeks flame with embarrassment. She pulled the necklace over her head, and thinking of her father and the day he had given it to her, she hesitated.

Then she thought of how alone Josi probably felt, and she put the necklace in Tao's hands, covering it with her own as she smiled at him.

"Tao, if you can do this and get her back, I'll owe you forever."

"We'll see, Chai. Don't get your hopes up, but we'll see."

He got up and put her necklace around his own neck, tucking it discreetly under his shirt. He turned and quietly left the room, sneaking back into the house to go to bed.

CHAPTER TWENTY

"Chai! Hurry up and get dinner ready and get these boys bathed! What is wrong with you? Why are you moving so slowly?"

"I'm doing the best I can, Mother." Chai smirked under the camouflage of the hair hiding her face as she peeled potatoes to fry with peppers. For the last two weeks, she had gradually gotten slower and more incompetent, much to the frustration of Mother, who couldn't understand what was wrong with her.

"Your best is not good enough. I'm almost seven months pregnant. What am I going to do when the baby comes? You'll have to do much more, and you can't even keep up now!"

Chai sighed as dramatically as she could muster. "I guess you're going to have to give up on the old tradition of a month of bed rest. I'm not a machine, Mother. I can't take care of four boys, a baby, and *your* husband all by myself."

She rinsed the potatoes and left them sitting in a pot of cold water, then moved on to slicing a green pepper into thin strips. They'd have their dinner—but darn if they wouldn't have to wait for it. Just like for the last few days Lao Chan had gotten his fishing socks washed, but not in time for them to completely dry before morning. The thought of him wearing damp socks in the chilly mornings brought a twinge of joy to Chai's heart.

Tao had come to her room the night before and told her he was ready to make the move. He'd sold her necklace to a Gypsy on the mainland and had been taking off early from fishing every night to pretend he was chopping wood for one of the farmers. He told his father he wanted to earn some money to buy his mother a present; he just didn't tell him the gift was in the form of one shy crippled girl. His plan today was to stop by and offer the family double what they had paid for Josi. He told her he had no doubts they would accept, especially because Josi had also conveniently come down with an extended case of laziness, making them just as perturbed with her as Mother was with Chai.

Mother passed behind her and swatted the back of her legs with the broom, not enough to hurt, but enough to say she was at the end of her patience. Chai stepped it up a bit—after all, she didn't want Mother telling Lao Chan she was causing problems. Chai had no fear of the woman, but Lao Chan was another story altogether. She was already feeling a bit shaky after an encounter with a girl at the neighboring floating house and her fear that their conversation would be repeated back to Lao Chan.

Chai had been out scrubbing the deck when she had seen a young woman hanging clothes at the house floating next to theirs. She'd seen her before, but that was the first time both of them had been alone. The woman appeared to be about twenty or so, and probably an *ayi* from what Chai could tell.

"*Ni hao*," she'd called.

The woman had lifted her face briefly and waved, then gone back to her work. Her face was chapped and ruddy from the cold and wind, and she worked fast to hang the wet clothes.

"*Qing wen*, excuse me. Can you come closer?" Chai had beckoned the woman to the edge so that she didn't need to raise her voice so much. She didn't want Mother to hear her.

The woman came near, her brow wrinkled curiously.

"I need your help. I don't belong to this family, and I want to go home. Can you tell me what cities the buses go to from here?"

The woman gave her a blank look and went back to hanging her clothes.

"*Qing wen!* Did you hear what I said?" Chai couldn't believe the woman's outright rudeness.

The woman turned back to her and nodded her head. "I know who you are. And you won't be getting any help from around here. Don't make trouble for the rest of us. Just do your work, and before you know it, you'll learn to like this life."

Chai stomped her foot. "But I will never like this life—I already have a life and a real family. I need to get back to them. What's the name of this place? Can you just tell me if there's a way to catch a bus from here?"

She waited another moment. As far as she could tell, the young woman wasn't going to be helpful, and she wasn't even alarmed to know that Chai was there against her will. Even though Chai didn't know which direction to take to get home, she still relished the thought of climbing aboard a bus and leaving; even heading out to the unknown was better than staying and being a slave. They should have left before Josi was sent away, but they hadn't had a plan, and until recently, it had never occurred to her to sell her necklace to get money. Now she couldn't go anywhere because she wouldn't dare leave without her best friend.

Finally the woman across the way spoke. "Talking to you about our situation will get me a beating, and it'll probably get you one, too. So go back to work and let me be."

Angrily, Chai had turned away and gone back to scrubbing the deck. At least a week had passed since then, and she was still hoping the woman would not tell Lao Chan of their conversation.

Finished with chopping the green pepper and cabbage, Chai began to clean the tall pile of fish for their dinner. She eyed the stack of chili peppers in the wire basket. That night their meal would be spicier than any of them would be able to stand. Even with the anticipation of *accidentally* ruining another meal and watching Lao Chan's face turn red as a beet, nightfall could not get there fast enough, for she didn't know if Tao would be successful or not, and she wondered if she would see Josi again.

CHAPTER TWENTY-ONE

Chai sat alone at the table, eating her dinner. She was brimming with anxiety. She had finished cooking the meal, cleaned everything up, and even bathed the kids; still Tao had not returned home. She had gotten a tongue-lashing about the ruined meal but had begged for another chance to try to do better—*quite a convincing and dramatic act*, she thought.

Even though Chai had saved herself a less-than-spicy share of dinner, she didn't feel like eating. But she knew in the morning she would have a full day of chores ahead of her and would need her strength, so she slowly ate her portion.

"Zhongfu, why is Tao out so late again?" Mother raised her voice so that her husband would hear her from the bedroom, where he lay sprawled across the bed.

"*Wo bu zhi dao.* He's still chopping wood, as far as I know," Lao Chan mumbled from his pillow.

Bo grunted his disapproval. "I don't know why he wants to work for someone else when Baba gives us all we need."

Just then the front doorknob rattled, and in walked Tao. Chai jumped to her feet but her anticipation was doused when he shut the door behind him. She didn't see Josi with him, and her heart dropped. She sat back down, stared into her bowl, and fought back tears. He had failed.

Tao didn't even look at Chai. "Mama, you know how you have said that you need more help, and now that the baby is coming you're going to be so tired? I've done something for you."

"Tao, what have you done? Have you made me something? I thought you were supposed to be chopping wood?"

"I *have* been chopping wood, Mama. But listen—I wanted to do something really big for you. Not only because you need it, but to show my gratitude for the good mother that you are to all of us."

Chai looked up and watched the door, wringing her hands and hoping.

"Well, tell me what you did, you fool son!"

Tao went to the door and opened it and gestured for someone to come in. First a moment of nothing, and then Josi's slight frame filled the doorway.

"*Josi!*" Chai jumped up from the table and ran to Josi, almost knocking her down with her uncontainable glee. She wrapped her arms around her and together they rocked back and forth, laughing and crying tears of joy.

Lao Chan quickly returned to the living area, his footsteps thunderous. Bo went to stand next to his father, the two making a formidable pair.

"What have you done, boy? Did you help her run away?" Lao Chan's eyes narrowed as he stared down his son.

Mother looked from son to husband to the girls and back again. She didn't know what to say—it was obvious that she wanted her best worker back, but not enough to defy her husband.

"Baba, she did not run away. I've worked hard to earn the money to buy Josi back for the family. I wanted to show you I can be a man and accomplish something on my own. Mother's too tired to keep up the heavy workload she's carrying, and Chai cannot do it all for her. Josi is the better worker of the two—and I only wanted to do right by our family." For just the right dramatic flair, Chai saw him bow his head to be humble.

"You imbecile, you cannot buy her back without permission from Baba," Bo said, his hands perched on his chubby hips. He looked toward his father for confirmation.

Before the man could answer, Mother stood up.

"Tao, you are a good son, no matter what your father's decision. Thank you for thinking of me, so tired and swollen from this baby. Now we must wait for his answer," Mother said quietly, then lowered her eyes and sat back down.

Chai and Josi stood still, waiting to hear if she would be allowed to stay. The entire room became quiet, everyone watching for Lao Chan's response.

Lao Chan cleared his throat, looking from the girls to his wife and back to his son. "She can stay through the birth of the baby and the recovery time after. Then we'll see if she is doing enough to earn her keep."

Chai and Josi began to laugh again, jumping up and down in celebration.

"And shut that cackling up and get to work. Do something." Lao Chan stomped back to the bedroom and slammed the door behind him.

Chai caught Mother smiling, unable to hide her moment of happiness for them and for herself that her life just got a bit easier again. But then Chai saw Mother look at the bedroom door and put on a stern expression.

"Chai, come over here and rub my feet. Josi, you clean up her dishes. Tomorrow, you girls are going to clean this place from one side to the other."

The girls scattered to do her bidding, knowing they'd soon be able to catch up. Chai passed Tao and gave him a wink as he turned his head to hide his shy smile. She knew that he'd be knocking at their door later to share in their celebration. She hoped he brought with him some of the fresh fruit she had seen Mother buy earlier that day from a passing vendor.

CHAPTER TWENTY-TWO

Chai finished her work on the netting and set it aside. She shook the cramps from her chapped fingers and stood and looked around the sparse room. She was hungry and restless—and tired of mending nets, shelling peanuts, and doing everything else she had done that day. She wanted to get away for a bit and think.

Even though Mother had given them some items to hang on their wall to make their room more comfortable and fitting for two teen girls, Chai felt claustrophobic and needed to get completely off the vessel. She had been waiting for months and was ready for her first attempt.

She crept out of the shed and around the side of the house. Through the walls of the wooden shack, she could hear the hushed laughter of Josi and the small children. *Mother must be taking her afternoon nap already. It's ridiculous how the lazy woman thinks being pregnant makes her totally incapable of anything.*

In the month since Josi had come back, Mother had let them take over all the housework, cooking, and caring for the children. Chai felt exhausted day in and day out, and she needed a break. Luckily, Lao Chan had started leaving the small boat tied up to the house in case Mother went into labor and they needed to make a trip to retrieve the midwife. Though many people on the mainland possessed cell phones, the old woman refused to come into the modern century and had to be hunted down when needed.

The first day Chai had seen the sampan there and the men had left for their workday, she had tried to talk Josi into getting in and running away. But Josi had settled her down and made her realize that they needed to form a plan, save some money and food, and then take off when they could make it as far away as possible. The biggest problem was that they didn't know which direction to go—all they remembered was their village was close to a canal, and that it could be one of hundreds outside the city. It was going to take some research, and so far, they were unable to ask Tao to help get them a map. So now they remained and bided their time, but Chai's mind was always thinking, strategizing, and planning.

After debating with herself for a few seconds the repercussions if she were gone while Mother unexpectedly went into labor, Chai decided to chance it. She went to the edge and deftly unwound the rope to the sampan. Quietly, she lowered herself in and began rowing toward the island. She'd just take a quick walk and return before Mother awoke. As her oars sliced smoothly through the water, she invented excuses as to why she was leaving her chores, just in case she didn't return before she was noticed missing. Josi would think her crazy for sneaking off, but she preferred to think of herself as brave.

Minutes later, she reached the community dock leading to the mainland. When her feet touched the ground, the pull toward the structure sitting high on the hill felt magnetic. To her, the majestic lines of the roof on the gigantic building were more beautiful than anything she had ever seen.

Chai imagined herself living there as a princess, possibly with a court of maidens to wait on her every whim. She would never have to scrub the deck again, or mend another net, or hold another child over the water to urinate. She would be able to do whatever she wanted. She'd be free to read and write, free to learn more about the world.

Daydreaming about her own personal fairy tale, Chai almost lost her footing when a woman dressed in a black robe quickly came around her and hurried up the path.

"*Dui bu qi.*" The woman murmured her apology as Chai stood aside to let her pass.

Chai was dumbfounded and stood staring after the woman with her mouth hanging open.

A foreign ghost, she thought as she held her breath.

The small, quiet woman wore some sort of black frock with a black headpiece, but wisps of the lightest brown hair Chai had ever seen escaped through the front and hung just over her eyebrows. She was definitely Chinese, but for the brief second they had looked at each other, Chai had seen eyes the color of the deepest water in the channel—a clear turquoise. The woman continued on her way as Chai stared after her, oblivious to the young girl's amazement at her appearance.

Chai had never seen a Chinese woman with eyes of that color. She wondered if this was one of those ghosts she had heard Mother warning the children about—threatening to take them to her if they misbehaved. This woman didn't appear to be such a monster, and Chai was encouraged by the kindness in her face.

Chai began to climb again, her eyes searching past the fast-moving woman to the building ahead of her that seemed to defy imagination. She examined the tall peaks and the large cross perched in the center roof. *It must be at least as tall as a person.* On either side of the cross were towers with stone points placed around the top, the way Chai had always thought a castle would look. The windows were unlike any window she had ever seen, tall and beautiful with arches framed around the casings, and an artistic diamond design at the top of each one. The windows opened out, bringing a cottage feeling to the huge structure. Surrounding the building was a tall wrought-iron fence, but the gate stood open, beckoning Chai to walk through.

This is not the frightening place Tao has claimed, she thought as she quietly crept around the enclosure. *I feel more at peace here than I've felt since I left home.*

Chai looked to the side of the building and caught a glimpse of a black garment disappearing around the corner. She quickened her pace and followed the woman, staying back just enough that she wouldn't be noticed.

The woman opened a side door and disappeared. Chai slowly made her way to the door, hesitated, and then opened it and peeked in.

The sound of chanting startled her, words unintelligible to her ears yet comforting in the hushed tone of many voices in unison. She saw only a long hallway with many doors leading to other unknown areas. Chai took a deep breath and entered the building. Once the door closed behind her, she stood still for a moment, deliberating what to do. She didn't see where the ghost woman had gone, but her curiosity was roused, and she had to find out more about the chanting. Treading ever so lightly, she crept down the hall toward the biggest door of them all.

CHAPTER TWENTY-THREE

Chai stopped in front of the door, hesitating as she realized that behind it was the source of the chanting that so mesmerized her. She wanted to peek inside to see what was happening, but she was also suddenly afraid of what she might find.

"Qing wen, wo keyi bang ni?"

Chai turned around, startled, only to face the woman who had passed her on the path. She began to shake, unsure even what to do or which direction to run. Before she could decide, the woman smiled and put a gentle hand on her shoulder.

"Are you lost?"

"Bushi."

"Well then, are you hungry? Thirsty? I can give you some water."

Chai hesitated yet again. She really was hungry and even thirsty after her long trek up the mountainside to the building. Yet she didn't know if it was safe to stay. On the other hand, she felt drawn to continue her exploration.

"Please, let me give you sustenance," the woman said, beckoning Chai to follow.

Chai found herself following the woman, her eyes glued to the long folds of the woman's robe swishing back and forth as she walked. They went through a door on the opposite side of the hall and entered a kitchen area. As soon as they walked in, Chai smelled a delicious aroma. She couldn't quite name the spices; she only knew that her stomach growled in anticipation.

As she trailed behind the woman, she looked around at the large room. The ceiling arched toward a very high peak, with beautiful oak beams accentuating the slopes. The stone floors were washed spotless, and another woman stood at the sink, cleaning a large fish taken from a pile of them on the counter beside her. The other woman wore the same black robe, with the white collar and headpiece. She turned and smiled at Chai, then resumed her work. Chai was relieved that the woman's eyes were the usual dark brown she was accustomed to.

The woman led Chai to one of several stone tables. "*Zuo xia.* I'll bring you a small snack and water."

As requested, Chai slowly sat at the table, running her hands over the glossy wood. She watched the woman go to a cupboard and remove a glass. The woman filled the glass with clean water from a pitcher on the countertop, and then stopped and pulled a small cake from a basket next to it. She brought both over and set them in front of Chai, then took a seat across from her.

Chai simply stared into the strange eyes—too overwhelmed to speak.

"*Nide mingzi shenme?*" the woman asked gently.

Chai didn't answer for a few seconds, but the woman waited patiently. "Chai," she finally said, letting out a long sigh.

"Chai? What a beautiful name! You may call me Sister Haihua. What brings you to our humble church?"

Chai wrinkled her brow, putting aside her sudden panic at muttering her real name to the stranger. "Church? What do you mean, church?"

"You don't know what a church is? Why, this is the house of God. This is where people gather to talk to Him."

Chai had heard of gods and such but was unsure if the woman meant the same god that her parents or Mother worshipped, or a different kind of god. "What is that chanting I heard?"

"That's the people saying their prayers."

"Are you a foreign ghost?"

Sister Haihua threw her head back and laughed—a sound both inviting and musical escaping from her mouth. Chai couldn't imagine laughing like that, or even feeling that kind of happiness. Before she could wonder how or why, Chai found herself giggling quietly. She felt a lightness she had not experienced in months come over her.

"No, my child. I am not a ghost; I'm quite real and have lived on this island my entire life. I suppose you're intrigued by my eyes, am I right?"

Chai stared, not saying a word.

"My mother was Chinese, but my father was American. I didn't know him, but he came to China many years ago and then left before I was born. My mother came to this nunnery to find refuge when her parents found out she was pregnant and disowned her. I grew up here—trailing along behind the sisters, running the halls, and helping to care for the less fortunate. When I grew up, I couldn't imagine living anywhere else, so I stayed. It is said my mother named me Haihua because of the color of my eyes, for *hai hua* means *beautiful sea*."

Chai felt a surge of comfort at the woman's friendliness, and she picked up the small cake and took a tiny bite. She tasted an unfamiliar sweetness and a look of surprise came over her face.

"It's called a muffin." Sister Haihua smiled at her reaction. "It is actually a foreigner's food, but I've found the children of Sandu'ao also like them. I like to experiment with different recipes. My treats bring the children to me, and with them come the rewards of my hard work. They are like sunshine on a day that has weathered many storms."

"Sandu'ao? Is that the name of this place?"

Chai tried to hide her excitement at the useful nugget of information. She continued to study the woman's interesting face—Chinese, yet different, with the contours of foreigners she had seen on television. Her skin was a beautiful tone of light brown, making her eyes even more vivid.

"Why yes. You do not know? So tell me, where do you come from? Do you have parents? We have had many children find their way here after becoming orphans."

Chai decided she had better not trust the woman too much, and she decided to volunteer the least amount of information possible. She hoped that giving her real name would not come back to cause her any trouble.

"*Shi*, I have parents. I live on one of the fishing boats, and today I decided to come to the island to explore."

Sister Haihua clasped her hands together. "Well, I'm very glad you did. It's always nice to have a new friend. You live in what we call the plantation on the sea—we don't see many visitors from there often. Usually your people mostly stay on the water. Does your father farm yellow croakers or prawns?"

Chai ate the remainder of the sweet cake and drank the entire glass of water. She set the cup down and stood to go. She realized time had gone by quickly, and she needed to hurry.

"Um...yellow croakers. Listen, I must get back. I have chores to finish." She shifted uneasily from one foot to the other, hoping that Mother was still sleeping. "Sister, can I take one of your muffins with me?"

Sister Haihua stood. "Of course. I'm so glad you like them." She wrapped up a muffin in a small piece of paper and handed it to Chai.

"Let me walk you back to the courtyard, then." Quietly she led the way out of the kitchen and down the long hallway to the door Chai had entered. "Chai, I'd love it if you would come again sometime."

Chai stuffed the muffin she planned to give Josi down in her pocket and then looked around the courtyard at the few locals wandering about. She hoped none of them knew of her or Lao Chan. If she was found out, she'd receive a memorable beating for sure. She moved her scarf over her head and tied it under her chin.

"Thank you for your kindness, Sister Haihua. I don't know if I can ever come back, but it was nice to meet you." She didn't wait for a reply; instead she quickly ran out through the iron gates and down the footpath.

* * *

Chai quickly returned to the sampan, untied it, and climbed in. She frantically rowed back home and climbed aboard. Just as she set both feet on the deck, she heard Mother calling out for her. Chai sure would be glad when the baby was born—and she expected it to be any day, making her spur-of-the-moment adventure all the more dangerous. Josi would be furious if she was left to deal with Mother in labor all by herself, so Chai hoped all was still well.

"Chai? *Ni zai nali?* My feet have swollen and need rubbing."

"I am here, Mother. I just finished mending the net. Are you ready for me to help Josi with dinner?"

"*Dui.* I forgot. Get in there and shuck the oysters. Tonight the boys will be home before dark, and Zhongfu will expect dinner to be ready."

Chai breathed a sigh of relief that her escapade had gone unnoticed. As she hurried toward the kitchen to help Josi prepare dinner, she couldn't get the taste of the sweet cake or the beautiful eyes of Sister Haihua out of her mind.

CHAPTER TWENTY-FOUR

Only a week after her daring adventure and chance meeting with the beautiful Sister Haihua, Chai peeked through the door into the master bedroom. The old midwife sat beside Mother, wiping her head with a wet cloth. She was glad Lao Chan had left her the sampan in case Mother went into labor, because Chai had used it to row to the mainland to get the old woman early that morning, right after he and the boys had left for work.

Ironically, the baby had come almost a year to the day that Chai and Josi had been brought to the fishing village. Its birth marked their anniversary of being abducted, a sign that Chai didn't know whether to take as bad luck or a good sign for her future.

Mother moaned, oblivious to anything going on around her. After only five hours of pushing, she had given birth, but she was still weak. On the floor beside her bed was a basket. Chai could hear the infant mewling softly from inside. She saw a tiny fist make an arc above the edge, but nothing else. Next to the basket was a huge pile of bloodied rags, making Chai feel faint as she studied them.

The midwife heard her and muttered some orders. "You! Go to the mainland and find the ingredients to make *lóng yǎn shuǐ yú tāng*. Hurry! Turtle soup will fix her right up and renew her strength."

"But what do I need? And what about the baby?" Chai didn't want to come closer; the old woman scared her just a little bit.

"You are stupid, child!" The old woman turned around, her bony finger pointed at Chai, who immediately pulled back, feeling as if she had just been cursed by a wicked old sorcerer.

Josi stepped around. "I know what's needed; I can tell her. And I'll care for the infant until Mother can hold it." She pulled Chai away from the doorway.

"Chai, we need a small turtle. You take the sampan and go to the mainland. You'll have to ask someone where the herb stand is. It can't be far because Mother gets her supplies there each week. When you find it, ask them for a bundle of dried longans, a foot of fresh yam, some ginger, a handful of red dates, and one fresh lily bulb. Don't forget the turtle, and tell them it needs to be from fresh water."

Josi went to the two little boys who sat huddled on the couch, fear on their faces. "It's okay, boys. Your mother is just fine, you'll see."

Chai rummaged through the kitchen drawer until she found the charcoal pencil and a scrap of paper, and began scribbling down the ingredients.

"Also get a baby bottle and some soy milk. I have a feeling Mother is not going to be able to nurse today." Josi spoke quietly. "Chai, quiet down—we need to try to keep some semblance of normalcy in the air for the boys."

"But I don't have any money. How will I pay?"

"Just tell them that Lao Chan's wife has had the baby, and when he returns home he'll come settle up. They'll let you charge it, I'm sure."

Chai quickly left the house, climbed into the sampan, and headed toward the mainland.

* * *

Josi quietly crept into the bedroom and went to the wicker basket. The infant had calmed and was quietly staring at the ceiling. Josi stopped in her tracks when she saw a gaping hole in the child's face where his top lip should have met his nose. Other than that, the child was beautiful, his dark almond-shaped eyes sparkling like tiny stars up at Josi. His cap of black hair peaked at the forehead, framing the tiny face perfectly, set off by the light blue colors of the receiving blanket he was wrapped in.

She bent and picked up the basket and turned to leave the room.

The midwife stood and followed her out into the living area, shuffling close behind her. The garlicky smell of her breath wafted all around the room, making Josi wrinkle her nose in disgust.

"She doesn't want that baby. I'll take it with me when I go."

Josi sat down on the couch, her knees weak. "What do you mean she doesn't want her son?"

"It is not a son. It's a girl, and a defective one at that. There's no place for an infant girl like that here with a fishing family. She'll be nothing but a burden; the missus knows what must be done."

"Well, that's the most ridiculous thing I've ever heard. You should watch what you say in front of the boys; you'll scare them." Josi reached in and pulled the baby girl from the basket and held her up to study her as Ying and Yifeng huddled around her. "That explains the beauty of this child—it's not another toad of a son, but instead a tiny princess. You'll not take her anywhere. Chai and I will care for her until Mother comes to her senses."

The old woman grunted and rolled her eyes. "You know nothing of caring for a baby, and no wet nurse will come for one who has this problem suckling. It will die anyway. Much more humane to let it go now; I have a system for children born like this and can take it away."

Josi looked around, wishing Chai had not left. She hesitated, gathered all her courage and stood as tall as she possibly could, then narrowed her eyes.

"Boys, go outside on the deck for a few minutes." Josi pointed at the door, and the boys grabbed their toy cars and left the house.

"Now let me tell you something, old woman. Tao has told us all about you and the evil things you've done. I can promise you that you'll have to pry this child from my dead fingers before you will take her out to the end of the bay and throw her in. She stays with me until Mother is fully awake. Once she sees her, she'll want her. It is her child. And I do know how to care for a baby; I've cared for them in my own family." She stopped, not daring to say more about her family in case Mother was awake and listening. She held the baby close to her chest and rocked back and forth.

"You are wrong, and you have no business handing out orders. Imagine, a child like you trying to tell me what to do!" The midwife laughed to herself while gathering up her things. "But I must go. I have another patient on the mainland to care for today. When that other girl comes back, hurry and make the soup and feed it to the missus as soon as possible. She'll be fine, though she's weak from so much blood loss. I stitched her up, but you'll need to change the padding between her legs at least once per hour, more if needed. Don't let her sit up until tomorrow, but I'll come back to check on her and to get the baby."

The woman gave one last look in at Mother, then grabbed her bag and left. Josi heard the splash of the midwife's oars slicing through the water as she moved away from the house.

Josi sat back down with the baby girl, cradling her in her arms. If not full, she knew her hands would be shaking from the feelings the woman's words had dredged up inside her. She'd struggled her entire life to bury her feelings of resentment that she was treated differently because of her leg. Among other names, she had been called a cripple many times by her school peers, village neighbors, and even her own father when he was drunk and spewing off at the mouth about his bad luck. If it weren't for Chai, most of the time she would have felt completely alone in the world. It hurt her to think that the baby girl would suffer through years of the same or even worse abuse because of something she had no control over.

She gave the baby a reassuring smile.

"Did you hear what she said? Don't pay her any mind, okay? She's just a haggard old woman with a hump on her back. You are precious and beautiful. There are doctors who can fix your lip, and then you will be just fine." She rocked the child back and forth and giggled softly as the baby girl stared back at her intently, her tiny mouth puckered in concentration.

Soon she heard Chai return and the familiar noise of her tying up the small boat. "I'm back! I got everything, except I had to buy milk powder for the baby. No fresh milk was available." Chai went to the kitchen area, set the bags down, and began unloading the items.

"Oh, I think powder is what we want anyway." Josi's voice softened. "Chai, Mother didn't have a son."

Chai turned around, her eyes wide. "Oh, no. She was so sure it was a boy. Does she know?"

"I don't know if the old woman told her or not. But it gets worse. Come here; look at her."

Josi turned the baby around for Chai to see. The girls were silent for a moment as they both studied the imperfection of the infant's mouth.

"Josi, what's wrong with her?"

"It's called *chúnliè*. My cousin had a baby with a cleft lip, and Mama said it was because she didn't get enough fresh vegetables in her diet while pregnant. Or it could have been because their water system isn't the cleanest. Sometimes it's worse, and there's a problem at the roof of their mouth, but from what I can tell, hers is only on the outside. The poor little girl. You know Mother's going to be so angry. She thought she was getting strong fisherman number five."

"Well, she's just going to have to change her thinking. And maybe this baby girl will grow up to be a great fisherwoman—she might just fool them all."

"There is nothing we can do about it for now, but we'd better take care of Mother before she wakes up like a growling tiger."

"Yeah, you're right."

Josi put the baby back down in the basket. "I'll start water boiling for the soup. You go check the padding between Mother's legs. There's a bag of fresh bundles at the end of the bed. When you come back, if you will chop the yam, I'll make up some milk for the baby. Once the water boils, we have to fry the turtle meat with ginger, and then throw it and everything else in the pot to simmer. It needs to cook for at least two hours, so I hope Mother doesn't wake up for a while."

Chai whistled, "Jeesh, Josi, and you say I'm the smart one? You're going to have to tell me all that again—I'm not going to remember everything you said, but I'll check on Mother and chop the yam for starters."

They both hurried to start their next chores, anxious to get back to caring for the baby girl but knowing that Mother had to come first.

CHAPTER TWENTY-FIVE

Chai sat on the edge of the bed, feeding Mother the turtle soup one spoonful at a time. The woman had awakened and was hungry from the exertion of childbirth. Chai was glad that Josi had told her the longan in the soup would make Mother sleepy once again. It gave her something to look forward to, for the woman was easier to handle when her eyes were closed and her mouth silent.

"It smells awful in here. Can I open your window?"

"No! It is one of the rules of *zuo yue zi*, the month after childbirth. If you open a window, I'll have pain in my joints and migraines in my old age."

"Well, tomorrow I'll wash your hair. It's greasy, and a thorough washing will help the room smell fresher. I'll even braid it, so it won't lay about you in such a mess."

"You or Josi can braid it, but I can't bathe or wash my hair for thirty days. More rules."

Chai's eyes widened. "What? You won't wash for an entire month? Mother—we will not be able to stand to be in the same room with you!" She held her nose, and the corner of her mouth twitched as she tried to hide her amusement. It was a rare treat to be able to poke fun at the woman while she was unable to discipline her.

"If I felt stronger, Chai, I'd slap you for your disrespect. I'll wash using hot water, alcohol, and salt. You'll need to soak a towel in the solution and help me to wipe my body. But no more talk of this. Feed me so I can go back to sleep."

Chai smirked, knowing the woman would not slap her, but letting her have the last word anyway. She did feel sorry for her; the labor had not been easy. At one point, Chai had asked the midwife why they didn't take her to a hospital, and the old woman had snapped back that the women of the fishing village were tough and didn't need to spend their husbands' money on needless hospital bills. During the labor, Josi had taken the little boys out of the house and tried to camouflage the sounds of their mother crying out, but they had still heard enough to make them silent and somber for the rest of the day.

Chai fed her the rest of the soup and stood to go. "Mother, do you want to see your daughter before you sleep?"

"I have seen her. I don't need to see her again."

"But don't you want to try to nurse her?" Chai used her sweetest voice, hoping to convince the woman.

"No. I can't. Didn't you see her mouth?"

"You *can* nurse her, or at least try! How will you know if you don't try?"

"Zhongfu doesn't want a girl. We can barely feed our own and cannot handle caring for a useless girl. He is going to be angry when he returns, and he will never let me keep her."

"Mother, she *is* your own. She isn't like Josi and me—she is your flesh and blood; she belongs to you and to Lao Chan."

"I'm tired of talking. When the midwife comes tomorrow, she will take the child away, no matter what I say. She knows who the boss of this household is, and she would never defy Zhongfu."

* * *

"Chai, what are we going to do? They're going to let that old hag take her, and you know what she'll do with her." They had returned the baby and her basket to the place beside the bed, but when hours went by without Mother showing the baby any attention, they had taken her out of the room.

"We don't know that for sure, Josi. Maybe the boys were just making up stories—but I don't want to take the chance. We have to find a way to convince Lao Chan that a girl will benefit his household."

Hours after the sun set, Lao Chan and the boys came in, tired from the long day fishing. When he discovered his wife had given birth, he was very excited, but his glee quickly evaporated when he looked at the child snuggled in Chai's arms.

"It's your fault. You with your stubborn ways and sharp tongue—you brought bad luck into our home." With that he stomped away, leaving Chai shaking and speechless.

He stayed behind closed doors with his wife for an hour before he came back out and told them the baby would leave in three days. He had heard from another fisherman that the old woman was tied up in an emergency case that would take that long before she could make it back out to the water village. Chai knew he'd wait for the woman, as he made it clear with his actions that he didn't want to touch the baby girl.

Chai tried to talk sense into him, but he shushed her up and told her to mind her own business, then slammed the door on his way outside.

Tao was the only one of them who showed the baby girl any attention or appreciation. He came and welcomed her to the family, and the baby wrapped her tiny fist around his finger and made him chuckle. But even he was too afraid of his father's wrath to voice his opinion on the status of the child's gender and imperfection.

Bo, once hearing that it was a girl, didn't bother to even look at her. Instead he taunted them with comments about the "swim" his little sister would soon be taking and how they'd better hurry and say their good-byes. Chai could see Josi visibly wince at the veiled threats Bo dropped as he paced around the room, doing his best to intimidate them as they hurried to finish their chores.

Even though the girls were tired from waiting on Mother, cooking for the family, and taking turns caring for the baby and the small boys, neither of them could go to sleep for want of looking at the petite infant. They had already worked out which of them would get up first with her and then would alternate shifts. But they both hoped she would sleep for at least a few straight hours. They had also whispered to Tao to stay away lest he wake her up.

"I'm so angry, Chai. They want to get rid of her. We can't let them take her."

The child lay between the girls on their pallet. The receiving blanket had disappeared, and they had wrapped her as warmly as possible in one of Lao Chan's old, worn shirts. After cutting a bigger hole in the bottle nipple, they had gotten her to eat enough to satisfy her big appetite. It took some practice, and the first session was a huge mess, but they had gotten the hang of squeezing a bit into her mouth, pausing to let her swallow, then squeezing again. Now she lay staring alternately at them, her eyelashes fluttering innocently.

"Look at her long fingers, Josi. She looks like royalty. Let's name her."

"We should really wait until her one month is up, then announce her name and give out red eggs—but I guess that won't happen. So what should we name her?"

Chai picked the baby girl up and cradled her close. "Hmm, you agree she has royal hands, right?"

Josi giggled. "Chai, I never know what you will come up with next."

Chai put her finger to the tip of the baby's nose. "I hereby name you Zetian, after the famous empress who became the first female emperor. She was known for her fairness to the lower classes, and she campaigned to raise the status of women. But we shall call you Zee until you grow into your majestic name."

The baby looked solemnly at Chai, as if she understood an important event was taking place.

"How do you know so much? Is that all true?"

"Yes, Josi. My father told me all about her, and then I read a book about her. Zetian even instructed famous scholars to write biographies of women, because she wanted more female history recorded. He said I'm like her because I'm headstrong and independent, and he told me I'm smart enough to be a leader myself one day. You, me—even baby Zee—we can *be* something, Josi. We don't have to be content to work as house slaves in this stinking village, or anywhere, for that matter. I'm going to be a writer, you wait and see."

"My father has always told me that I need to be able to cook and clean better than anyone, because no one will want to marry me, and I'll be lucky to get work as an *ayi* in a rich household."

"Josi, your father is old-fashioned and sees things the way it used to be. Outside of our village, in the bigger cities, people think differently. There your limp won't even be noticed. You can do anything you want! Have a career, get married—whatever. Do you know that my aunt is a manager in a bank in Ningde? She has her own apartment and isn't even married. All we need is an education. Don't let anyone tell you to settle for less, Josi, because you're smart and beautiful."

Josi smiled shyly. "I don't dream to be a manager or have a big career or anything like that. I just want to find someone who will love me for who I am. You give me hope, at least. And I agree with your father, Chai. You're very smart—and stubborn." She laughed briefly, but then her smile fell, and her eyes filled with tears. "Do you think our families have looked for us?"

"Josi! Of course. Why would you even doubt that?"

"*Wo bu zhi dao.* My father always said he wished I were a boy, to help him more with the chores. I think it would be easy for him to forget me."

"Well, I know my father will never forget me. And I know he's looking for us and will never stop. If he doesn't find us in this stinky fishing town, we'll find our way home one day, Josi."

Between them, the baby girl let out a long, throaty burp and then started at her own noise. The interruption lightened the mood, and the girls giggled again.

"She's got a lot of personality, this one." Chai tickled the tiny foot that continued to kick right next to her nose.

"I love the name Zee. But do you think we should really name her, since she'll be leaving so soon?"

"Yes, she is officially our little Zee. Believe me, Josi; we won't let them harm her. Trust me. I'm working on a plan." Chai pursed her lips together, thinking through the details. She wasn't ready to share them yet, for she was still deciding if it would work.

"She looks like a tiny doll." Josi used her finger to stroke Zee's eyebrows until the little girl's eyes slowly shuttered closed, her long eyelashes lying softly against her cheeks. Josi nudged Chai and put her finger to her lips, telling her to be quiet. They both snuggled down under the covers and moved as close to Zee as possible to share their body heat.

"Good night, Chai."

"Good night, Josi," Chai whispered back.

"Goodnight, Zee," they both whispered in unison and then giggled softly.

CHAPTER TWENTY-SIX

Jun and Josi's father sat outside their houses, leaning back in their bamboo chairs, smoking their long brown cigarettes. Jun had waited until his friend stopped bragging about the new business venture he was putting together and the car he had finally been able to afford before he brought up the subject of the girls. He was tired of pretending interest when all he wanted to do was discuss their next steps to finding their daughters.

"We have to find them, Shen." Jun blew smoke rings and watched them float toward the moon.

"I know, but what else can we do? The police are no help at all."

"There has got to be something else—someone else that we can call. I have followed the path from where I was working that day, through town and back home at least twenty times. I have asked every shopkeeper, and no one saw them. How can that be?"

"When do you find time for all of this, Jun? Aren't you working?"

"Yes, I'm working. I go in before the light of day and get off at dark, but in time to talk to the shopkeepers before they close for the night. They all know me by now and start shaking their heads when they see me in their doorways." Jun used the heel of his boot to dig a small hole in the soil—back and forth he dug, deeper and deeper, lost in thought.

"Last week I called that man from Beijing who started a website for missing children. He posted Chai's photo on there, and you need to get me one of Josi to send to him, too. He also drives a van around with the photos blown up and posted on the side of it—he stops in different cities and hands out fliers. Maybe someone will see her photo and recognize her." Jun leaned forward in his seat. "They found a little boy last week who was stolen from outside his mother's shop. Some man had brought him home and told his wife the boy was his child, born from his mistress. Can you believe that? Just stole the boy and tried to pass him off as his own! But he's home now. I saw the reunion on the local news. It was something, Shen."

Shen sighed. "Jun, I must tell you, people in the village say you bring too much trouble with all of your coming and going to the officials. They've asked me to talk to you and convince you to let it go. Do you think maybe they ran away? We worked Josi fairly hard, caring for the little ones and helping out her ma. And she had full responsibility for the animals while I worked. Perhaps she was tired and wanted to be free."

"*Bushi.* At fourteen years old, you think they would do that? Chai would never run away. She was happy, even doing her chores. And she is much too smart to do something so stupid. Chai is destined to be a great woman."

"*Aiyo*, Jun. How do you know this? They are but girls, and though we are very sad to lose Josi, it is not like losing a son. It has been over a year now. You must let go and move on with your life. You have aged so much—you're killing yourself with this useless chase." Shen took a final drag on his cigarette and flicked it into the grass.

Jun stood and faced his neighbor, his eyes flashing with anger. "Never say that to me again, Shen, or I must cease to call you friend. I will never give up looking for Chai. I don't care what my neighbors think. Don't you know the saying 'A wise man makes his own decisions; an ignorant man follows public opinion?' And the world is different now. Women hold up half the sky. Where would you be if not for your mother? Would you let something terrible happen to her and then go on with your life like it never happened?"

Jun's hands hung in tight fists at his sides, shaking with rage. "Josi is your child, man. Speak sense when you talk to me, or keep your mouth closed. My daughter is as good as any son, and probably better. And what have you done to help find them? Nothing!"

Shen stood up, nose to nose with Jun. "Don't tell me what to say. We have lost more than you, for who is there to help us now with all of our children, and to cook and clean? Feed the pigs? You only have one other child in the house now—not much work to do. You didn't lose much." He turned and stomped away, back to his own home, muttering one final shot, "You need to let this go, Jun."

Jun sat back down in the chair and stared at the moon and the stars. Only his shaking hands gave away his barely controlled anger at his ignorant neighbor. He had always been a peaceful man, but he was changing. There was a fire building in him as each day passed. For just a moment, he wished he could put his hands around Shen's throat and squeeze—just for one glorious instant. As a matter of fact, he was fighting a strong urge to run through the path and down to the canal, a need to demolish everything in his way.

Why am I the only one still trying to find the girls? Why? He fought to calm himself, not wanting to wake his youngest daughter. Finally, after many deep breaths, his heart rate slowed, and he leaned back.

He whispered, "Chai, I know you are out there somewhere, maybe even staring at the same moon. I won't forget you, and I will *never* give up. Be strong, and be smart, like a mighty emperor. Take care of Josi, and find your way home, daughter."

Hours later, when Wei came to check on her husband, she found him asleep in the chair facing the moon, the same place she had found him every evening since that day—keeping watch and waiting for Chai. She sighed, then went back inside and returned with his heavy quilt, tucked it around him, and returned to bed.

CHAPTER TWENTY-SEVEN

Wei stopped at the guard shack and showed the young man the photo pass hanging from the lanyard around her neck. He feigned interest and then waved her through. He yelled and beckoned for her to hurry and get out of the way for the dark sedan that was coming around to pull through the gates.

Watching him stand at attention in his rumpled and too-large suit, Wei marveled at how the guards for the rich expat houses continued to get younger and younger. *Do the foreign residents really think the boys are any good as security when a strong wind could literally blow them over?* However, Wei knew that for the young men, who most likely did not have the means for an education, getting this work was a windfall for their families.

Now pushing her bicycle, because according to the property rules the hired help couldn't ride inside the gates, she quickly made her way past the rows of identical houses to the one labeled B6. Unlike the rich Chinese who lived in swanky apartments in tall high rises, the foreigners preferred freestanding houses. Like all the others around it, her boss's home looked like something out of a fairy tale, the concrete painted warm beige and trimmed with a pastel peachy color. The house was two stories high with tall columns bordering the elaborate front porch. She shook her head and thought again how her entire family could live in just the space the flowers and front bench took up. They could probably house half the people in her village inside the spacious home. After propping her bike against one of the columns, she used her key to enter the home.

"Xiao Wei, is that you?" the woman called from upstairs. The woman had been through several Mandarin immersion programs and still had a weekly session of private tutoring. All her efforts had benefited them both. Though Wei spoke a local dialect, their mutual understanding of the basics of Mandarin had helped them work out a language all their own. Some Chinese and some English—as well as some words that couldn't be recognized from either side without lots of hand signals—but usually they got the message across and understood each other well enough.

"*Dui*, it's me. I'm sorry I'm late. There was a bus accident blocking the entrance." She moved closer to the garage door, looking down at her watch and frowning at the time. It read eight fifteen; she was fifteen minutes late.

"Couldn't you get around it on the sidewalk?"

Wei sighed. "No, *tai tai*. They ran over some old man and his wheelbarrow of fruit. The police wouldn't let anyone around until he finished his paperwork. I'll be back in just a second; let me put my bike up. *Deng yi xia*."

Wei opened the door to the garage, pushed her bike in, and leaned it against the wall, frowning at the broken kickstand Jun had promised he'd fix and never gotten around to. She turned and went back into the house. At the door, she took off her dusty shoes and lined them up under the foyer bench. From the basket next to it, she selected and put on the ragged cloth slippers that were designated for her indoor use. Moving quietly in case the big boss had not left for work, she went to the laundry room and got a basket, then climbed the stairs.

Outside the master bedroom Wei knocked gently.

"Come in," the *tai tai* called out.

Wei shuffled in and went straight into the bathroom and gathered the soiled clothing and towels from the day before. She set the heavy basket at the door and returned to the sleeping area, relieved to see the boss was gone. The missus sat at her computer, still in her pajamas as usual, and didn't turn as Wei began making the bed behind her.

"Wei, today I want you to scrub down the front patio and clean off the furniture that's on it, please."

"*Hao de*, but I usually do that every Tuesday. Is there some reason you don't want me to wait for tomorrow?" Wei kept a daily schedule of indoor and outdoor tasks and didn't particularly like to throw it off the usual rotation. The house was so huge it required a lot of work to keep it up and a tight schedule to fit it all in.

"We have company tonight, and I want the front entrance to be immaculate. I've got some other things I need you to do, too. I'll need you to run to the supermarket for some items, and don't let me forget to show you which wine to buy. I'll get with you later this afternoon for specific instructions."

"*Hao de.*" Wei dropped her shoulders in defeat as she plumped and arranged the silk pillows on the bed. It sounded like another late afternoon to her. She hoped Jun would get home in time to pick up Luci from the neighbors before they began their supper. With Chai gone, they had come to depend on their friends next door way too much for her comfort, and she didn't like to feel indebted to anyone.

Opening the heavy curtains to let the sunlight in, she finished tidying up the bedroom and picked up her basket. The missus never turned around. She continued to peck on her keyboard as Wei softly shut the door behind her and headed downstairs to start the laundry.

* * *

Wei finished cooking the stir-fried spicy pork and turned to grab the platter. The *tai tai* stood behind her, hands on her hips while she surveyed the spread of food laid across the glossy marble counter.

"Great job, Xiao Wei." She inhaled deeply over the heaping dish of pork. "Oh, this is Jack's favorite dish. It smells so good and spicy. He'll be pleased. One of these days, you have to teach me how to cook this."

"Do you want me to stay to serve?" Wei asked. She dished the beef dumplings out of the wok and arranged them neatly on the shiny plate, then covered them with a lid. She didn't understand why the family liked their dumplings with beef instead of pork or the many other options, but once told, she had found a way to make them as tasty as beef could be.

She looked up at the clock and cringed when she saw how late it was. She hoped she didn't have to stay much longer. After washing the laundry, cleaning three bathrooms, mopping all the floors, and using the hose and scrubber to clean the front patio, she was thoroughly exhausted.

She had passed the girls getting off the school bus when she was leaving for the supermarket, what felt like an entire day before. When she'd returned with all the bags of vegetables, meat, and wine, she had spent another two hours prepping and cooking a seven-course meal.

Wei leaned on the counter to take the pressure off of her back for a moment. She just wanted to go home and put her feet up.

"No, no. The girls can help do that. You're already three hours late leaving. You need to get on home. I appreciate you staying. Why don't you come in late tomorrow?"

Wei shook her head. "No, I'll be here at eight. I have some ironing I didn't get to today, and I need to finish it before more comes out of the laundry. I don't want to get behind."

"Oh, Xiao Wei, I stacked some of the girls' outgrown clothing in their hallway for you to go through later this week. Some barely worn jeans in there may fit your oldest daughter, and there are some smaller shirts for your youngest. Take what you want for your girls, and give away the rest."

Wei's eyes filled with tears, and she turned to hide it from the missus.

The *tai tai* inhaled sharply and covered her mouth. "Oh, Xiao Wei, I'm so sorry. I didn't even think! Please forgive me. I completely forgot about your daughter being missing. "

"It's okay." Wei began washing the stack of pans, letting her hair drop around her face to hide her tears. She was embarrassed at her lack of control over her emotions, and she blamed her exhaustion.

"No, it's not okay. How thoughtless of me. How's the search going, anyway?"

Wei turned around to face the woman. "It's not. They don't care anything about our daughter. The police are useless unless you're rich or know someone in the government."

The missus wrinkled her brow. "Is that true? Even in the case of a missing child? That's absurd. Is there anything—anything I can do at all—to help?"

Xiao Wei finished washing the pans and began to dry them, carefully putting each one away as she worked. She hesitated, then put the towel down and turned around. She'd never before shared her problems with the woman, and the only reason the *tai tai* even knew about the situation was because Wei had to give a reason for why she had uncharacteristically missed a few days of work after Chai had disappeared. She reminded herself that even though a year had gone by since Chai disappeared and the woman had not once offered her assistance, this might be Wei's only chance at doing something to help her daughter. So she gathered her courage and took a deep breath.

"*Tai tai*, if you really want to help, can you ask your husband to put a word in with someone at the precinct? Does he know anyone who can help? The search has all but stopped for Chai. We need a way to push them to take her disappearance seriously. My husband is doing everything he can, and he's driving himself to exhaustion. Since you're a *waiguoren*, foreigner, maybe your husband can help?"

The missus shifted from one foot to the other nervously. "Hmm, I don't know, Xiao Wei. Honestly, Jack doesn't like to get involved in the epidemic of bribery that goes on around the city, and bribery is exactly what it would take for him to get anywhere. I remember when we first came to China; he had to turn his head quite a bit to ignore what was going on. It was an ordeal just to get all the proper approval and permits to start the construction of the factory. But I'll talk to him and see what he says." She patted Xiao Wei on the arm and left the kitchen.

Disappointed but not surprised by the lack of interest the missus showed in helping them find Chai, Xiao Wei finished cleaning up and went to the foyer to pick up her jacket and shoes. She was mad at herself for even asking; she knew the woman wasn't really interested in anything that didn't involve herself or her family. Her concern was fake.

She retrieved her bike from the garage and walked it up and through the gates, then hopped on. All around her, people on other bikes, electric scooters, and cars competed for positioning on the narrow roads as everyone hurried to get home.

Wei stopped at an intersection to wait for the light to turn. As she stood there with one foot on the ground to balance her bike, she examined all the faces around her, as she had every day since Chai had disappeared. She looked at all the girls who had even a slight resemblance to her daughter's build or hairstyle, and some who simply caught her attention by the sounds of their voices, which reminded her of her carefree child. But so far, the crowds had not produced the answer she searched for.

The young couple beside her laughed loudly at something, the girl almost falling as she balanced herself on the back rack of a bike. Wei remembered when she and Jun had been that way, years ago, before the complexities of life had made them grow apart. She'd hop on the back of his bike and sit sideways, just like this girl, arms wrapped around him as he pedaled them around town.

Wei smiled at the couple's display of happiness. Their clothing and the shabby condition of the boy's bicycle told Wei that they were not well off. Unless they found a way to be a part of the select population that climbed their way out of poverty, they had no idea the hardships of life they were in for.

She looked at her watch and imagined what Luci was doing. She knew that the little girl was probably wishing her mother would hurry up and get home. Lately, she felt more and more like a failure, to her eldest daughter and to her youngest.

Her mother had tried to convince her to let the girls come live with her while she and Jun saved some money, but her mother lived so far away, and they didn't want their girls to grow up without them. Even if it was normal for grandparents to raise the children while parents worked, they had decided it was worth the effort for them to keep the family together. If she had only known—if she had sent them, her daughter would have never disappeared. Her heart lurched as she thought about Luci waiting, and she hoped again that Jun had gotten home hours ago.

She sighed. Eventually they were going to have to find a way to go on with life without Chai. In addition to the strain on her marriage, she knew that Luci was also suffering from the constant atmosphere of grief she and Jun had created.

She lost her smile when her thoughts about the poor shape of their marriage continued. Admittedly, most of the problems stemmed from the fact that she couldn't discuss Chai's disappearance with Jun. Coming from a very traditional family, she'd been raised to suppress her concerns, fears, and even her opinions. The few times she had cried in front of her father still brought back memories of some of the worst beatings she had endured.

Even though her husband was a man who treated women fairly, years of growing up without verbalizing or showing her thoughts had left her emotionally crippled. She loved her children dearly and they knew it by everything she did for them—their favorite foods she cooked, the precise braids she wove, the neatness of their home, and the occasional touch of affection she forced herself to give them as she put them to bed. But actually *speaking* of her love—or of any feelings she had—that was too hard. Jun had always known this about her but he pushed and pushed until she just felt like running away. But she never would. Her girls needed her.

It's days like this one that I wish I could snap my fingers and be home, she thought as the light turned, and along with the mass of people around her, she pedaled furiously through the intersection.

CHAPTER TWENTY-EIGHT

"Would you like to watch some television?" Chai had just finished giving Mother a sponge bath. The bedroom contained the only television in the house, though the home-made antenna on the roof only brought one fuzzy channel to the tiny box.

"No, it's not allowed. Neither is reading, so don't offer."

"Well, these after-childbirth rules are downright crazy, if you ask me," Chai responded, rolling her eyes. "And your midwife has ordered us to make *zhu jiao jiang* tonight!"

Mother managed a small smile. "Pigs' feet with ginger and vinegar sounds delicious to me. Chai, I've missed your spunk in the last few days. You might be a thorn in my side, but you're also an unexpected breath of relief from the constant boredom of this fishing life."

Chai grinned and continued to neaten the bed around the woman. The truth be told, she found the childbirth traditions fascinating. In their village, it was such a sacred yet secretive time after the mothers gave birth that Chai really never knew what went on during their forced seclusion. At least now her curiosity was being appeased.

She turned to see Mother's eyes scan the room and watched as her smile disappeared, making the woman look somber again.

"Where is she?"

"Who? Josi?" Chai asked her.

"No. You know who I mean."

Then Chai understood. The woman couldn't even bear to call the infant *her* child. "Josi has her; she's taking a bottle." The girls took turns feeding her, both of them loving the interaction with the sweet-natured infant.

"You mean she can eat?" Mother asked weakly.

"Yes. It takes some extra time and patience, but she has a healthy appetite. She eats like a greedy little piglet. We got her some soy milk from the mainland, and a bottle. And we named her, too."

"Don't tell me." The woman gave a long and tortured sigh. "Can you bring her to me?"

Chai got up and crossed the room, opened the door, and went into the living room. Josi was the picture of motherhood with the baby in her arms and the little boys gathered at her feet playing with their toys. Zee was looking around, content to be held and unaware that, so far, her own parents had not claimed her. Chai stopped in front of them.

"She wants her."

Josi's eyes opened wide with surprise. "She *wants* her?"

"Well, for the moment. Here, let me take her." She took her from Josi's arms and carried her into the bedroom, kicking the door shut with her foot. She brought the baby to the bed and laid her in the crook of her mother's arms, wary but relieved that perhaps the woman had found a change of heart.

Mother stared down at the baby girl, her eyes filling with tears. "Why did she have to be born like this? He might have let me keep this one." She traced the baby's jawline, then her eyebrows. When Zee locked eyes with her and turned the corner of her mouth up, Mother smiled back and then reached over and took Chai's hand. "She looks just like Tao."

"Ha. I told him that. He thinks she's cute, too. But Bo won't even look at her; he's too afraid his father will see him show an ounce of compassion. You know, you need to stand up to Lao Chan. Tell him he needs to accept his daughter."

Mother didn't respond to that. Chai wasn't surprised. She knew Mother wouldn't speak against her husband or her sons for any wrongdoing. She was much too old-fashioned and didn't realize she had a voice, too.

"Chai, there have been others." Mother spoke the words in such a low, quiet voice, it was almost inaudible.

"What do you mean, *others*?" Chai pulled her hand back, horrified by what the woman's words brought to mind.

"I will only say this. Please do not let the old woman take her away. Enough is enough, and this one should be allowed to live out her destiny. I know you are strong. You will find a place for her, and then come back. Tell Zhongfu you laid her to rest yourself. He will not ask where. He will never ask about her again; this I know for sure. Do this for me, Chai. Please."

Mother did her best to lift the baby up to Chai, holding her there until she had no choice but to take her.

"What do you want me to do with her?" Chai couldn't believe the woman was going to brave her husband's wrath by concocting such a story.

"I don't know, and I do not want to know later. But you must do this before my mother-in-law comes, or she will take her, and this one will be no more. That is all. I am tired." Mother turned her face toward the wall and closed her eyes.

Despite the woman's efforts to hide her face, Chai saw a tear escape and make a trail down the woman's cheek. She turned to leave with the baby, and she sighed as Zee struggled to turn her tiny head toward her mother, almost as if to get one last look for their final good-bye.

CHAPTER TWENTY-NINE

Chai swaddled Zee in the towel and put her down in the bottom of the big fishing basket. She smiled when she saw that Josi had layered it with one of Tao's red-checkered shirts. Josi was such a little mommy, always thinking of ways to bring comfort to others. Mother didn't realize what a gem she had taking care of her children.

Chai was so tired. She and Josi had stayed up all night, discussing options until they had both agreed on the destination for the baby girl. Their plan was for Josi to stay with the boys while Chai took the baby to the mainland.

"Chai, I don't want to say good-bye to her."

"Then don't, Josi. If it works out the way I hope, we can sneak away to see her once in a while. But we have to get her out of here before that old hag returns, or Lao Chan's mother comes and something terrible happens." Chai carried the basket outside and set it down. She took off her slippers and pulled on Mother's water boots. They never had gotten their own shoes back, and so far they had not been given new shoes of their own, as Lao Chan thought they had no need of ever being off of the floating house. He'd have a fit if he found out that Chai had already made a few trips to explore the mainland—all during Mother's extended naps.

"Are you sure they'll take care of her? What if they don't know how to care for a baby with her problem?"

"I'll explain it to them, Josi. Don't worry."

"Will you tell them not to squeeze milk into her mouth too fast, or she'll get choked?"

"Yes, I'll tell them." Chai picked up the basket and set it down in the bottom of the sampan. She settled herself on the bench and grabbed the oars. "Untie us, Josi. I need to hurry before the men return and find me gone."

Josi handed her the bag of milk and bottles. "Okay, but lift the edge of the basket and let me see her one more time. Please."

Chai lifted the wicker flap and Zee peered up at them, her dark eyes sparkling. She was such a happy baby. Both Chai and Josi had fallen head over heels in love with her.

"*Zai jian*, Zee. I hope I'll see you soon. *Wo ai ni*," Josi whispered her love to the child. She untied the boat and stood back.

"She'll be fine, Josi. I gotta go. I'll be back as soon as I can." Chai closed the basket and reached up to pull the scarf over her head and tie it under her chin. She didn't want any of the neighbors to know who she was. She looked around and then began moving the oars to back away from their house.

"Tell them she doesn't like her milk too hot!" With one last wave at the fading boat, Josi went back into the house.

Chai watched her go as she paddled backward. She knew Josi planned to bribe the boys to go to sleep so that she could have some time to herself for a bath.

Chai shook her head—Josi was going to have to hurry if she was going to bathe, wash her hair, and have it dry before it was time to start preparing dinner. Chai felt sorry for her. Josi's monthly had come for the first time and she knew she felt dirty, but they couldn't bathe with the men at home. Even though they only used a bucket of soapy water, they still needed to undress, and their door could not be locked from the inside. They knew they could trust Tao, but Lao Chan and Bo were unpredictable.

Chai hoped Josi wouldn't obsess over the journey to find Zee a new home. They were going to miss the baby girl—Zee had been the one bright spot in their dark days.

* * *

As Chai methodically rowed the boat, she thought about the new strangeness of her life. Just over a year before, she had been a child, living a child's existence. Now she felt far older than her years, having lived through a kidnapping and made to be the caretaker of a family she wasn't a part of, working her fingers to the bone to make them comfortable every day. *It could be worse*, she thought. At least she had Josi, and so far Lao Chan had not made good on any of his threats of beating them or throwing them to the depths of the sea.

If he ever found out that she was the one responsible for the sudden mishaps around the house, he'd skin her alive. Chai grinned as she thought of his yell of indignation the morning he woke to find all his bait buckets knocked over during the night, or the morning he put his boots on, only to be pinched on the toe by a tiny crab stuffed down deep inside. He even thought it was simply bad luck when his fishing boat was found drifting off into the bay one morning; he was sure he had tied it up, and he was right. It just hadn't stayed tied up once Chai had snuck out during the night after begging Tao to leave her door unlocked from the outside.

The family had become quite comfortable ordering her and Josi around, but now they had grown confident that the girls wouldn't try to run so were granting them more freedom.

Chai snorted to herself. Mother thought she had given up the yearning to go home, but she didn't know Chai and how stubborn she could be. She *would* get home, someday and somehow. And that night, Chai had a special trick planned for old Chan. She planned to take his favorite Sunday trousers in a few inches at the waistline. She couldn't wait until that weekend, when he attempted to wear them and discovered he had gotten a lot fatter in the last seven days. If she could find the time, she even planned to take an inch off the legs. Then he'd think he was not only fatter but taller, too. It might mean an hour or so of sewing for her, but she and Josi would laugh over the results for days, so it was well worth her time.

Chai rowed faster and was soon at the main pier. She tied the boat and then reached for the basket. Zee had not made a peep, so Chai had not taken the time to look at her during the trip. She lifted the flap and saw the baby was sound asleep, probably from the motion of the water. Chai reached over the side of the boat to set the basket and the bag of supplies on the pier then climbed out to stand beside them.

On the other side of the pier was a man tying off his own boat, but he paid Chai no mind as he began unloading his crates of crab and setting them on the weathered wood.

Pulling her scarf lower over her face, she picked up her precious cargo and followed the dock to land. Jumping off, she quickly began the climb up the steep hill to the huge church.

CHAPTER THIRTY

As Chai got closer to the church, she heard a chorus of wailing. Perplexed by the eerie sound, she hurried up the winding path.

At the gate, Chai stopped when she saw a procession of children and adults wearing white following four nuns carrying a short wooden box. All expressions were sad, and the song they sang—and some hummed—sounded so mournful. Bringing up the rear were a few more nuns, and one of them did a double take as she passed Chai. She dropped behind the procession and turned to backtrack until she was standing in front of the girl.

"Sister Haihua, what is this? Why are all these people crying?"

"*Ni hao*, Chai. It's nice to see you again, friend. But your visit falls on a sad day. One of the children has died. We are marking her passing."

"Whose child is it?"

"Why, she's God's child. It doesn't matter who her parents were. All children are a gift, and if they come to us, we love them until they are sent off into the world, or in Ping's case, until they leave the world."

"What was wrong with her?"

The woman placed her arm around Chai's shoulders. "Nothing was *wrong* with her, Chai. Everything was just right. But she was born with a weak heart, so she was called home early. Now she's rejoicing in her new body in a wonderful place."

Chai looked down at the basket, suddenly uncertain about the decision she'd made the night before, and completely bewildered at the explanation of the child's death and new home. She had never been taught religion—the most she knew was to burn candles for her ancestors a few times a year—and all the god talk made her extremely nervous.

"What do you have there?" Sister Haihua looked down at the basket. "It must contain something important, for you are cradling it so protectively."

"Um, can we go inside?" Chai looked at the procession again as it moved closer to the church.

"Of course. I need to attend the memorial, but I tell you what, I'll settle you in the courtyard, and you can wait for me there. I won't be long. Come on; follow me."

Sister Haihua led Chai around the side of the church and along a cobblestone path until they entered a courtyard surrounded by a short stone wall. In the middle of the enclosure, Chai's eyes were drawn to a huge marble fountain—empty, chipped, and scarred now, but in its day, it was probably quite the masterpiece.

In a corner, under the protection of a group of huge willow trees, sat four elderly women, all in wheelchairs, facing each other. Each held a corner of a wide blanket with one hand, while their other hands worked to stuff it with padding.

"They're preparing blankets for everyone in the complex," Sister Haihua explained. "Boxes of old, tattered coats were donated to the church, and they are using the stuffing from them to fill the blankets."

"Complex?" Chai looked to Sister Haihua for an explanation.

Sister Haihua pointed to an old building to their right. "That used to be a nunnery, but it's mostly used for housing the elderly now. It's called *Tianlao Yuan*, Heaven's Garden for the Elderly. Some of these people had nowhere to go when they became too old to fish or do other work. We take them in here and give them a safe home. But the winters are cold in this old stone building, so we use all that is given to us for resources."

She guided Chai to a bench and gestured for her to sit. "I'll be back very soon, I promise. Then we'll talk about why you are here and how I can help you. I feel you are carrying a heavy burden today, Chai. We'll see what we can do about that." She winked at Chai and quickly walked away toward a door in the side of the church.

Chai looked over at the group of old women and saw their heads bent and eyebrows raised, as if they were talking about her. She turned her back to them and opened the flap of the basket to find Zee wide awake and fidgeting—and by the looks of it, preparing to launch a fit for a bottle.

Great, what am I going to do now? They're going to see her if I bring her out. Chai looked around her for a place to escape to.

Zee let out a long, pitiful wail. Chai sighed, knowing there was no way to hide her secret from the women now.

"*Ni hao.* You over there. Is that a kitten or a baby we hear? Come closer so we can see."

Chai turned and saw one of the old women waving her handkerchief at her to get her attention, squinting her way to see her better. She debated getting up and walking back down to the boat with Zee, but she couldn't return to the house with her, so she stood and brought the basket over to the nosy women.

"*Ni hao lao ren.* Yes, it is a baby. Her name is Zee." She opened the flap and the ladies all struggled to get a look. Chai waited to hear them condemn the baby girl for her facial imperfection.

The woman wearing the yellow scarf who had called her over—she appeared to be the one in charge—exclaimed and covered her mouth with her hand. Chai prepared herself to defend Zee, feeling her cheeks flame with indignation over the insult she felt sure was to come.

"What a beautiful baby!" the woman finally said.

Chai was shocked into silence by the compliment. As she stood there holding the basket out, the ladies one by one took turns declaring Zee to be a special child, a little princess, and all sorts of other flowery compliments, until finally Yellow Scarf Lady reached out and plucked the basket right from her hands. Chai was surprised—for such an old woman confined to a wheelchair, she was strong!

"I want to see the rest of her. You got a bottle in that bag? I believe someone is crying for their lunch." The woman pulled Zee from the basket and cradled her against her shoulder, cooing to Zee as she thumped her on her back repeatedly. The other women all looked on, waiting their turns for a chance to hold the baby.

Chai reached into the bag and grabbed the bottle Josi had prepared and pushed into a thick sock from Tao's collection. She shook the contents and handed it to the woman, who promptly began the squeeze-pause-squeeze method to feed little Zee.

Yellow Scarf Lady looked up at Chai. "It's been a long time since we had such a little baby here, but not so long that I forgot how to care for one. And this little frog is hungry!" She cackled at her own words, her friends joining in with her as Chai looked on with a straight face.

The woman's gleeful expression turned sour and she wrinkled her nose. "Aww...*dabian*...she has left you a little gift, in her britches. That's why when my babies were tiny, we didn't put those useless diapers on them. Which one of you old cronies wants her now?"

The old woman looked around at the others, who all shook their heads at her. They began their cackling again as Yellow Scarf Lady handed Zee back to Chai so that she could tend to the baby's soiled bottom.

CHAPTER THIRTY-ONE

Yellow Scarf Lady gave Chai one of the ragged coats from the bag at her feet. Chai spread it on the ground and gently laid Zee on it. Luckily, Josi had also packed all the torn pieces of material they had been using as diapers, and Chai pulled one from the bag. She recognized the material as another of Lao Chan's thick shirts, and she chuckled when she thought of him trying to find it later in the week. She'd love to be able to tell him it was doing a fine job keeping his daughter's bottom warm. Instead he'd probably think the ocean winds blew it off the line and into the bay.

Chai could feel the many eyes on her as she worked to clean Zee. She expected for one of the old women to tell her she wasn't doing it right, or fast enough, or some sort of unwanted advice. Working through the split in the baby's pants, Chai used the edges of the soiled diaper to clean the rest of Zee's little behind and then rolled it up and put it in the bag.

Free from the binds of her diaper, Zee kicked her chubby little feet in the air and gurgled her glee. Chai gave her a minute to enjoy the freedom in the brisk air, then slipped another piece of material under her, covered it with the torn piece of plastic, and tied the rope around it just as Sister Haihua returned. She straightened the tiny pants on Zee's legs and set her up on her lap to look around.

"Oh…" She smiled gently at Chai. "I see now what was in your basket."

"Um, yes. Can I talk to you? Alone?" She added, quickly looking at the gathering of old women who watched them.

"Of course. Let's go to the kitchen, and we can have some privacy." She picked up the basket and bag while Chai cradled Zee close to her and followed behind.

Entering the kitchen, Chai once again felt a calmness come over her. She was still infatuated with the cavernous room and the feeling of quietness it prompted inside her. She really liked it there and was anxious to find out if it could be a place of retreat for their baby girl.

"Sit down. Would you like something to eat?"

"*Mei guen xie.* Some water would be nice, though." She was much too nervous to even try to put anything in her stomach except for liquid. Chai settled herself at the table and propped Zee in her lap. The infant looked all around the room, finally settling her eyes on the high beams over her head.

Sister Haihua returned with a tall glass of water and set it in front of Chai.

"Here, let me hold her. You look a bit tired." She reached across the table until Chai handed over the baby. The sister laid Zee down the length of her lap and began to expertly move her legs back and forth in a soothing motion.

Chai wasn't sure how to start the conversation. After a few times of opening her mouth and then closing it, Sister Haihua interrupted with a question. "Is this your child, Chai?"

Chai wrinkled her head in confusion. "Mine? What? No, she isn't mine! I swear."

"Because if she is, I won't judge you." She looked at Chai imploringly, compassion the only thing evident on her face.

"Zee is not mine, Sister Haihua. But I've been caring for her because her mother doesn't want her."

The sister sighed. "I see. Well, that is sad news. She is quite the little beauty and will be more so once her tiny mouth is repaired. I love the name you've given her. How old is she?"

Chai looked up at the young woman, beseeching her with her eyes. "She is less than a week old. Sister, the midwife—or maybe even Zee's grandmother—is coming to take her away tomorrow. We know what will happen to her, and I don't know what to do to save her." Chai was shocked at herself for being so quick to trust this woman, a virtual stranger.

Sister Haihua cuddled Zee close to her. She slowly began to tell Chai a story.

"Chai, many years ago, before I was ever born, Sandu'ao was a booming place. Fishermen were becoming rich, along with the shopkeepers and restaurant owners. Spanish missionaries came and built this church, and later the Americans added the nunnery behind it. In the beginning, it must have been magnificent, let me tell you. I've been told it was the pride of Sandu'ao, and fishermen can still see its steeple from miles away as they fish in the ocean."

Chai smiled, for even she could feel the special atmosphere of the place, and she had been drawn to it herself.

"Then the war came, and the Japanese were intent on razing Sandu'ao to the ground. And they did, killing thousands of people and completely wiping out every house, business, and boat. Everything was gone—everything except for this church and the building behind it. It was protected by something unseen, something that bombs and bullets couldn't penetrate. Since then, it stands as a beacon of hope to those who are experiencing hard times. And it has been used for the good of many people, especially those who have nowhere to call home. Your child—or whoever she belongs to—will have a safe place here. On that you have my word, Chai."

Zee looked up at the beautiful face of Sister Haihua, and the corner of her mouth lifted, almost as if she understood that she was accepted. Chai breathed a sigh of relief. Regardless of what she had told Josi, she didn't have any other ideas of where to take Zee and had hoped that her only plan would work.

"Would you like to see where Zee will be staying? There are other children there, too."

"Other children?"

"Yes. We have some who have found their way here, one way or another. Come on. I'll show you. It's nothing fancy, mind you; but to us, it is home." She stood and, holding Zee over her shoulder, led Chai out of the room.

Chai felt the burden she was carrying suddenly disappear from her shoulders. Zee would be safe there; Chai had done a good thing by bringing her.

* * *

Chai followed the sister through a long hall and out a back door. They crossed through the courtyard, and the gang of old women tried to wave them over again.

"We'll bring the baby back to see you shortly!" Sister Haihua called out to them as she went on by and out a gate located at the back of the yard.

She led Chai to a door at the building in the back, the one she had pointed to earlier. Ferocious-looking but chipped lion statues guarded the shabby entrance.

"I thought you said this was an old folks' home," Chai said.

"It is. And what better place to house the children, where their infectious joy can improve the quality of life for those who have lived so long they will soon be leaving this world? Our nursery is located right in the middle between the men's and the women's wards. It's a popular place for the elderly to go and feel needed. There they can drop in and use their years of experience and gentle ways to teach our children, give them comfort, and make them feel loved."

"But where do the children come from? Where are their parents?"

The sister sighed. "Oh, like little Zee, some are unwanted because of a simple physical issue. We have also had a few perfectly healthy girls whose fathers wanted boys. Some of our children have more complicated disabilities—but nothing that can't be handled."

They walked down a long stone corridor that had many smaller apartment-size rooms leading off of it, most with the doors standing wide open. Above them, red paper cutouts of dragons and birds hung by threads, swaying in the draft and adding the only burst of color to the gray surroundings.

As they passed the individual rooms, Chai caught glimpses of elderly people doing various things. Some were sitting in wheelchairs, staring off into space. Some knitted, and others were napping on their beds. Other than being bundled up in hats and mittens for the cold, for the most part they appeared to be content. The halls and rooms were sparse but clean—they even passed a woman using a strong solution to mop wide arcs back and forth as she walked backward down the hall.

Sister Haihua's voice echoed around them as they walked.

"Many of the men are outside, wandering about. In the spring and summer they like to work the gardens. The ones who can still get around walk down the path a piece so they can smoke. We don't allow tobacco inside or even out in the courtyard. It's a hard concession for them, but they do it because they have nowhere else to live." She turned and gave Chai a wink. "Honestly, we have some who keep a pinch of snuff in their cheeks, but I don't think that does anyone else any harm, so I pretend I don't know."

Sister Haihua turned the corner with Chai right behind her, and they came to a huge wall covered with windows. Unlike the gray walls of the halls and smaller rooms, the nursery walls were painted a bright yellow, with cartoon posters and red good luck tassels hung on all sides. Through the window, Chai saw children playing on beds, a few toddlers in cribs, and several elderly women walking around tending them. In the corner, a wrinkled old man sat in a wicker rocking chair, his *Mao* hat pulled low over his eyes as he rocked a tiny boy to sleep in his arms. Chai wasn't sure which one looked more content, the old man or the toddler.

Nothing in the room was new or overly special, and from what she was seeing, it was just as cold in there as in the other parts of the building. The children were bundled up, their cheeks flaming red, and their bodies lumpy with layers of clothing. But Chai could feel that they did have something that was missing from her own life: a sense of security.

Sister Haihua opened the door and led the way in. At the sound of her voice, the children flocked to her like bees to honey. When they saw that she carried little Zee, they were even more anxious to get close.

"*Deng yi xia*, little ones. Let me find a seat, and you can all look." She carried Zee to a small table and chairs—child-sized and painted a multitude of colors, with a scattering of books across it—and she sat down. Chai knelt beside her, still a bit wary of letting so many strangers touch the baby.

A little boy was sitting on the floor on a red square pad, his legs crossed and a serious look on his face. His hair was trimmed short in a little buzz cut. Chai giggled. "He looks like a little Buddha."

"Yes, but you should have seen him when he first came to us a few months ago. He was left in the courtyard, with a note attached to his shirt saying that he was seventeen months old, yet he couldn't even sit up on his own. His head was completely flat from lying on it all day, and he had not a bit of muscle tone in his arms or legs. He couldn't even hold on to a cookie! I'm glad they brought him here; now he crawls all over the place and will soon be walking. They catch up fast with some tender loving care, you know."

One small girl held her hand out close to Zee, and Chai saw that the girl did not have any separate fingers. Instead her hands appeared to be split down the middle, the fingers fused together. Chai looked away, not wanting to show her shock at what looked to her like lobster claws.

Sister Haihua saw her looking, anyway. "This is Lin. She's six years old and was born with ectrodactyly. Her hands are malformed, but she is one of the smartest children here. And oh, what a little mommy. I promise you, she'll be trying to take care of Zee from the first minute, and she'll do a good job, too."

"But what can she do, with her hands like that?" Chai studied the little girl's hands.

"Anything that another child with normal hands can do. She is very accomplished, for she has never known anything else." Sister Haihua patted Lin on the head and was rewarded with a huge smile.

"How do you know so much about it? That name sounds complicated."

Sister Haihua laughed, and Chai could see all the children look her way, as if the sound were magnetic. "I know about many genetic birth defects. I do a lot of computer research to read up on what some of the children are afflicted with."

Chai's eyes grew big. "You have a computer?"

"Yes. I even have an office to hold it in. It was actually donated by a visiting pastor. You wouldn't believe how organized I am now that I have it, and it helps me to communicate with the rest of the world. It's been very beneficial to me when I'm trying to find help for some of the children's medical issues." She lowered her voice. "Can you keep a secret, Chai?"

"Sure."

"I'm a bit enthralled with learning about *Meiguo*, America. It probably has something to do with the American blood running through my veins. I've even made online friends and have learned some English. I'm not fluent by any means, but I can communicate well enough."

Chai was amazed. She had always wanted to own a computer or even be able to work at one. She'd only seen them on television, but she dreamed of going to university one day and having access to computers and other technology—and to even think of learning how to speak English was more than she could imagine. She didn't know anyone from her village who had learned more than the alphabet and counting to ten, the standard English studies in every primary school.

"Can I see your computer?" Her interest with the children waned a bit as she thought of the glorious secret room somewhere near her that housed a window to the world.

Sister Haihua laughed again. "Not today. Maybe on your next visit, *hao-bu-hao*?"

Chai suddenly found herself the center of attention when a little boy brought her a puzzle and dropped it on her lap. She set it on the table and picked the pieces off the backing, then helped him and a couple of others put it together again. When she turned around again, Zee was being cradled by Lin, and very happy to be there by the looks of it.

"So how many children do you have?"

"Well, right now we have only about fifteen. They come and go."

"What do you mean come and go? Where do they go if their parents don't want them?" She felt a moment of panic as she worried about Zee's future and second-guessed her decision to bring her there.

The sister gave Chai a sympathetic smile. "Chai, there *are* kind people out there, even here around Sandu'ao. We have some families who foster the children and even adopt them. Nothing official, mind you—it's not needed here to have documentation. What's important is a family, and many of our children over the years have been placed in homes near here."

Chai lowered her eyes. Other than Tao and the sister, she hadn't met any kind people in Sandu'ao.

"Do you want to talk about your family? You said you live on the water in the fishing village, right?"

Chai looked away, over Sister Haihua's shoulder.

"I don't want to talk about it right now, if you don't mind. I want to spend some time with Zee." She got up and went to Lin, who reluctantly gave up the baby girl. Chai still didn't fully trust anyone and was afraid of what Lao Chan would do if he knew that she had been talking about their arrangement.

Sister Haihua gave her another sympathetic look and changed the subject. "So—I think we'll give Zee the crib closest to the window so everyone can see our new addition as they're going by. She's now the youngest here, so I believe she'll get more than enough attention." She pointed to a painted pink crib. It contained a soft duvet, and Chai saw a wide strap lying across the material.

"What's the strap for?" She didn't like the looks of it and wondered why a strap would be needed in a crib.

"We must put the straps over the babies at night to keep them from kicking their covers off. It's very cold in here, and they would freeze. We're lucky to get most of our food donated from the farmers and fishermen, but paying to heat this monstrosity is another story. We do what we can, but it never really gets warm inside until spring."

"Zee is not going to want that strap; she likes kicking her feet in the air."

"She'll get used to it, Chai. Believe me, it's better for her to be warm than to have room to kick."

Zee must have known she was the center of attention again, for she started to whine a bit and then let out a shrill cry.

"She's tired," Chai said. "She's usually napping at this time of day."

"Would you like to lie down with her? Then when she goes to sleep, you can sneak away, and it won't be so difficult."

Chai looked doubtingly at Sister Haihua, then at Zee, not sure now if she had made the right decision. It was going to be harder to walk away than she had imagined.

"I don't know…"

"Well, Chai, what are Zee's other options? Do you have another place for her to go?"

Chai shivered as she thought of the deep blue water stretching in front of the mainland for miles. She didn't want to believe that someone could harm such a sweet child as little Zee, but her gut told her differently.

"No. This is it."

"Then have no fear, she will love her new home here. And you can come to visit her whenever you like." Sister Haihua put her arm around Chai and led her to a longer bed in the back of the room.

Chai felt her heart constrict at the thought of leaving the baby girl behind, but she knew that it had to be done. First, though, she wanted a few more minutes with her. She laid her on the bed and then snuggled up beside her. Soon, they were both asleep, and Sister Haihua covered them with a blanket and shushed the other children as she hurried them to their beds for their afternoon naps.

CHAPTER THIRTY-TWO

Jun looked at his watch and sighed when he saw it was half past ten. Wei would be annoyed that he was out again so late. Pride kept her from calling to see where he was, but he'd suffer her anger later with her silence. These days she was silent more and more—a punishment far worse than if they could just say the angry words they were both holding inside.

He jumped to the side as a passing scooter clipped his elbow. Everyone else appeared to be on their way home for the night, but he couldn't bring himself to go. He wanted to check one more street—one that was way off the path home, but one that still held a remote possibility the girls could have taken a wrong turn and landed there.

At the corner, he turned and was immediately overwhelmed with the lights and higher sense of energy of the street. The after-hours nightlife had begun in this part of town. Shop after shop boasted pretty girls, many even standing outside to get the attention of customers and bring them in. The black-and-white barbershop poles were misleading; what should have indicated a simple hair salon really meant much more on this side of town. Looking around, Jun grimaced at the unkempt walkways. He maneuvered around a pile of overflowing trash cans and a heap of bicycles, and then stepped back onto the sidewalk.

At the first shop, two girls stood in high heels and short skirts under a red barbershop light.

"Haircut? Massage? Please come in..." One of the girls rubbed his arm for emphasis. Her childish bangs, cut straight across her forehead, contradicted the skimpy clothing she wore.

Jun stopped and pulled Chai's photo from his pocket. It was over a year old and he could only imagine how much she had changed, but it was all he had, and he carried it everywhere he went. "Have you seen this girl? She may have been through here several months ago."

The girls curiously studied the photo. The shortest one looked up at Jun through the fringe of her Japanese-style bangs.

"Is this your party girl? She is very young." They grinned at him with a knowing smile.

Jun narrowed his eyes. "No, she is not my *party girl*. She's my daughter, and she's lost. Have you seen her?"

"No, we have not seen her. No massage, no haircut. *Zaijian*." The girls gave him a sarcastic wave good-bye and turned away.

"Maybe you girls should go home to your parents, ever think of that?" Jun was sickened by the young age of the girls and only prayed his daughters never ended up in such a predicament. Even though he had suggested they return home, he knew that most of those girls had been sold by their families into the industry. He shook his head at the sad state of the world and the desperate acts many parents were brought to just to keep going.

He continued along the street, stopping occasionally when the girls looked friendly enough to approach. A few asked how old Chai was, where she was last seen, and a few other questions, but ultimately they were only curious and didn't know anything.

Jun stumbled along, exhausted from carrying load after load of bricks for twelve hours, and then three more hours of walking and searching. He was really feeling his age—even more than his age if he was truthful—and his feet hurt terribly.

He stepped off the curb in front of one of the shops when a trio of rumpled men in suits emerged from the door and almost ran him over. The oldest one, in the middle, was so intoxicated that his friends held him up as they guided him to a waiting taxi.

The end of the street proved less seedy, and a few official massage shops spotted the block. At the last one, a girl sat outside on a small stool, watching the pedestrians walk by. Her clean face and simple clothes were a welcome improvement over the colorful women he had seen so far. Jun decided she would be his last stop.

He pulled the photo out again, sighed, and then asked her. "*Qing wen*, have you seen this girl?" He hoped the answer was no.

The girl took the photo from his hands and studied it intently. Unlike the others, she seemed to take the time to really look.

"*Bushi. Ni yao jiao anmo?*"

"No, I don't want a foot massage." Jun shook his head and put the photo back in his pocket. He needed to get home, and he wasn't looking forward to explaining to Wei why he was so late again. Lately she had been losing patience with him more and more. The silence between them was getting louder each day.

"Please, sir. If I do not bring in one last customer, my boss is going to be very angry. Half price?" She held her breath, waiting on his answer.

Jun looked at the pitiful girl and was reminded of Chai. Though pretty, she wasn't overly beautiful, but it wasn't the attractiveness he saw that brought his daughter to mind; it was the intelligence in her eyes. And his feet were killing him.

"*Hao de.* Half price. But I'll give you a good tip."

He followed her through the door and into the dimly lit shop. The front room was already full, with three other men sitting in small green overstuffed chairs, their feet being kneaded by two girls and one wiry boy. They passed by them, and the girl led him to another room down the main hall. She beckoned him toward the row of three blue chairs, and he chose the one on the end.

Jun sat down and removed his shoes and socks. The girl took them and put them in a cubbyhole located on the wall. She pointed to the tiny television mounted behind her. "*Dianshi ma?*"

"No, I just want peace and quiet for a few minutes," Jun answered.

The girl disappeared and returned a minute later with a large bucket of scalding water. She directed him to put his feet in. Despite his first reaction to pull them out because of the scorching heat, he suffered through until it began to feel soothing. While his feet soaked, the girl stood beside him and kneaded the knots in his neck.

"You are very tense."

"You don't know the half of it." He closed his eyes, relishing the painful pleasure her fingers were causing.

"So what is the matter? Hard day at work?"

Jun opened one eye and looked at the girl. She had moved back in front of him and sat on the stool in front of his chair. She picked his left foot out of the bucket and wrapped it in a steaming towel and set it in front of her. Then she did the same with his right. She stood up and gently laid a steaming towel around his neck. Then she returned to her seat and unwrapped his foot and began to massage it.

"I always have a hard day at work—but that's not why I'm so tense."

"So talk." She expertly massaged his foot, using her middle knuckle to find the pressure point in the center of his sole.

"*Aiyo*...too hard." Jun pulled his foot toward himself, and the girl yanked it back and laughed.

"Wife troubles?" she asked.

"For such a young girl, you are very nosy, do you know that? What happened to just letting me relax?" He leaned his head back and shut his eyes, thinking of Wei and how far south their marriage had gone since Chai's disappearance.

"You are my last customer, so I can talk. And I'm nineteen—not a young girl." Her forehead wrinkled, then cleared. "Oh, I know. The girl in the picture. You're upset because you cannot find her. Who is she?"

Jun sighed. "My daughter, Chai. She disappeared and I'm trying to find her."

"How old is she?"

"She's thirteen. Wait, she's fourteen now." His heart lurched when he remembered that an entire year plus some had passed.

"Where was she last seen? I hear there are a lot of girls disappearing from around here—probably taken to the big cities or something."

"She and her best friend were walking home from my work site. They would've had to pass within a few blocks of here. But I doubt they would have ventured too far off the path, because her friend has problems walking long distances."

"Oh? What kind of problems?"

Jun rolled his eyes. Every time he answered the girl, she popped out another question. He was much too tired to dissect this again with someone who couldn't help him.

"Josi was born with one leg much shorter than the other. It puts pressure on her hips, and she walks with a very pronounced limp. She tires easily."

The girl instantly stopped rubbing his foot.

Jun looked up at her. "What?"

"Did you say they were together when they disappeared?"

"Yes, that's what I said. Why?"

The girl started rubbing his foot again. "Oh, never mind. Probably just a coincidence. It's nothing."

"What's nothing? Something is not nothing. Anything is something." He sat up and jerked his foot out of her grasp.

"What? You're talking in riddles, *lao ren*." She reached for his foot again but he put them both on the floor, out of her reach.

"Tell me what you just thought of. Let me decide if it's nothing."

The girl sighed. "Okay, fine. Many months ago, my grand-mother came home and told me that she saw a couple of girls being led into an empty apartment building not far from here. She said one of them was limping along, looking pitiful."

Jun was instantly alert. "Where was this? What did the other girl look like?"

"I don't know what they looked like! And it was at the apart-ment complex that hired my grandmother to sweep their parking lot. She doesn't work there now. Her arthritis has gotten too bad."

"Where? Take me there! Take me to your grandmother." Jun jumped up and quickly crossed the room to look for his shoes in the cabinet.

"Wait! I have to finish your massage, or I will have to stay for one more customer."

Jun opened his wallet and threw a fifty-yuan note at her. "Here. Take me to your grandmother." He stood waiting, shifting from foot to foot impatiently.

The girl stood up and grabbed the pail of water and towels. "You're going to have to wait until I clean my station. Then I'll get my coat and take you to speak to my grandmother, but it was probably nothing."

Jun put on his socks and shoes and then watched her impatiently, tapping his fingernails on the doorframe and silently urging her to hurry. He felt a ripple of hope, and he wanted to hang on to it as long as possible.

* * *

The girl, Ruju, poured him another cup of green tea and sat down with him at the small table. Jun wrapped his hands around the mug, relishing the warmth. The room she had led him to was over the massage shop and was bitterly cold.

"So, this daughter of yours, why was she running around town, anyway? You said she was seen not far from here. This isn't a good area, you know?"

"I didn't say she was seen around here. I said she was *near* here. She came to see me at work to ask if she could go swimming." Jun didn't like her insinuation that he was a negligent parent. "If it's so bad, what are you doing working down there?"

The girl hesitated. She lowered her eyes and began picking at her nails. "I don't have much choice. My parents left me with my grandmother when I was three. They went to work in Ningde and never came back. *Nai Nai* says they sent money for a while, but when it stopped coming, we had to find a way to survive. *Nai Nai* used to live downstairs, but when the businessmen started opening their massage shops on the street, I talked her into doing the same. Except ours is legitimate—we only offer foot massages and none of that other creepy stuff. *Nai Nai* will shut us down before she allows any of that in her house."

Jun frowned. The girl obviously was a smart one. He felt sorry that she had been forced into an industry she wouldn't have chosen if life hadn't dealt her an unfair hand. But then he knew many families who participated in unsavory careers just to survive. It didn't always mean they were bad people, after all.

His thoughts were interrupted by stomping on the stairs. An old woman stumbled in, a flurry of gray in her long dress and scarf. She pulled up a stool and sat in front of Jun.

"What is it you want?" she asked, looking from him to her granddaughter.

"Your granddaughter—Ruju—was telling me that many months ago you saw a strange encounter with two girls. They were being led into an apartment or something? Can you tell me about that?"

Ruju smiled at him as she picked at her cuticles, as if she knew he was speaking slowly and more patiently than he actually felt, just for the benefit of her old grandmother.

"Nah. I don't know what you are talking about." The old woman chugged her tea down and held the cup out for Ruju to fill it again.

"*Nai Nai*, remember, you told me that it was strange, because a woman took two girls up to an apartment in a building that hadn't been finished yet. Yet you said she left without them."

The old woman squinted her eyes and looked at the ceiling, as if her memory were located up there amid the cobwebs. "When?" she grumbled.

Jun waited. He felt like shaking the old woman but knew it wouldn't get him anywhere.

"The place you were working at, *Nai Nai*. Remember, you said one girl limped really badly. You said it reminded you of your niece."

Jun reached into his pocket and withdrew his wallet. He pulled fifty yuan from it and laid it in on the table.

The old woman smiled as she grabbed the bill and stuffed it in her pocket. "Oh, yeah...I remember now."

"*Nai Nai!*" Ruju's cheeks flushed until they matched the scarf around her neck. "He already gave me—"

Looking intensely at the grandmother, Jun held his hand up to interrupt the girl. "Can you take me there?" He stood, unable to sit quietly any longer.

The old woman shook her head stubbornly. "No, I'm not going anywhere else in this cold tonight, but if you have a phone, I can call the man who owns the building. My granddaughter told you I used to work there. I even know what apartment that was—I remember, you see, because later that night I saw those girls tapping on the window at me. I can even tell you what they were wearing. You see? I'm not senile. I still have my wits about me."

She cackled at her own joke, showing a mouth full of darkened teeth stained with tobacco. Jun had no doubt she had a memory like an elephant and could probably tell him what she'd had for breakfast way back in the Cultural Revolution.

"You saw them tapping at the window, and you didn't call the police?" Jun threw his hands in the air. "Why?"

The old woman gave him a stern look. "When you are old like me, you mind your own business, that's why. Now do you want me to call him, or do you want to leave and let me be?"

Jun groaned and pulled his cell phone from his pocket.

CHAPTER THIRTY-THREE

"Chai, stop pulling so hard! *Aiyo*, you are killing me." Mother struggled to loosen the bandage gouging into her sore abdomen as Chai pulled the end of it even tighter.

"You heard what that old hag said. If we don't pull it tight enough, your belly won't be flat; instead you'll have a jelly belly like Lao Chan. Is that what you want?"

"No. Pull it." Mother sighed as she once again planted her feet wide apart to try to be ready for Chai's tugging. "I should be used to this; I've sure had to wear it enough over the years."

I can tell it, too, thought Chai as she grimaced at the ragged and stained material in her hands. They ought to at least invest in a new one after each child.

Together they worked to get the bandage just right, a difficult accomplishment considering it was more than ten meters long and at least forty centimeters wide. Chai couldn't erase the mischievous expression from her face as she gave it one final jerk just for good measure.

Josi watched from the doorway, a small smile on her lips at Chai's antics as she waited to be called in to brush and braid Mother's hair.

"Maybe we should let you stay fat so you'll stop making babies." Chai stood panting from her exertion, hands on her hips. She really didn't think the woman was fat, but it was fun teasing her.

"Don't be silly, Chai. Lao Chan will still want to make babies whether I am fat or not. I have a few years left to give him another son or two."

Chai rolled her eyes at the back of Mother's head as the woman slowly waddled over to her bed to sit down and waved Josi over to start on her hair. Since her mother-in-law had canceled her visit a week before, she had gotten even more dependent on them.

"Josi, you can come do her hair now. Good luck." The hair was another source of bickering between Chai and Mother, for it hadn't been washed in weeks. Chai refused to touch it.

Josi quietly went to the bed and sat down behind the woman. She began brushing the hair back to pull it together for a braid.

Chai wasn't quite done giving Mother a hard time. "If I'd have known you were going to go weeks without clean hair, I wouldn't have suggested you grow it out long."

Mother wiped the sweat from her forehead. "Okay, Chai. Enough. I'm so hot today—and I feel a bit nauseous. I think I may be coming down with something."

"You're fine, Mother, I told you—you are just too fat. Anyway, I don't understand how you can have all these babies; isn't it against the law?" Chai wanted to bring up the possibility that Mother might produce even another daughter, but she didn't want to get her too riled up before asking her if she could have a few hours off to go to the mainland. She was hoping to sneak a visit in to see how Zee was doing. So far, since asking her to take the baby away three weeks before, Mother was giving Chai a lot more freedom without questions, but Chai had only been able to make one other trip to see Zee. Though Chai wished she could see her more often, she was pacified by the fact that at the visit Zee looked to be strong and happy—and was being totally spoiled by everyone around her, especially her new *jie jie*, Lin.

"We don't register all the children—only Bo and Tao are documented and have a *hukou*. The family planning office also gives us villagers some flexibility. They know we need to have extra hands to bring in the farming or fishing. It just depends on what official is currently over the area and if they are willing to work with the people to smooth the way. If we get unlucky, we just give more money until the wheels are oiled enough for them to forget. The ones that come after the older boys will not be able to attend school, but that's a fair exchange for building our family line. What good is school anyway for a bunch of fishermen? They learn everything they need to know from their father."

"Well, where are you going to put more children? This house is already too small for your family. I hope you don't think they're going to bunk down with Josi and me. Oh, never mind, old man Chan would never let his sons freeze in our tiny shed. They must be coddled like princes."

"Chai, you're getting way too mouthy for your own good. You'd better be thankful to have a roof over your head and food in your belly. And one day, you'll be married to my finest son."

Chai bent her face to hide the fire in her eyes as she mumbled to herself that she had once had a better roof and tastier food in her belly before she had been stolen.

Mother pretended not to hear.

CHAPTER THIRTY-FOUR

"Oh, oh! I'm dying."

Chai rolled her eyes at the ceiling and prayed for patience. "You aren't going to die, Mother. You only have a virus of some sort. Once your fever breaks, you'll be fine."

Mother tried to slap her hand away but gave up. "Yesterday you said I didn't feel well because I was too fat. Today you admit I have a fever. Which is it, Chai?"

Chai ignored her rambling. She dipped the cloth back into the pan of water, wrung it out, and laid it across Mother's forehead again. Her back ached. She had been up and down for hours nursing the woman and longed to close her eyes. "I told you being exiled to this room for so long wasn't good for you. It made you fragile. No wonder you caught a flu bug."

Josi had covered all the other chores for the day, allowing her to focus on Mother. The woman refused to allow anyone but Chai into the bedroom with her. She said that Josi was weak and would only make her worse, and she didn't want Lao Chan to see her looking so wretched, so he was camped out with the others in the living room, where he'd moved the television.

"Mother, it's way past midnight, and I need to go back to my room and sleep. I'll be back to check on you first thing in the morning."

Mother struggled to push up to her elbows, causing the wet cloth to fall from her forehead. "No. I want you to stay. Please don't go."

Chai sighed. "Mother, you'll be fine. Josi doesn't like to sleep alone. How about if I come and check on you in a few hours? If I don't get some rest, I won't be able to care for you tomorrow—"

"No, Chai. I'm begging you; don't leave me. You know Zhongfu won't send the boys in here. He's too afraid they won't be able to work if they get sick. No one will come if I call out. Josi knows I'm sick; she'll understand. I swear to you, if you don't stay, when I am well, I'll make you regret it."

Chai knew only too well that Mother would stand by her threat. She'd probably withhold food other than rice for a week. Still, she didn't want to leave Josi alone all night. She debated about what to do as Mother watched her carefully.

"Fine. I'll stay. But only until three o'clock, and then I'm going to wake up Tao to come in here so I can go back to Josi. Lao Chan will be good and asleep by that time, so he'll never know." She didn't mention that the old man had consumed an entire bottle of *bai jiu* and was more than asleep—he was passed out cold with the television blaring out a late-night soap opera. Chai didn't know how the boys were able to rest with the racket, but obviously, it had lulled them to sleep.

Chai held up the cup of warm water and urged Mother to take a few sips. "I hope you're better by tomorrow. I heard on the radio that Typhoon Keso might bring some heavy rain and wind our way. I definitely can't leave Josi to sleep out there alone in a storm."

Mother lay back down, and Chai readjusted the cloth again. She swiped a few pillows from the bed and laid them on the floor, then lay down.

"Chai, you can get a blanket from the chest at the end of my bed." Mother sounded much more pitiful than she should have, in Chai's opinion.

Chai got up and crossed over to the chest. She opened it, and the first thing she saw was the blue receiving blanket Zee had been wrapped in after she made her entrance to the world. Chai had wondered where it was. Feeling a touch of compassion for the mother who was probably silently missing her newborn, she moved it aside and pulled out a thick blanket.

"Mother, how come you have never asked me where I took your baby girl?"

The woman was quiet for a moment. Then she turned over and faced the wall, giving Chai all the answer she was going to give. "Good night, Chai."

Chai sighed as she returned to the pillows on the floor and groaned as she lay down—her back really ached. She spread the blanket over her body, tucking it in all around her to fight against the cold draft she felt along the floor. She planned on staying awake, but before she knew it, she was snoring lightly, exhausted from her day of playing nursemaid.

* * *

Josi tossed and turned on their pallet, wishing for the hundredth time that Chai would come to bed. She was cold, and because she was afraid to turn off the lantern, she couldn't go to sleep. *If Mother would stop being such a baby, I wouldn't have to be out here alone.*

Finally, giving up on getting any rest, she pulled out the book that she and Chai had started the night before. She knew Chai would not like that Josi was reading on without her, but she had to do something to pass the time until she could go to sleep. After just a few pages, she heard a light knock on the door. Mother had ceased locking them in after Zee's birth, and knowing Chai would have just come in, she realized who it was.

"Go away, Tao," she whispered. "Chai is still with your mother."

While she would have loved to have his company, she was still too shy to visit with Tao without Chai there to help keep conversation going. It also wasn't proper to have a boy in her room with her alone, and Tao would understand that.

He knocked again, more insistently.

"Tao!" she hissed. "Go away—you're going to wake everyone up and get me in trouble!"

She knew Tao wouldn't enter the room without permission, so she was startled when the door slowly opened, allowing a sliver of moonlight to sneak through.

"What are you—" Her question was cut off when Bo stepped through the door, a sneaky grin on his face, his blue fishing cap pulled down low just above his eyes.

"Ha. You thought I was Tao, huh? Did you think I didn't know he's been coming out here and messing around with you girls? I'm not stupid."

"Uh, wh—what do you mean?" Josi was terrified. She had never been alone with Bo before and couldn't imagine what he wanted. She hoped he couldn't see her begin to tremble. She also didn't want to admit anything about Tao's visits. He would be in big trouble, and his visits were the only highlights of her boring life.

"I've seen the way he looks at you two. And the way you and your bossy sister flirt with him. You treat him nice, but you look at me like I am dirt under your long, ugly feet."

"Bo! What are you talking about? My *sister*? Leave my room right now, or I'm going to scream!"

Bo dropped to his knees and immediately clamped one arm around Josi's neck, with his hand over her mouth. He grabbed her sweatshirt and with one quick move, ripped it open down the front, exposing her breasts.

Josi screamed and fought to get away but he threw her down and straddled her body. He leaned in close enough that his hot breath made the hairs on her neck stand up. When she felt his tongue on her throat she struggled harder, kicking but making contact with nothing but blankets.

He was all over her, and Josi felt nauseated from the strong smell of fish that emanated from his pores. She was light-headed from the lack of air but not ready to give up. She clawed at his hands, but his grip was too strong.

He growled through his teeth as he struggled to unbutton his trousers. "I'm going to teach you to go around tempting my little brother. You want to see what a real man is like? You're going to find out right now."

He reached down and grabbed her flaying hand, forcing it between his legs and holding it there tightly. "Feel that throb? That's a man, not a boy like Tao."

Josi kicked and yelled, desperate to be heard over the pounding rain and wind. She felt like her fingers would break, but she finally got her hand loose from his crotch and pushed against his chest with all her might, trying to move his unrelenting body off of hers.

Bo snarled in her face, his spittle flying into her eyes. "If I didn't think Baba would kill me, I'd have gotten Chai first. But you'll do, at least until they officially give her to me. You might be a cripple, but you've still got all your female parts, and you'd better be a virgin." He grabbed her hard between her legs to prove his point.

He clenched her so violently and the pain was so intense that a wave of dizziness overtook her. Bo took advantage of her hesitation to yank at her clothes. His brute strength overpowered her, and her body began to give up. When he ripped the blouse right off of her shoulders, she whimpered, too exhausted to cry out any more. Then she thought of her best friend asleep in the house only feet away.

Chai would never give up.

With a burst of energy, Josi kicked, making contact with Bo's groin.

He hunched over and grabbed himself. "You're going to pay for that!" he snarled as he lunged and grabbed her hair.

"No—please!"

Using his free hand, he struck her across the face. The blow was hard, and again she felt a wave of weakness, giving Bo another opportunity to sprawl over her squirming body and get into position again. With one hand he pulled his erection free from his pants and frantically tried to guide himself between Josi's splayed legs.

"No, Bo, please, stop!" Josi begged, crying loudly.

The door flung open. "Bo! What are you doing?" Tao stood in the opening, his eyes wide with shock.

"Tao!" Josi cried, kicking and flailing. "Help me!"

Bo's thick arms held her down as he turned to Tao with a menacing sneer. "Get. Out."

Rage filled Tao's eyes. "The hell I will! Get off her right now, Bo!"

Bo continued his tug-of-war with Josi's clothes. A large rip sounded as her trousers and panties came off in his fist, exposing her to both boys. "We—bought—her. I can use—her!" He huffed through each word, never relenting in his struggle to make her cooperate.

Tao dived for Bo, knocking the breath out of Josi. She rolled out from under them and ran to the door, crouching to cover her naked body. She yanked at one of their blankets until she freed it from the fray and wrapped it around herself. Even more than the pain of the beating, she felt mortified that Tao had seen her naked. She looked out the door but decided not to run for the house. She was too afraid to go for help, sure that Lao Chan would blame her. Tears ran down her face as she grabbed clothing from the corner and struggled to pull it on and catch her breath.

"Damn—you—Bo!" Tao used too much energy to cuss at his brother and not enough to get the upper hand. They wrestled, trying to overcome one another.

"*Tamade!*" Bo cursed, now out of breath and heaving hard. He finally maneuvered himself on top of Tao, pummeling his face. He outweighed his little brother by at least fifty pounds and used his weight as an anchor. Still barefoot but at least semi-dressed, Josi cried harder and the two continued to fight viciously. Tao showed signs of slowing down, terrifying Josi even more. Bo might kill his own brother if he didn't stop punching him. The fury on his face suggested they could be the last few breaths Tao would ever take.

"Stop! I'm going to go get Lao Chan if you don't stop!"

Josi was too afraid to really go after the old man. She looked around desperately for anything to use as a weapon. Their ceramic toilet bowl sat in the corner, and she ran for it. Bo saw her only a split second before she tried to crash the bowl on his head. He rolled left, tipping over the crate they used as a table, loaded with books and the lantern. The bowl shattered, and the spilled kerosene ignited the bedding.

Bo went back to pummeling Tao as Josi screamed at them to stop, her cries drowned out by the wind and rain, but still she tried.

"Stop! Please—please stop…" Josi sobbed. She jumped on Bo's back and wrapped both her arms around his neck and squeezed.

Shocked at the sudden heat from the fire and another set of arms in the fray, Bo hesitated long enough for Tao to slip out from under him.

Coughing and choking, Tao stood up, pulled his leg back, and let loose, kicking Bo's nose with the heel of his shoe.

A sickening sharp crack filled the room and Bo fell face-first onto the pallet. Other than Tao's ragged breathing, silence filled the room until Josi sprang into action.

"Tao! What are we going to do? Oh my God—did you kill him?"

"Get some water, quick!" Tao yelled. He grabbed Bo's legs and pulled him out of the room and onto the deck.

"Tao, wh—what are you doing?" She was afraid to hear his answer. She was seeing things. *This isn't really happening.*

Tao stopped at the edge of the deck. Bo stirred and slowly opened his eyes.

Tao kicked him again. "You've beat up on your last victim, Bo." He pulled his leg back to give another kick and Bo caught his foot in midair, jerking Tao off his feet. Tao fell on his hind end. The fight was on again.

"Stop!" Josi hissed. "You're going to wake up Lao Chan!"

They wrestled closer to the edge, and Bo tried to get to his feet. Tao shoved Bo, and he slipped on the wet deck. He waved his arms around like a windmill in an attempt to regain his balance before falling backward into the bay. A loud splash broke the night air.

"Now. You can cool off in there," Tao slurred, his breath coming in short pants. He bent over and put his hands on his knees as he struggled to breathe. He shook his hair like a wet dog as he tried to clear the water from his eyes.

Josi stood in the pouring rain and watched Bo splash while he tried to reach the edge of the platform and pull himself up. "He was going to rape me," she mumbled.

Tao ran back to Josi and put his hands on her shoulders, then shook her.

"Josi. Snap out of it. I don't want this fire to get out of control. Hurry. Get the hose."

Without a word, Josi ran for the hose that was hooked to the side of the house. She pointed it at the doorway to their room and unclenched the vise that was used to cut off the flow. The water began to spurt inside the structure. Even though the rain was coming down in sheets, she knew there was still a chance the decking could catch fire. She thought about the boys sleeping in the house and knew she didn't want that to happen.

"Tao, what about Bo? Are you going to help him up?"

Tao took the hose from her and moved closer to the inside of the shed. "Bo can get himself out of the water—maybe by then he'll have settled down."

The small fire was out in a few short minutes, and Josi turned around to see where Bo was. She didn't see him anywhere. "Did he get out of the water?"

Tao turned around. "I don't know. I was busy helping you, but I heard him splashing just a minute ago."

Tao dropped the hose, and they both ran to the edge of the deck and peered over the side. Bo was nowhere to be seen.

"Tao, where is he?" Josi turned all the way around, looking in every direction for Bo. "Tao, answer me!"

Tao stayed on his knees, staring into the dark water toward a trail of bubbles lingering on the surface. He stared a minute longer, not saying a word or even looking at Josi.

Josi went to the room that had at the least become a private sanctuary for her and Chai, but it was now nothing but a charred mess. Nothing could be salvaged. She began to shake violently again. Her mind was not able to take in everything that had happened in the last few minutes. How could she look Mother in the face when she had stood by as her son sank to the bottom of the bay? Even if he was a cruel bully, he was still her son—her favorite son, no less.

She returned to the deck. "Tao? Did Bo drown? Please tell me he got back up?"

Finally, Tao turned to her. "Get in the boat, Josi."

"The boat?" She looked at the sampan and then back to him, confused. "Why?"

Tao picked up his extra fishing boots and tossed them toward Josi. He reached into their room and quickly picked up the remains of her ripped clothing, tossing them into the water where they immediately began to sink from the weight of the pelting rain. He grabbed her coat from the mess inside and dropped it into the tied-up sampan, his expression sadder than she'd ever seen it. "You have to go."

CHAPTER THIRTY-FIVE

Chai struggled to open her eyes. Faintly she heard someone moving about the room. She sat up and rubbed at her neck, looking around.

"Well, *zao shang hao*, Chai." Mother stood over the bed, folding her blanket, and woke Chai with a greeting of good morning.

"Ugh. I slept here all night?"

"You sure did, and thank goodness I didn't need you any more last night. I don't think I could have woken you."

"Have you seen Josi? She's going to be so mad at me. I bet she barely slept at all. Is it still storming?"

"It's only five o'clock, and it's still raining. No one has stirred yet, but Zhongfu should be getting up any time to head out for the day with the boys, unless the weather reports have gotten worse. And yes—I feel a lot better, thank you for asking," she added.

"What do you want from me? I took care of you all day yesterday and half the night!" Chai was sore and grumpy and didn't feel like catering to Mother that morning, even if she did have to lose her supper privileges.

"Get up and start making breakfast, that's what I want. You think you're getting a morning off just because you—"

A piercing scream filled the house, shocking Chai and Mother into silence. Chai jumped to her feet and ran out of the room, Mother right behind her.

In the living room, the two little boys sat up in their pallet, startled and looking around them to find the source of the noise. Chai and Mother ran by them and out the door. On the deck, they found Lao Chan struggling to pull Tao from the bay. He barely looked conscious, but he was alive.

Mother shrieked and threw her arms in the air. "What happened?"

Chai ran to help Lao Chan pull Tao all the way onto the wooden deck. "Tao, are you okay? What happened?"

Chai turned his head to the side as he coughed water up. The bruises along his entire face made his mother gasp. Chai turned to look at the open door to their room. "Where's Josi?"

Then her eyes landed on the charred remains of their blankets and books. "*Josi!* Where is Josi, Tao? There's been a fire? Where is she?"

Lao Chan pushed Chai away from his son. "I found him in the water, barely holding on to the side. That useless girl is not here—neither is Bo. Shut up so he can get his breath and tell us what happened out here."

Chai frantically ran around the floating home, checking all over for Josi. She wasn't anywhere to be found. She quickly scanned the other houses, but she found only a few gawkers, no one that looked like Josi or Bo.

Tao got to his knees and coughed and spit water. "They're gone."

"What do you mean, they're gone?" Lao Chan demanded. Mother stood behind him, wringing her hands and pacing back and forth, the rain plastering her hair to her head.

"They're gone! I came out because I heard a noise, and I saw them getting into the small boat. I tried to stop them, and Bo hit me across the face with the oar, knocking me into the water. He must have given me a concussion because I blacked out, and when I woke up I couldn't get the strength to climb back up. I've barely been holding on for hours."

"Why would they leave? This doesn't make sense." Mother looked around, muttering to herself, for she knew that her eldest son wouldn't just up and leave, especially with the less favorable of the two girls.

"What are you saying, boy?" Lao Chan shook Tao's shoulder, his anger building to an explosive level. The two youngest boys ran to hide behind their mother's legs.

Tao refused to look his father in the eye. He waved his hands in the air toward the water. "I'm saying they ran away! I tried to stop them; I did!"

His father wrinkled his brow. "Ran away? Why would Bo run away? With the crippled one? *Aiyo*...I don't believe it!"

In frustration, Chai stopped in front of Tao and slapped him across the face. "You know Josi wouldn't run away with that pig! Stop lying and tell me where she is. Now!" Tao was hiding something—Chai could feel that he knew more about where Josi was or what had happened. She struggled to stand tall, though her head was spinning and she felt faint. Her fear for Josi was paralyzing. She felt her usual energy sap away until she had to lean against the shed just to continue standing.

"I'm telling the truth." He looked at Chai, trying to convey with his eyes what he couldn't say aloud.

Lao Chan pushed her aside. "How did this fire get started, and who put it out?"

"*Wo bu zhi dao*, Baba. I told you. I heard a noise and came out to see what it was, but the room was already like this, and they were climbing in the boat. I guess Bo put it out—but I don't know what started it, and I don't know where they were going."

CHAPTER THIRTY-SIX

Jun flicked his cigarette into the dirt and paused in front of the door to his house. Finally he had something. Even if it turned out to be a false lead, it was at least somewhere to start. His heart felt lighter, and though he still carried a heavy sadness, he finally had a glimmer of hope to pursue.

He turned the door handle and walked in.

He wanted to wait until Luci was asleep before talking to Wei about the old woman he had met, but the spot where Chai's books usually were caught his attention—especially evident, because it was a now-empty clean spot in the middle of the dusty table. He looked around and saw that Chai's clothes no longer hung on the metal bar with everyone else's. He looked down beside the door, and his fears were confirmed: her small red house slippers were gone.

"Luci, where are your sister's books? And her other things?" He had made it clear before that he wanted all of her stuff to stay where it belonged, so that when she returned she would know they had not forgotten her. Her books were her most prized possessions, and Jun knew that wherever she was, she had to be wishing they were with her.

Luci looked at her father with wide eyes. "I don't know. Ask Mama."

Wei was at the counter, dipping soup into bowls, and didn't turn.

"Wei? Where are Chai's books?"

No answer came. Only the stiffening of her shoulders indicated she had heard his question.

He strode across the floor and grabbed Wei's shoulder to pull her around and face him. She dropped the bowl she was filling, and the crack of the pottery hitting the floor was like a discharged bullet in the quiet room. The brown soup seeped across the uneven floor, traveling down a deep groove like it was following a tributary to a river. Wei stared at it, not moving or even looking at her husband.

"Wei. I asked you a question: Where are Chai's books and the rest of her things?"

Wei sighed loudly. "I still have the books—they're in the trunk for Luci when she can read them herself. I gave away her clothes and slippers. I don't want Luci to ever wear them."

"Don't be ridiculous. What about when Chai comes back? What will she think?"

Wei went to the edge of her bed and sat down, lowered her face in her hands, and began crying.

Jun threw his hands in the air in frustration. "Why won't you talk to me about her? Chai is your daughter. She is still out there somewhere. Going through God only knows what!"

He paced the floor, waiting for his wife to stop her sobbing and answer him. He was glad to at least witness some emotion from her. For months, she had refused to speak of their eldest daughter and would leave the room, her face set in stone, whenever he mentioned her.

Luci huddled in her bed, listening intently while she clutched her doll.

Wei sat up straight and glared at Jun. "Because I can't! I don't want to think about what could be happening to her—if she is cold or hungry, being beaten or…or…worse. Don't you understand? I cannot put myself there; it is too agonizing. It has been over a year, Jun! And you're making me hate you because you won't allow me to forget!"

Jun went to Wei and knelt on the floor in front of her. He took her shaking hands in his, his eyes pleading with her to understand.

"Wei, we cannot forget her. We are her only chance, and she is waiting for us to find her. " He swallowed past the lump in his throat. "I can't fail her again. Wei, I have something to tell you. I found a woman who may have seen the girls that day. She led me to an apartment she thought she saw them enter the day they disappeared. It's empty now, but I have traced the person who rented it, and I know where her home village is. I have a name, Wei! I have something!"

Wei looked at him, confused. "But how do you know it was the girls? It could have been anyone. How do you know? Since Chai left, there have been many people telling me stories of missing girls who are never found again."

"Wei, Chai didn't *leave*. She was taken. The woman said she saw two girls, about the same age as Chai and Josi, and one of them walked with a strong limp. She said the next day she remembers them tapping on the window to get her attention, but she was afraid of the owner so she didn't respond." He didn't mention the only part of the story that didn't fit—that the girls were wearing bright-colored dresses. He knew they hadn't been wearing dresses that day, but he didn't want to let that detail deter him and decided to keep it to himself. "I have to go find the woman, and her home is at least a week of travel from here."

Wei's sudden intake of breath was loud, but she didn't respond.

"Please, Wei. Let me do this, and if I come back without her, then I will work on letting it go. But I have to try. Lao Tzu tells us that 'A journey of a thousand miles must begin with a single step.' This might be the lead we've been waiting for. Can't you see? It is my fault she's gone. I told her she could go to the canal that day. If I had told her to go straight home, she would never have disappeared. I'm her father—I was supposed to protect her, and I failed." Jun stood and turned away from his wife.

Luci pulled her covers back and crept over to stand in front of her parents. "Baba. Go find my *jie jie*. Please find her." She burst into tears and crumpled to the floor.

Jun gently picked her up and sat on the chair with her cradled in his lap, rocking her back and forth. "Now, now, Luci. *Bu ku le.*" He told her not to cry as he used his hand to wipe the tears from her cheek.

Luci's anguish cut him right to the heart, for he knew she had been holding it in for so long. She was too much like her mother, usually refusing to show her emotions. It hadn't gone unnoticed by him that Chai's disappearance had made their usually rambunctious daughter afraid to even go outside alone. He knew she was silently suffering as much or maybe more than he, but it was hard for him to comfort her while his own pain was so overpowering. It was sad what their family had come to—each of them shutting the others out and wallowing alone in their grief.

Wei stood and turned away as her own tears began to slide down her face. "Fine. Go. When you come back without her and we've lost everything because we cannot pay our bills, then don't complain to me. I guess we'll have to sleep with Shen's pigs."

"I would rather lose it all than give up on finding Chai." Jun carried Luci to her bed, tucked her in, and kissed her on her forehead. He gave his wife one last look and opened the door to go sit in his usual sentry post. "I'll leave in the morning, Wei. When I return, with or without her, I want to see all of Chai's things put back exactly where they should be. If you gave them away, you'd better get them back."

As the door closed behind him, Wei walked past the mess in the floor, past the dirty dishes, and went straight to her daughter. She crawled under the covers, filling the empty spot still left for Chai each night. She pulled Luci close and buried her face in the sweet little-girl smell of her hair.

As she drifted off to sleep, her voice was a whisper in the room, pleading quietly over and over, *"Please find her. Please find her."*

CHAPTER THIRTY-SEVEN

Chai sat on the charred remains of her bedding with her arms wrapped around her legs, her chin resting on her knees. She'd stayed that way for hours. After they'd pulled Tao from the bay and he had told them about Bo and Josi running away, Lao Chan had slapped her and accused her of somehow being a part of all of it. She was a mess. She was terrified for Josi, her cheek throbbed, and her pride stung because he had thrown her in the shed and locked the door. No one had yet returned to let her out. Even if she had wanted to, she couldn't read; all their books had been ruined by the smoke and water. So Chai sat and listened to the heavy rain, thinking about the disaster her life had become.

She should have been hungry considering she hadn't eaten since the day before, but she wasn't. More than anything, she was sick to her stomach, worried for Josi, and wondering what had happened. She didn't care what Tao said; she knew that Josi would never run away with Bo. They hated him, constantly talking about how mean he was. They couldn't wait to find a way to leave the fishing village, especially to avoid the plan of Chai marrying Bo one day. They had both said they'd rather die than become a bride to someone like him.

Chai thought she heard the splash of oars in the water and rushed to the door. She knelt on her hands and knees, peering under the crack.

"I'm going to kill that girl!" She heard Lao Chan's thunderous voice and felt the structure move beneath her as he climbed from his boat to the deck. She jumped up, scared of what he was going to do. *Who is he talking about? Me? Josi? It has to be one of us.*

Chai heard the door slam and Mother's voice. "Zhongfu! No! Do not touch her again! Chai was with me all night, lying right beside me. She could not have had anything to do with this."

Chai kept silent, and she saw Mother's slippered feet under the crack of the door, as if she had put herself between Lao Chan and the shed.

"Dead—he's dead! Our son is dead!" Lao Chan thundered, and Chai heard buckets and other items being kicked out of his way.

Mother began to wail. "What do you mean, dead? Bo can't be dead! You heard Tao. He left with Josi!"

Chai heard him say that Bo was found dead and she froze, too shocked to move or speak. If Bo was dead—what did that mean for Josi? She closed her eyes to stop the sudden tears.

"You stupid woman! I told you we couldn't keep both of these girls. Now the crippled one has killed our son. I have seen it with my own eyes—someone found him floating in the bay only an hour ago. I just saw his body. They have pulled him in and covered him."

Mother's wailing increased, then hushed.

"You are a liar. My son is not dead." Her voice took on a low, deadly tone.

Chai heard the lock being taken from the door. She stepped all the way to the back, crossing her arms over her body for protection. Mother jerked the door open, and Mother and Lao Chan both glared at Chai.

Chai saw the murderous look in Lao Chan's eyes and tensed, wondering if now was finally the time he'd follow through on his many threats of violence.

Lao Chan stepped forward and grabbed her arm. He yanked her out of the shed and shook her. "What happened? Tell us!" In his anger, spittle flew from his mouth and dripped from his chin. Chai struggled to get free from the excruciating grip of his fingers.

Beside him, shivering under a tattered umbrella, Mother stood crying and shaking her head from side to side as if to say, "No, no, no."

"I—I don't know, Lao Chan. Please, tell me. Did you see Josi?" Chai was scared for herself but more terrified that they had also found Josi floating in the bay.

Mother turned to her husband and between sobs asked, "Well? Was the girl there, too?" Mother held her hands around her stomach as if she was suddenly in a lot of pain. Then with unusual bravery, she reached out and slapped at her husband's hand until he released Chai.

Tao came from the house and stood beside his mother, looking at his father for an answer.

"No. Only our son. And his face—it was beaten." For the first time, Lao Chan looked weak and defeated as he dropped to his knees and cradled his face in his hands. His loud sobs sent chills down Chai's spine.

Mother went to him and knelt with him as their smallest sons joined them. She reached up and pulled two handfuls of hair from her own head, rocking back and forth on her knees as she wailed. At this the little boys were even more terrified, and soon the four of them were all crying. Tao and Chai stood nearby, their expressions as solemn as soldiers' as they watched the drama unfold.

Chai looked around at the other houses and saw neighbors as far as she could see, standing and staring at their unfolding drama. To the people on the water their sudden tragedies were nothing but a welcome break in the monotony of boring days. If they held any true concern, it was for Bo, the eldest so most revered child of the Chan family. No one even considered Josi. They didn't know who she was or what she meant to Chai—what she meant to her family. Suddenly too weak to stand herself, Chai dropped to her knees on the deck.

"Oh, where is Josi. Where is she?" She began to cry into her own hands as Tao remained standing silently in front of her. She could feel him above her and knew he didn't move when she fell. She wanted to strike out at him but somehow controlled herself. Instead of standing there staring at her, she wanted him to hurt like she hurt, cry like she cried, and feel the sense of loss she felt. She didn't want to be alone in her grief. Most of all she didn't want to face the truth that she had failed to protect Josi.

CHAPTER THIRTY-EIGHT

Ruju turned to Jun and held out her hand. "Give me eighty yuan for the bus tickets to Xiapu. From there, we'll have to change buses to get to Sandu'ao. Near Sandu'ao, we'll climb the mountain to a small village where the woman who maybe had the girls is from."

Jun looked at Ruju doubtfully, wondering if he was getting scammed. The old woman had proved to be a huge help. After her call to the property owner, she had found out who had rented that apartment, and though he said it had been empty for months, the woman had gotten the man to tell her where the original renter was from.

Luckily for him, the old woman knew of the village and its exact location. She offered her granddaughter's services—for a small fee, of course—to escort him there to question the woman. Without some connection to the village the people surely would not tell him a thing, so he had felt forced to accept her offer. With the useless help he'd gotten from the police so far, this time, he was going to do the investigating himself. In person, but with Ruju as a mediator.

Ruju let out a long breath of exasperation. "Fine. Don't give me any money, and I can go back to work rubbing feet. You know I'm only doing this to ease my grandmother's conscience." She turned to walk away, indignant at his skeptical expression.

"Deng yi xia."

Ruju turned back around, crossing her arms impatiently. "I don't want to wait a minute. What do you want to do?"

Jun dug in his wallet and handed her a hundred-yuan note. It still sounded very expensive to him, but he rarely traveled anywhere, so he wasn't sure. Ruju walked up to the window and paid for two tickets. The attendant pointed over her shoulder, and Ruju turned. Both Jun and Ruju saw their bus at the same time. It looked like it was on its last leg, but what could he do? This was his best tip so far, and he was going to see it through.

They both sighed, picked up their bags, and climbed aboard the bus.

Jun looked for an empty seat for two, but the bus was already crammed with local people. One old woman, toothless and gray, smiled and patted the spot beside her. Jun walked on, holding his bag to his chest. Ruju slipped in beside the elderly lady and stuffed her bag on the shelf over their heads. She sat down and immediately became engrossed in her fingernails.

A few rows back, Jun found a seat being taken up by one small toddler. He moved in and sat next to the boy, sure that the boy would later disappear to find his mother, leaving Jun the entire seat to himself.

More people squeezed onto the bus, and Jun wondered where all of them were going to sit. A man carrying a bamboo pole with baskets dangling from each end sat opposite his seat and laid the pole and baskets down in the middle of the aisle, making it even more difficult for others to traverse. In his baskets were a variety of fruits, but he watched over them very carefully to ensure none were plucked out—a tedious chore, considering how many children were wandering around and climbing over the seats.

After an eventful loading of a small goat by one traveler, the driver finally shut the door and declared it was time to go. Jun was relieved when the boy beside him did exactly as he'd expected and ran along to find his mother, leaving Jun a bit of room to stretch out. He leaned his head against the window and stared at the passing scenery. Before he knew it, with his head bumping repetitively against the window, he was fast asleep.

* * *

Jun opened his eyes to find Ruju hovering over him, one hand shaking his shoulder. Next to him, an old woman sat, holding a basket of fresh oysters. She had obviously snagged a seat when he had closed his eyes. Jun wrinkled his nose at the overwhelming assault of the fishy aroma on his senses.

"Come on, Lao Jun. *Dao le.* We have arrived in Xiapu."

"Already?"

"Yes, already. It took almost three hours because of a problem with the gear shifting in the bus. And the roads are bad because it has been raining. You have slept the entire trip."

Jun stood and shook his head, trying to clear his grogginess. He knew he was tired, but he didn't think he was *that* exhausted. The atmosphere on the bus was so crowded and noisy that he couldn't believe he had slept so deeply. He picked his bag up off the floor and held it to his chest again. He shuffled behind Ruju, one painstakingly slow step at a time, behind about fourteen other people, until they were finally off the bus.

Jun waited on a bench near the attendant window of the bus stop while Ruju asked for new tickets to take them to Sandu'ao. She returned to sit beside him. "Lao Jun, there are no bus tickets to Sandu'ao until at least tomorrow because of the weather. We can stay in a local hotel tonight and leave in the morning."

Jun sighed. He was anxious to get to the village and ask the questions he hoped would lead to his daughter.

"Fine, Ruju. Before we do anything else, let's go eat some lunch."

They spotted a small noodle shop on the other side of the street and made their way across the small road. Inside they sat at a table near the window and waited for the server to take their order. The server finally arrived, and they guessed he was also the cook, judging by the spattered and stained white apron he wore around his middle and the sanitary cap over his head.

"*Ni hao.* What do you want to order today?" He pulled a notepad out of his apron pocket and reached for the pencil behind one of his overly large ears.

"What do you have special here?" Jun asked.

"*Yumian.* Fish noodles here are the best around."

"Okay, fish noodles it is. Two bowls, please."

The chef-waiter returned shortly with their steaming bowls and ceramic spoons. He set the dishes and spoons on the table and with a flourish of his hand, beckoning for them to start eating.

Jun was hungrier than he had first thought. Around his spoon he twisted the fresh seaweed that floated over his noodles and took a big bite. While he chewed the tasty green vegetable, he searched through his noodles but didn't find any bits of fish.

The chef waited beside their table. Jun figured he wanted their approval, but then the man spoke.

"Nori seaweed. And you won't see any fish in that bowl. It is minced and mixed in flour to make noodles," the chef said proudly and pointed at their bowls, then switched subjects again. "I saw you get off the bus. So, you want to go to Da Jing Ancient Village?" he asked, his eyebrows raised.

Ruju laughed. "*Bushi*. We are going to Sandu'ao in the morning, as soon as we can get bus tickets."

The man frowned. "Da Jing is a much better place to see. You can see the castle there that was built to fight the foul Japanese!" For emphasis, he made an unsettling noise in his throat and spit a large blob onto the floor in front of him. "For a small fee, my friend can show you some of the parts of it that still stand—though most of the stones were taken down and used for local houses."

Jun smiled uncomfortably; he didn't want to offend the man by appearing uncaring about their one claim to fame, but they needed to go. Any other time, he would have liked to see a part of ancient history—especially any involved with fighting the Japanese—but right now, he wanted to get to Sandu'ao and information about Chai.

"*Xie xie*, but no. We really need to get to Sandu'ao."

The man lifted his chin. "Then my friend will take you in his taxi. Only fifty yuan more than the bus. Each."

"No way, that is rob—"

"*Hao de*. We'll pay," Jun interrupted Ruju. He didn't relish the thought of getting back on another bus, so he was willing to pay the extra fare and didn't want to take the time to barter. "But we go now, not tomorrow." Mentally he counted how much money he had spent in the last few days, and he again hoped that Wei did not find out how much he had been taking from their dwindling savings account to fund his search.

Ruju shook her head.

"Fine, Lao Chan. If you want to be robbed, it's your money, not mine."

The chef-waiter looked out the window and gave a thumbs-up to a small, raggedly dressed man standing at the curb beside a tiny taxi. Basically just a small enclosure with benches built over a three-wheeled motorcycle, it was so beat-up that Jun wondered if it would really run.

"You know, tomorrow they say Typhoon Keso will visit Sandu'ao." The chef pushed his thumbs through his belt loops and hiked his pants up higher, showing his mismatched socks.

"Another adventure to look forward to." Jun raised his eyebrow, lifted the bowl to his lips, and began to slurp his noodles.

"Want to turn around and go back?" Ruju asked hopefully.

He shook his head no as he drained the last of his broth from the bowl.

Ruju sighed. "This must be one special girl you are chasing around."

CHAPTER THIRTY-NINE

With a full belly and his nerves frayed from anticipation, Jun climbed into the mini taxi and made room for Ruju. He pulled the curtains open on each side so he could look out at the people and passing scenery. Ruju set her bag in the seat next to her and got busy cleaning her fingernails.

The driver got comfortable behind the wheel and, with a clanging sound, started the motor and took off. With the compact shape of the tiny vehicle, he was soon weaving in and out of traffic.

They made small talk about the weather first, and then Ruju hesitated. "Lao Jun, you said you have two daughters. Were you sad they were not sons?"

Jun thought a minute. "Of course I wanted a son. Every man wants a son. But when each of my daughters was placed in my arms, I loved her. I don't know if I love them more or less than I would a son—I only love them as my children."

"You are the first man I've ever heard declare love for his daughters. It's very strange to hear. But what about when you get older and your daughters are married off? Who will take care of you and your *tai tai*?"

"If I raise my daughters right, they will make sure their mother and I are cared for, even if they are married off. The old Chinese way is to drill a sense of responsibility into a child, but I want my children to *want* to do it out of love and respect."

"What about your wife? She is happy, only giving birth to girls?"

He sighed. "Wei loves our daughters, too. But she, like all mothers, still hopes to have a son. When Chai was born, she was very disappointed. But she got over it, and when our little Luci came, Wei was resigned to the reality she may never have a boy."

Jun remembered the day Wei had given birth to Chai, and the deep sadness his wife could not conceal. Everyone waiting outside had quickly returned to their homes at the news the baby was a girl, their congratulations dissolving before being spoken. After only a split second of disappointment, Jun had fallen head over heels for the baby girl that had been created from the love he and Wei shared.

Looking over at her furrowed brow, Jun could see his answers were hard for Ruju to accept. By the circumstances surrounding where he had met her, he was aware that she had been treated badly because she was not born a male. He felt sorry for her, but there was nothing he could say to ease her mind.

Ruju changed the subject. "So, when we get to Sandu'ao, we must stay the night there and wait until morning to climb to the village."

Jun narrowed his eyes at her. "*Weishenme?* Why not go tonight?"

"Because of many reasons. One being that it will soon get dark. The other reason is I am not even sure if you can make the climb. Perhaps I will need to go alone."

Jun laughed. "You have to be kidding me. You think *I* am too old and fragile? Do you know what I do for a living, girl?"

"No, and I didn't say you were fragile. But you *are* kind of old."

"Compared to you, maybe. Listen, Ruju. I am not proud of it, but I work as a laborer. I haul bricks from one pile to another. I clean up huge messes of construction. I build scaffolding for the painters. I drywall apartment walls of huge complexes. You name it, and I do it. Believe me; I can handle a little stroll up a mountain. I am only thirty-five years old—far from what I consider an *old man*." He flexed his muscle to show her his sturdiness.

Ruju watched him quietly. Finally, she nodded. "Okay. But we go in the morning—and only if Keso changes course like it's supposed to. The path is too treacherous for evening climbs. This I insist."

"*Hao de*, Ruju. You win that one. We'll get a hotel room."

Two hours later, the driver stopped in front of a small hotel in the tiny coastal village of Sandu'ao. Jun and Ruju climbed out, anxious to be on solid ground again. The small car ride had been even worse than the bus ride, the road full of deep potholes and mud bogs. The tiny vehicle was so close to the ground that they had been bumped and thrown around until they were both sore. The splashing from the mud puddles had at times reached their feet, and they were both soiled and wet. At each lurch, the driver had guffawed and thrown apologies behind him as he fought to get his vehicle under control.

The only enjoyable part of the trip was the show of scenery they were treated to, mostly of artistically laid rice plateaus and high mountains. Jun was mesmerized by the village of floating houses in the bay. Behind the dwellings stretched miles and miles of fishing nets and cages that could be seen from his perch on the backseat. With the backdrop of the magnificent sea stretched behind it, the floating village had created quite a picture and almost made up for the misery of the travel. He wondered about the people who lived the fishing life. *Were their lives easier? Simpler than his? Or were their lives just as hard but in a different kind of way?*

As Ruju collected their bags, Jun paid the taxi driver. They stepped out, and the man took off again, in search of customers to take back the way they had come.

Inside the hotel, the desk clerk was sound asleep on a pull-out cot behind the desk. Jun rapped on the counter with his knuckle until the young man jumped up, disoriented for a moment. As Ruju covered her mouth to hide her amusement, the clerk pulled himself together and tried to smooth the wrinkles from his crumpled uniform. He gave up and asked to see Jun's identification, and then took his money for one room with two small beds.

Ruju followed behind him as he climbed the stairs to the third floor.

"Look at all these cigarette holes in the carpet." She *tsk*ed behind him.

"I just hope we don't burn up alive in here," Jun answered, out of breath at the last landing.

"Well, you smoke, right?" She pointed to the pack of cigarettes peeking out of his front shirt pocket.

"Yeah, but I don't throw my lit cigarettes down on the floor, especially not on carpet." He found the room labeled 303 and fumbled with the key, then opened the door. Inside the room he looked around to find just what he expected—a shabby room with exactly what he paid for. Two beds, a small table between them, and nothing else.

Ruju groaned. "*Mei you weishengjian.*"

"Yes, they do have a bathroom. I saw it just down the hall." Jun threw his bag on the bed and sat down beside it. He reached for one of his feet and began to knead it.

"Do you want a foot massage?" She plopped down on the bed, already studying her fingers.

He looked up at the girl. "Ruju, no. I do not want a foot massage. You don't have to do that. You're doing enough to help me by escorting me to the village." He didn't want her to think he was some old man, out to take advantage of her youth. "And that reminds me, we need to talk about your future. You can't be working in a massage house for the rest of your life. Don't you have any other options?"

"Foot massage half price?" She joked and laughed as she pulled some clean clothing from her bag. "I'm going to wash up, Lao Jun. We can talk about my *future* later. I suppose we're going to go out for some dinner, right?"

Jun sighed and leaned back on the pillow from his bed. He was so tired. "*Hao de.* I'll wash up when you come back, and then we'll go. And stop chewing on your fingers, already!"

He hoped they could find a cheap meal. He still had to make sure he had enough cash to get them home. "*Wo hen lei.*"

He murmured that he was tired and closed his eyes. He heard the door open and softly shut behind Ruju. He thought briefly about calling to check in with Wei, but he knew their conversation would most likely consist of dead silence between them or be uncomfortable at best. He hoped his youngest daughter was being well cared for by the neighbors while Wei was working. His last thoughts before he drifted off to sleep were of Chai and what she might be doing at that exact moment.

CHAPTER FORTY

Chai finished scrubbing the rice cooker and wiped the counters down. She stacked the clean bowls up and put them in their place. Mother had let her out of the room hours before and told her to get to work. She had to weave in and out of all the mourners to even get to her tasks—and the word had spread about her best friend being accused, which made her the target of several tongue-lashings and dirty looks. The people from nearby houses pulled up in their boats, and some huddled under umbrellas on the deck, looking miserable in the bad weather. If not for Josi being out there somewhere, she would have been grateful for the rain because at least it probably kept away some of the villagers.

Through it all she had kept her head held high and refused to let anyone know how upset she was. She wished she could tell them that their cries were wasted on Bo, that he had been a mean-spirited, hateful bully. But she kept her mouth shut and did her work.

Despite her nearly paralyzing fatigue, she had managed to clean the house and organize all of the food brought by the neighbors for their evening meal. She was tired—so very tired—and hungry, but she knew she was skating on thin ice; and until she could find a way to go look for Josi, she needed to do what she was told. Otherwise they'd only keep her locked away, and she'd never have a chance to escape.

Tao passed behind her and whispered, "Need to talk to you tonight."

Chai didn't turn or acknowledge him, and he continued across the room and out the door to sit with his grieving father. She was still furious at him, because he surely knew more than he was saying. The entire story he gave them was too unbelievable, no matter how much he continued to repeat it. She stood by her belief that Josi would never leave willingly with Bo—or anyone else, if it meant she had to leave Chai behind.

"Chai. Sit down and eat before you fall down." Mother came into the kitchen and laid her hand on Chai's shoulder. "I'll bathe the boys tonight."

"You? You cannot bathe them. What about your stomach?" Chai looked down at the band wrapped tightly around the woman's abdomen—another chore she had been made to do when she was allowed out of her room.

"Don't worry about that. After you eat, go clean up that mess in your room. Everyone should be leaving in the next few minutes. You'll need to remove everything and mop up the ashes. I'll get you some clean bedding. It's even older than what you had before, but it will keep you warm." She patted her arm gently. "And Chai, tomorrow we have to plan the funeral for Bo…"

Mother paused and swallowed back a fresh sob. "But after that, I'll see what I can do about finding Josi. Let me talk to Zhongfu. Like you, I do not believe Josi murdered my son. That girl doesn't have a mean bone in her little body. Something has happened that we do not understand, and I'm worried about her being out in this storm alone."

Much to Chai's embarrassment, her eyes filled with tears at the unexpected kindness from the woman. She bowed her head to hide the emotion from Mother. She couldn't stop thinking of Josi, but she had tried to put aside the thoughts of their wrecked room. Besides the loss of the bedding and the books borrowed from Tao, the disastrous condition of the little space she and Josi had made their own was hard to think about. They were back to nothing again—or at least *she* was back to nothing.

Josi was gone. *I will not let them see me crumble.* She sucked her breath in to hold back the crying that threatened to come, and she took her bowl of rice to the table.

CHAPTER FORTY-ONE

Jun's ragged breaths came faster and faster. He finally stopped and leaned against a tree. "Let's stop for a minute, Ruju."

Ruju turned around and came back to join Jun. She dropped her bag on the ground and sat atop it. "*Hao de.* I'm tired, too. I told you this was a treacherous hike." Other than one old, wet farmer leading a goat down the rocky path, they had seen no other people, and to make matters worse, the rain continued to fall.

"I'll be fine once I catch my breath. It's just steeper than I expected." He took the bottle of water from his bag, opened it, and took a long swig. He held it out to the girl.

"I've still got some. Thanks." She got her own bottle out and took a quick sip. "You know, it's starting to rain harder. Maybe we should go back down to the hotel and wait until the weather clears."

Jun ignored her suggestion and looked out over the mountain. "What are those buildings down there?" He pointed below.

"You didn't see those when we went through the town? It's an old church and nunnery, built way back in the nineteen hundreds."

"Hmm. It sure is huge. Do they still use it?"

"My *nai nai* told me that it's a shelter for misplaced people now."

"Misplaced? What do you mean? Homeless?"

"Something like that. So, Lao Jun, what if we find nothing up there? What is your next plan?"

"I don't really have a plan." Jun didn't even want to think of the possibility that they were following a dead end. He had all his hopes stacked on this one lead.

"Well, you know they may not be too welcoming here. *Nai Nai* said these people are very private; even the foreigners that visit Sandu'ao are not allowed to visit this village. They may refuse to talk to us. You need to be ready for that possibility."

"We have a name, and I'll go to every house to ask for her if I have to."

Ruju picked up her bag and began to climb again. "Then come on, you stubborn old man."

* * *

Hours later, Jun and Ruju sat on a rock under a huge tallow tree, sharing their packed lunch of crackers and the small container of rice the hotel breakfast attendant had given them. It was still raining steadily, and though the tree offered some protection, it wasn't much. Jun shivered as he watched Ruju reach up and squeeze the water from her hair. *She is a tough one, and definitely not a complainer.* But he was discouraged and it showed. They had not had any luck in the small village. The few people who would talk to them claimed they didn't know any woman named Bai Li—or even anyone by the family name Bai.

It was obvious the people were either afraid or simply protecting someone. Because of their dialect, they had been pegged as foreigners right away, and most of the villagers wouldn't even look at them. They were also both insulted by the amount of doors that were closed in their faces when they mentioned the name Bai.

"Let's rest for a few minutes and head back down to the hotel and get a room. It's getting dark, and it looks like the storm is getting worse. I'm tired of being wet." Ruju pulled the hood of her raincoat farther down over her eyes.

Jun raised his eyebrows. For her to finally admit her misery he knew she had to be at the end of her patience. He sighed. "I guess you're right. And I need to get you to a real shelter. It doesn't feel like the storm is retreating any."

They both began eating faster, anxious to get going again and find some warmth. All around them, the village people were busy covering their windows with tarps and odd pieces of plastic, some even nailing boards across the glass. The small children ran around in a heightened state of excitement, not understanding that the break in their routine was not for a good thing. Everyone worked at a frantic pace around them—everyone except the village fortune-teller.

Jun watched him sitting across the way, playing with his tiny bird. The man didn't look overly concerned about the impending weather, and he even appeared to be in a peaceful state of mind. When he wasn't petting his bird or feeding it small seeds, he was stroking his long white beard.

"You know he's blind, right?" Ruju whispered to Jun.

"Well, yes, it's fairly obvious by the way he's staring into space. I just don't know how he gets that bird to stay there on his hand or around him without it flying away." The tiny black bird hopped all around the small table, going in and out of its small cage and on and off of its master's hand, scattering cards in a flurry of activity all around him. "I wonder if he realizes his cards are getting rained on?"

Ruju chuckled. "My grandmother told me about him before we came. He tells fortunes using his *bai ling niao*. She said I should take you to talk to him. He's very famous far and wide—people come up here all the way from Ningde just to have him declare their lucky wedding dates and have their futures told with the help of the bird."

"I don't believe in that stuff." Jun shook his head, but he did feel a bit sorry for the old man. He popped another cracker in his mouth. "How can one insignificant little bird tell someone's future?"

"*Nai Nai* said he began the process of enlightening his bird from the day it was conceived as an egg. It was incubated and, once hatched, was fed spiritually and physically by only the fortune-teller. Every day for forty-nine days, the chick was placed on the altar in the temple while the master did his daily chanting.

"Actually, he started with two birds' eggs that were hatched from the same nest. The chosen one was not determined until the end of the process, and the one not chosen flew away free."

"Ruju, that's nonsense."

"*Nai Nai* doesn't speak nonsense, Lao Jun," Ruju answered, challenging him with the serious tone she used.

Jun looked back over at the old man and was surprised to see the fortune-teller lift his gnarly hand and wave to him. "*Guo lai, pengyou.* Come over here, friend."

"Oh, no," Jun said to Ruju in a low voice. "Now he wants us to come over and give him some of my hard-earned money. How did he even know we were over here in the midst of all this chaos?"

Ruju laughed. "He must have very good hearing. You might want to see what he has to say. He seems insistent."

The fortune-teller continued to wave at Jun to join him. Not wanting to show the man any disrespect, even though the fortune-teller couldn't see them, Jun stood and stretched his aching back, then walked over. Ruju followed at a distance.

"*Zuo xia.*" The man gestured for them to sit on a small wooden stool next to his. Jun sat down, running his hands nervously through his damp hair. Ruju stood behind him, holding the umbrella over both of them.

"*Ni yao shenme?* What do you want, *lao ren*? I'm sorry, but I have no extra money to pay for a fortune today."

"I don't want your money. You are searching. *Dui?*"

Tao looked up at Ruju, and she raised her eyebrows questioningly.

"You heard us talking from all the way over here? Yes, I'm looking for a woman named Bai Lu. I would like to ask her some questions. Do you know of this woman or her family?" They had not talked about Chai, so the man had to be fairly ignorant of *why* he was searching.

"My bird tells me you are searching for peace. Would you like to hear more?"

"Well, I guess you could say if I find what I am after, I'll find peace. But the first step is finding the Bai woman." Jun sighed, wishing once again that his nightmare would end and he could go back to the way his life had been a year ago.

The man said a few words, and his bird hopped back into the cage, seeming to calmly wait on further instructions. The old man shut the cage door, picked up his deck of cards, and shuffled them, then fanned them out in front of the birdcage. He then said a few words that Jun could not understand and opened the small door again.

"What's your bird going to do?" Jun asked.

"*Anjing.*" The old man scolded him to be quiet.

The bird hopped out, picked up a card in its beak, and held it up for the old man. The man took it and turned it toward Jun.

"What card is this?"

Jun looked at it and searched for words to describe it. "It shows a mountain, a waterfall, and an eagle."

The old man appeared to be deep in thought. Then he put the card back down and said a few more words to the bird. The bird picked up another card and held it in its beak. The man reached down, took the card, and held it up for Jun.

"And this one?"

Jun squinted his eyes, looking closer at the card. "It looks like a building sitting in the hills of a valley."

Ruju inhaled deeply. "It's a church, Lao Jun. Look, there's the steeple."

The old man laid the card on the table, and his bird hopped back into the bamboo cage and shook itself to scatter the water droplets from its feathers.

"As I said before, you are searching for peace. Perhaps you should examine your heart. The first card shows that you have been through a hard journey, still have more to go, but that you have the courage to reach your destination."

A warm feeling spread through Jun despite the cold chill of the falling rain.

"The second card tells us that you must find refuge from the storms in your life, and then you will find peace."

"That's it?" Jun asked impatiently. "Will I find what I'm looking for or not?" He still didn't want to mention Chai, for that would give the fortune-teller too much information.

"If you trust your heart to lead you to the right place, you will find peace. Now you must go. My bird and I should return home." The old man stood and began deftly packing his things in a large bag sitting at his feet. He latched the door to the birdcage and turned to go.

Jun and Ruju watched him walk toward a thick grove of trees, the small birdcage dangling from one hand and the bag in the other. It amazed them both how he knew exactly where he was going and didn't need assistance to get there. As he stepped into the woods, he stopped. Without turning around, he spoke.

"Your daughter is a strong woman. Have faith in her ability to protect herself." Then he disappeared through the trees.

CHAPTER FORTY-TWO

It was close to midnight, and the pounding rain and leaky roof ensured that Chai was still wide awake when she heard Tao at her door. He knocked and waited for her to tell him to come in. Chai wanted to punish him by ignoring him, but she was too anxious to see if he would tell her anything different.

"Come in, Tao."

He entered the room and lowered his eyes, staring at his shoes. His shoulders slumped even more than usual. "Chai, I'm sorry."

"What are you sorry for? Do you know something more about Josi and how your brother died?"

Tao continued to hang his head for a moment. Then he looked around and saw the small bucket on the floor, catching the steady stream from the ceiling. "Are you warm enough? Do you want me to bring you some of my socks?" Most of their things had been ruined by the small fire or the smoke. They hadn't had much to begin with, and he knew that now Chai was back to almost nothing.

"You didn't answer me, Tao. What do you know?"

"I'll bring you more books, Chai. Tomorrow—I'll go first thing in the morning. Tell me, what kind of book do you want me to bring?"

Chai sat straighter and narrowed her eyes at the boy. His guilt was showing all over his face, glaring like a beacon.

"What are you hiding, Tao?" She felt that there was more—lots more—that he was holding inside.

Tao hung his head again. Then his shoulders began to shake. Chai realized he was crying and went to him.

She put her arms around him. "It's okay, Tao. Let it out. Please, talk about it."

He continued to look down at his hands. "I killed him, Chai."

Chai dropped her arms to her sides, her eyes wide with shock. She'd felt like he knew more about what happened, but never had it crossed her mind that he was responsible for his brother's death. He just wasn't that type of person, and Chai couldn't—wouldn't—believe it.

"Tao. What do you mean?"

"I killed Bo. I left him in the water and didn't pull him out, so it's my fault he drowned. But Chai—he tried to rape Josi. He beat me and would've killed me if he could have. But now he's dead, and it's my fault." He began to sob loudly and rock back and forth, his hands covering his face.

"Shh! I don't know if your father is asleep. Tell me exactly what happened. And if you did this, you must know where Josi is. Tell me, Tao. Now."

Tao cried for a few more moments and then sat down on the floor. Sniffling and looking embarrassed at his show of weakness, he told her the whole story. As he described the scene he had walked in on, Chai felt sick. She winced, remembering that she had decided to stay by Mother's side so that they wouldn't lose eating privileges. If Chai had only returned to Josi and been with her when Bo came, he would have never tried to hurt her.

By the time Tao got to the part where they couldn't find Bo and he instructed Josi to run away, Chai was dizzy with fear. "Why didn't you tell your father, Tao? Explain that Bo was trying to rape Josi? And tell him it was an accident, and Bo fell in the water? There is a chance he might have believed you. It was worth a try, Tao!"

"Chai, you know Baba would never believe anything bad about Bo. He'd probably insist that Bo walked in on me and Josi, or some other twisted story. He'd turn it around and make Josi look like the guilty one. Don't you understand? He would never take Josi's side—right or wrong—or even mine, his own son. Bo could do no wrong in his eyes."

"But your face? Bo didn't knock you into the water?"

Tao winced. "He did this to my face, but not with the oar. He used his fists. I put myself in the water to make the story more believable. I stayed in there for hours waiting on someone to find me. I was terrified something—maybe even Bo—was going to get me from beneath the water."

Chai stood up and began pulling on her coat and mittens. Now over her initial reaction, she was calm and determined. "That's quite a story, Tao. I would thank you for finally telling me the truth but you've waited so long that by now anything could have happened to Josi. For your sake, you'd better hope she is okay. Tell me where she went. I'm going after her right now."

Finally Chai had the *real* story—one that made more sense. Now that she had something to go on, she wasn't going to wait around any longer. She didn't care if ten hurricanes were in her path, she was going to find Josi, and anyone who got in her way had better watch out.

"That's just it, Chai. I don't know. I told her to run as far as she could before Bo's body was found. I didn't even give her any money or food. All she had was my boots and the clothes on her back. I'm so scared something has happened to her. They found the sampan floating in the bay—empty. What if she drowned, too?" He lowered his face into his hands.

Chai nudged him hard with her foot. "She did not drown, Tao. I refuse to think like that. And I bet I know where she went. Come on; we're going to find her. Tonight."

"You're right. The storm is getting worse. Before he went to bed, Baba told me to stay up and listen to the weather reports. I just heard on the radio that we might get more than strong winds, and to stay tuned in case the fishing village has to evacuate. We need to find Josi." He stood up and headed for the door.

"Get us some rain jackets, Tao. We're going to get drenched out there. Hurry, before your baba wakes up!"

Tao quickly left the shed and pulled his and Bo's yellow slickers from the pegs under the porch overhang. The slickers were already wet from the sheets of rain but would provide a little bit of protection. He returned to find Chai pulling on his mother's boots. He threw her a coat and put his own on over his clothes.

"What about some food, in case we have to stay on the mainland all night? You go back in the house and get us some fruit; I'll wait out here in case Lao Chan wakes. Hurry, Tao!"

Tao quietly entered the house as Chai stood peeking out of the shed, ready to hide in case anyone else came out. She clutched the door with both hands, anxious but relieved to finally be doing something to find Josi, even if she did get caught and punished by Lao Chan later. She wondered if Josi might be hurt, or if she was hiding somewhere, too scared to come out. The possibilities were terrifying, and Chai had to find her.

When Tao returned with a plastic bag of oranges and a few bottles of water, he beckoned for her to climb into the sampan. He gave her the bag, and he bent to hold the boat steady, a difficult chore with the swells the wind was making.

Chai climbed in and pushed back the thoughts of Josi being there just a short time before. Lao Chan had brought the boat back, and all day it had floated there, an eerie reminder that only it knew the secret of where her best friend had landed.

"We have to hurry. I just heard another alert on the radio and will need to get back and wake up everyone. They said Keso was bringing gusts up to a hundred seventy-eight kilometers per hour and is moving at twenty-five kilometers per hour toward us. They have already shut down the Fuzhou airport and are announcing evacuations. It's expected to make landfall tomorrow morning," Tao said, grabbing the oars and setting them up in the wooden holders.

"What will everyone do?"

"Most likely the families will all move to higher ground on the mainland, unless it changes direction by morning. At least the women and children—but many of the men won't leave their boats. Because Sandu'ao is mostly landlocked, we usually don't see much damage from the ocean squalls, but this time might be different. It sure feels different." He pointed at the line of floating houses rocking violently in the wind. "Look at that! The wind feels like it's coming from every direction. I've never felt it like this before." He began to paddle them quickly away from the house and headed for the mainland.

* * *

About halfway to the mainland Chai heard voices calling through the wind. She turned around to find a group of children stranded on a few rocks near the edge of the bay. She could just make out their silhouettes in the dark, but they sounded young.

"Tao, look! There's some kids stranded over there on those rocks!" She pointed behind his head.

"Chai, we barely have room in the boat, and I don't even think I can get in there near those rocks without turning us over. Someone else with a bigger boat will be by to help them soon. What possessed them to get out there, anyway?"

Chai squinted her eyes, peering through the rain to make out more of the scene as Tao paddled faster. Chai could make out the sound of the youngest child's pitiful wailing. It struck her that just because she hadn't received any kindness from the people of Sandu'ao didn't mean she had to be like them. Her father would expect her to do something—anything—to at least try to help the children.

"It looks like they've got bundles of stuff with them. They must be from the fishing village and were left there while their parents went after more stuff—a lot of families are evacuating now. Tao, we have to help them; the water's rising fast, and what if no one comes for them?"

Tao stopped paddling and looked where Chai pointed. He reached up and pushed his wet hair out of his eyes, straining to see the children.

"Fine. I'll try to get over there. I just hope Baba doesn't wake up and come after us before we can even make it to the mainland," he shouted over the wind, paddling the sampan toward the rocks.

As they got closer, the children called out louder, excited to see someone coming for them.

"Bo and I used to play here—but it looks like the water has covered up the smaller rocks so much they can't make it back to shore. Chai, I don't know if we're going to be able to get them or not."

"Keep going, Tao. We can't leave them."

Tao rowed until he got the boat as close as he could to the children, but it was still too far for them to reach. There was a series of other rocks between him and them, blocking the boat from coming closer. He looked at the floor behind him and saw the rope that was used to tie up to the dock.

"Chai, we can throw them this rope. They'll have to jump in and follow it to the boat."

Chai looked at the children: two girls of around eight to ten years old huddled around a toddler boy. They were terrified—she couldn't imagine they'd get in the choppy water, even to reach safety.

"Which one of you is the oldest and strongest?" she called out to them.

"*Wo shi jiu shui*. I am nine," the tallest girl called back.

"We're going to throw you the rope! Catch it, and then your brother and sister will need to use it to come through the water to the boat while you hold the other end. Okay?"

The girl shook her head from side to side, her eyes huge with fear. Chai realized she wasn't old enough or strong enough for what needed to be done.

"I knew it. They aren't going to do it. Chai, we'll have to go get help."

"No, Tao! I'm not leaving them." She looked over the edge into the dark water, and a chill at the unknown traveled the length of her spine. *I don't want to go in—I really don't. But what else can I do?*

Tao picked up his oars and began to back away from the rocks. "We're going to get help. Now."

Chai stood up and pulled the life jacket from under the seat. "No, we're not. They'll be drowned by then. I'm going after them." She struggled out of her raincoat, put her arms through the life vest, and began tying it up in the front.

"Chai! You can't swim! I can't either. We do not need to get into this water! We have to find Josi. Someone else will be by any minute. Everyone is evacuating."

Chai looked at the children huddled together and could hear the little boy crying. She thought about her little sister and how terrified she would be in that situation. She stared down, but the water was too dark to see below the surface. *What's under there? Sharks?* Feeling like she was starting to hyperventilate, she reminded herself she couldn't drown—*I have a life jacket and a rope.*

"Chai?" Tao called to her, his voice carrying a warning.

She grabbed the end of the rope and stood up, then jumped over the edge into the water.

She went completely under, and the coldness paralyzed her for an instant. She gasped and immediately swallowed a mouthful of salty water.

Even while choking, instinct kicked in, and she fought to get back up to the top. She was freezing, and she didn't know how to swim—but she and Josi had made a pact to learn how, and how hard could it be? She began to use her feet and, still holding onto the rope, frantically waved her arms around until she started making progress.

She broke the surface, sputtering and looking around for the boat.

"Chai! Are you okay? Get back in here!" Tao stood over the edge, wildly waving her back toward the boat.

She looked to the children and began to use her arms to get farther away from the boat. She had seen older boys swimming before, and using the actions she remembered, she was getting somewhere. The thought of what lived under the waves near her feet moved her faster than she would have thought possible for a first-time swimmer.

Though exhausted, she soon made it to a rock that was big enough for her to climb on. Using arms that felt like jelly, she climbed up and paused to get her breath.

"I'm coming," she called out weakly, still panting. She was shaking—but from fear or the cold, she didn't know.

She gathered the rope in her hands and began to hop from one rock to the other and almost slipped back into the water as she moved from one slippery surface to the next.

Before she could get to the rock that the children stood on, she ran out of rope.

"You're going to have to come to me!" she called out to them.

The girls started inching across the rocks, pulling along the little boy behind them as he cried. They finally made it to the rock next to Chai and stood waiting for directions.

"Why are you out here?" Chai asked them as she wound the rope around her arm to pull it tight across the water.

The older girl answered for them. "Our baba put us out here and told us to wait; he forgot the weather radio. Then he didn't come back, and the water got higher and higher." She broke into sobs.

Chai fumed that a parent would be ignorant enough to leave his children in a situation that was growing more dangerous by the minute—rising waters, high winds, with not even the protection of rain gear. She kept her fury to herself and tried to focus on the problem at hand.

"Okay, enough crying. You need to be strong; you are the *jie jie*. Right?"

The girl sniffled. "*Dui le.*"

"Then you have to help me coach your brother and sister to do as I say. Nothing will happen if they follow my directions. Okay?"

"Okay." More sniffles.

"You." She pointed at the younger sister. "You look very brave to me. Am I right?"

The girl gave a timid smile through the rain and her tears. She nodded her head up and down.

"Can you swim?"

"I can float." She wrinkled her brow, a worried look filling her eyes.

"Guess what? You're in luck. If you can float—you can swim. I want you to ease yourself into the water, and do not let go of this rope. You don't even have to swim much; just pull yourself along all the way to the boat, and don't let go. Okay?"

"I don't want to." She began to cry more.

"*Bu ku le.* You're scaring your brother with all that crying. Dry it up. See that big boy wearing the red cap over there in that boat?"

"Yes." She sniffled and lifted her head to look at Tao. Though he let the rope stay tied to the hull, he kept his hands on it for added security.

"He is amazingly strong. Like a fierce dragon. He will not let go of that end of the rope. And I won't let go of this end— because I am a warrior princess. I promise. Go on; get in."

The little girl hesitated and then dropped to her bottom, and grabbing the rope, eased into the choppy water.

"It's okay, *mei mei*. You can do it," her sister encouraged her.

The little boy watched, his eyes huge with fright.

"Okay," Chai called loudly to be heard over the wind as she struggled to keep the rope taut. "Use your hands and pull yourself to the boat." After a few seconds of hesitance, the girl began using the rope to drag herself through the water. "Go ahead—that's right." Chai nodded her head, relieved the little girl seemed to know what to do.

With the added weight on the rope, the boat began to rock side to side precariously. Tao looked scared, but to his credit, he didn't say anything.

Hand over hand, the girl began pulling herself through the water. Despite her constant choking and spitting out water, she made good progress and got to the boat. Tao pulled her in.

"Send the next one. Hurry, Chai! The rain's coming down harder."

"Okay, *jie jie*. Your turn. I'll make sure your brother is fine. Go."

The girl peeled herself away from her brother, sending him into shrieks of hysterical crying. Chai reached down and pulled him close to comfort him.

"*Mei guan xi. Mei guan xi.* I got you. We're next. Okay?"

He clung to her legs and whimpered as he watched his sister drop to her bottom and take her place in the water, clinging to the rope. As Chai held on, the girl quickly crossed the twenty or so feet of water faster than her little sister had, and Tao helped her into the boat. He looked up at Chai.

"Now what? You can't send him alone," he yelled across the water.

"We're coming over together." She reached down and tied the rope around her waist and knotted it tightly.

"Chai, you can't. He'll drown you if he panics!"

233

"What do you expect me to do, Tao, leave him?" At those words the boy cried harder, pulling on Chai to pick him up.

"Shhh…I'm not leaving you. Listen to me!"

The boy shuddered and tried to stop crying. He looked up at Chai, his tiny lip quivering.

"You have to trust me. In the water, you must be very still. Just wrap your legs around my waist, hold on to my neck, and don't move, okay? *Mingbai?*"

"*Hao de.*" He sniffled again, nodding in agreement.

The boy calmed down, and Chai sat down and scooted closer to the edge on her bottom. "Wait until I get in, then it's your turn. Okay?"

She looked over at Tao. "Keep the rope taut. Then when I get in with him, pull as fast as you can, and I'll use my feet. Don't let us sink, Dragon!" She tried to keep the fear from her voice. She was doing everything she could to give the boy confidence in her ability to get him to the safety of the boat.

Tao shook his head and gave her a thunderous look across the distance. Chai glared back, refusing to back down. She watched as he wrapped his hands around the rope at the boat and prepared to pull as fast as possible to keep from rocking them all out of the sampan.

Once more, she took a deep breath, then lowered herself into the cold, swirling water.

CHAPTER FORTY-THREE

J un held his arm out for Ruju to take as they attempted to climb the slippery path to the church nestled in the valley on the mountain. The rain poured down and entered through opening in his jacket and trickled down his neck, causing him to shiver uncontrollably. After their long trek back to the hotel, they had found the door posted with a note on the glass that stated the hotel was full for the storm. Inside, two security guards stood blocking the way. A man camped out in front under a tarp said the owner wouldn't let anyone else in because he was afraid his hotel would get trampled from everyone trying to evacuate the water village and the coastal area next to it. He told them that there were no other options in town. Disheveled and cold, Ruju and Jun followed a group of other misplaced people to the only remaining refuge, the church on the hillside.

Though talk on the street said the news report was that the typhoon was going to divert from their coast at the last minute, the edges of the storm were already causing more damage than most of the poor families could handle.

"Ahh…my feet are sticking in this mud." Jun stopped to pull one of his shoes out of a particularly sticky bog.

"What? I can't hear you?" Ruju yelled through the howling wind.

"Nothing. Never mind."

Being soaked to the bone and tired were his physical complaints, but more than anything Jun was disgusted with himself and his lack of progress in finding the woman named Bai. He'd used up a large chunk of his family's savings for this trip and probably lost his job for missing work, giving Wei more ammunition in what had become the first silent war of their marriage. Now he was trampling along in the pouring rain to find somewhere to take cover and sleep—at a church, no less!—until the next morning when he would try to find a bus out.

"Are you okay, Lao Jun?" Ruju moved closer and squinted up at him, trying to stay under the cover of the umbrella.

He sighed. It wasn't her fault, and actually she had been a fairly pleasant guide, considering the conditions she had traversed with him and that she had rarely voiced any complaints.

"*Shi*, I'm okay. Just disappointed."

"You aren't giving up, are you?"

"Nah, I'll never give up. But I am sorry I dragged you all this way and got you caught in this storm." He slowed down as they found themselves directly behind a family of five on the path, all of them headed to the same place. The children were sliding all around, and the parents' arms were too full of belongings to help them. He and Ruju both offered their arms to the children and began helping them up the hill. The parents muttered their appreciation as they continued to trudge ahead, their exhaustion evident.

"I'm tired, too. If we had known we weren't going to be able to get back in the hotel, we could have stopped at the church on the way down. Now it's after midnight. I'm wet—*you're* wet.

And we'll be lucky if we don't get blown away in this typhoon." Beside them the trees along the trail bent in the wind, almost touching the ground and becoming useless as shelter against the rain.

"At least I had the good sense to wear boots on this trip. Your feet are going to rot by the time they dry out," she mumbled, barely heard under the howl of the wind and the heavy rain.

"I can't even feel my feet, so that's the last of my worries right now." He thought of Luci and how disappointed she was going to be when he returned home without any news of Chai. He had let her down—just like he'd let Chai down when he'd told her she could go swimming that day. He had forgotten the encouragement from the fortune-teller hours ago, and all he was thinking about was that he felt like a failure.

"Lao Jun, please don't get discouraged, or you might make me feel sorry for you and actually have to be nice to you." Ruju clutched the child she was leading more tightly as they both slid a little way back.

"Well, we don't want that, do we? You know, you sort of reminded me of Chai the first night I met you, and the more sass you show, the more of her I see in you."

"And you know what, *lao ren*? If I had ever known a father, I would have wanted him to be just like you. I hope you find your daughter one day."

At that Jun smiled slightly. He didn't mind her calling him an old man—coming from her it almost sounded like an endearment.

He grabbed the youngest child as the boy began sliding back in the mud once more, and after straightening him up, they continued their treacherous climb.

CHAPTER FORTY-FOUR

At the mainland, Tao climbed out of the boat and onto the dock. He tied the rope securely and began helping the children out one at a time as Chai assisted from inside the boat. He was still shaky from the fright Chai had caused him and the girls when she'd disappeared under the water with the boy. Tao had almost upset the sampan trying to pull them in—and when their heads had finally popped up again—gasping and sputtering—he wanted to throttle her for scaring him so badly.

He had to admit, she was something else. He'd never known a girl so brave. She had flipped over on her back, and with the boy holding onto her like a baby monkey, she had pulled both of them to the boat. He still couldn't believe it.

"Good work, Dragon." She punched him on the arm as he helped her out of the boat. She looked down at her hands and frowned at the white, puckered skin along her fingers and over her palms.

"Back at you, Warrior Princess," he grumbled, rolling his eyes.

When all five of them stood safely on the wooden dock, he looked up at the scene on the bank. At least twenty or more people, women and men, were busy filling bags with sand and piling them against the bank. The people were soaked from the rain but continued to work hard, most of them not giving them even a glance.

"*Ni hao!* Can you help us?" one old man called out to Tao as he and Chai stepped off the wooden planks, her holding the clingy little boy, the girls following along like soggy ducklings.

"*Dui bu qi*, we cannot," he mumbled as he grabbed Chai's hand and pulled her along, afraid she'd feel called to be a hero again if he hesitated. He heard insults behind him as the old men grumbled their displeasure at his refusal to help the village. If he was going to help anyone, it would be his own family, but until they found Josi he was going to have to leave their fate with his stubborn father.

"The reports must have gotten worse if these people are out this late. It's after midnight, Tao. We've got to get these kids to shelter. They're soaked and are gonna get deathly sick if we don't get them dry." Chai had carried her slicker from the sampan and she wrapped it around the boy, guiding his tiny hands through the armholes.

Watching her, Tao shook his head and then pulled off his own coat and handed it to the big girl. "Put this on your sister." Looking at Chai, he raised his voice so she could hear across the howling wind. "I'm afraid you're right. And we might not have much time before Baba comes to look for us. If he finds you, I don't know what he might do, Chai. Do you want to go back before we are in too much trouble?"

"No. I have an idea of where Josi might be, and we need to find her before Lao Chan does. It's also a good place to leave these kids so we know they'll be safe from the storm. We'll check there first." She stepped in front and began leading Tao up the hill toward the church.

"Where are you going? The church? You know she wouldn't go there, after all the superstitious stories I've told you two about it."

"I've been there, Tao. It's not a scary place. Trust me—that's where she probably went to find shelter." Chai pulled at the wet strands of hair in her eyes. She didn't tell Tao about taking baby Zee there. If Josi was there, she had no doubt he'd soon find out for himself.

* * *

With Chai in the lead, the children between, and Tao holding up the rear, they made good time climbing the hill to the church. Chai led them through the gates and up the path. At the elaborate entryway, she gathered the children in front of her and herded them through as Tao held the door.

A woman dressed in a long black robe welcomed them in and immediately brought out her notebook and pen. By the looks of all the writing on the paper, she had been logging names for quite a while.

Chai recognized her as the woman whom she had seen preparing food in the kitchen what now seemed ages ago. She recognized Chai as well and gave her a warm smile.

"*Ni hao.* I remember you. You and your family, please come in."

Chai looked down at the straggly children, shaking her head.

"Oh, we're not together—except for him." She nodded toward Tao. "I'm looking for someone else. We just helped these kids climb the hill. They need shelter, and I think someone will probably be here to look for them shortly."

The woman nodded, her forehead wrinkled with worry. "They're not the first ones to arrive without parents. I need to get their names so that we can have a record of them when the parents come looking. Then we'll get them dry and help make them a little bit more comfortable."

With a nudge from Chai, the oldest girl stepped back into her role and began giving the woman their names.

"Do you have a Josi on your list?" Chai asked as she peered over the woman's shoulder to look at her paper.

The woman used her pen to skim names quickly.

"*Bushi.* No Josi."

Chai looked around the small group in the largest part of the church, searching faces. Knowing Josi, she would have been too afraid to give her real name. She took a second to get her raincoat back and then she took off, weaving in and out of the groups of people huddled together around the halls.

Tao barely had time to peel the little boy's hands loose from where he was still clutching Tao's legs before running after Chai.

With her face set in determination, Chai deftly maneuvered around the people camped out in the halls and to a back door at the very rear of the church. Stepping out into the wind and rain again, she struggled into her raincoat and headed straight to the building behind the church.

"Chai! Wait!" Tao called, struggling to catch up to her as he held his coat over his head in an attempt to block some of the torrential rain.

Chai couldn't hear his voice through the wind, but at the door to the building she hesitated, giving him time to join her.

"What is this place?" Tao opened the door and peeked in, only to be met with more curious faces camped out in the large front entry.

Chai ignored his question and led the way in and down a few halls until she stopped in front of a huge room enclosed with glass. Tao stopped next to her, breathing hard to catch his breath. He looked down and grimaced at the puddles of water both of them were forming on the stone floor at their feet.

Chai's eyes stopped searching and a small smile crept over her face. She pointed at the window.

"There. See her, Tao?"

Josi created quite the picture—sitting in the nursery with a half dozen children huddled around her and Zee snuggled comfortably on her lap. Chai's smile disappeared when she looked closer and saw the fading bruises coloring her best friend's face—but Josi looked perfectly at home and content to be helping the kids put together a puzzle.

Tao sighed loudly. "Well, there she is. How did you know she'd be here, Chai?"

He squinted and got closer to the glass.

"And is that—*don't tell me*—yes, that's Zee. I'd recognize her little dumpling face anywhere. What is going on?"

Chai snorted. "Of course it's Zee. I'll fill you in later. Come on, Josi's going to be so happy to see us." Chai tapped on the window, and Josi and some of the children looked up. Clutching Zee, Josi jumped to her feet and ran out to the hall.

"Chai! I knew you'd figure out where I went and come after me!" Josi exclaimed. With Zee cushioned between them, they hugged and danced around together. Chai felt the fear and worry drop away in an instant.

Finally, she heard Tao clearing his throat to get their attention, and she nudged Josi. They broke apart and Josi turned to him.

"Tao, hi. Um…thank you for coming with Chai."

"We've got a lot to talk about, you two," Chai interrupted, sensing that Tao was unusually tongue-tied. A lot had happened—and the two of them had turned a bad situation into a worse catastrophe by all the lies. They were going to need time to figure out what to do next.

At the sound of footsteps, they all turned around to find Sister Haihua coming toward them.

"Chai! As you can see, we've met Josi. She gave me quite a surprise showing up here and claiming Zee. We've been taking good care of her, though—or maybe the other way around. She's quite the nurturer."

Josi blushed, shaking her head in denial at the sister's praise.

Sister Haihua smiled at Chai. "She said you'd come. I'm glad to see you made it. It's terrible out there, and Josi's been very worried about you. I almost had to tie her down to keep her from going out in the storm to find you."

Chai frowned as she wondered exactly how much Josi had shared with the sister. "That would have been a very bad idea, Josi. Lao Chan would have been waiting."

Josi's eyes filled with fear.

Tao dropped his head. "It's all my fault, and Josi's stuck taking the blame. Look at what Bo did to her; she didn't deserve that."

When Josi reached up and touched her bruised cheek, Chai felt the anger fill her up and threaten to spill over. She squeezed her hands into fists at her side. "I wish I could kill him myself."

Sister Haihua put one arm around Tao, and with the other she reached to stroke Chai on the cheek. "Shh. Don't get yourselves all worked up. I understand you're all weathering some storms, but first let's get through the one outside our door, and tomorrow we'll talk about everything else. Have faith and get some rest; we'll figure all this out."

Sister Haihua led them back into the nursery to wait and returned a few minutes later with a rolled-up pallet for Tao. She beckoned for them to follow and showed them where he would be sleeping—in one of the main halls with the other evacuees. Josi and Chai trailed along to help him settle in.

Tao held his arms in front of Josi. "Let me carry Zee. And I want to hear how she came to be here. I'm glad she didn't meet the fate my father planned for her, but I just don't know how you two did it."

CHAPTER FORTY-FIVE

Chai sat on Tao's pallet on the floor, sharing it with him and Josi as Zee held center court. So far they had given her everything within reach, and she was still looking around to see what else she could hold her fat little hands out for. They had laughed as they peeled the oranges and put them to her lips to taste the juice. It was so cute to watch her wrinkle her tiny nose at the sudden bursts of flavor.

"I can't believe how fast she's grown." Tao smiled at his little sister. "And she looks happy here."

"She *is* happy," Josi said as she reached over and rubbed Zee's little head. "She's the youngest here, so she's treated like a little queen."

Chai laughed. "You mean empress. I guess her name fits after all."

Josi smiled at Chai. "I'm so glad you came, Chai. I knew you would—I just didn't know you'd bring Tao."

"Oh, admit you're glad he came along, Josi," Chai teased, giggling when her prompting brought a blush to Josi's cheeks.

"Chai, stop it," Josi mumbled.

Tao changed the subject quickly. "So, I guess I knew that when you two supposedly got rid of Zee, she'd end up somewhere like this—somewhere safe. I didn't want to ask, because I didn't need to know. I just felt that you'd do the right thing."

Chai smiled at him. "You knew we were in love with her from the start, didn't you?"

"Well, it was fairly obvious. But can Zee stay here? Forever?" Tao asked.

"Sister Haihua said if it is needed, this can be her home. But she also thinks that as beautiful and smart as Zee is, after her surgery, the sister will soon find a new home for her." Josi plucked the baby up from between them and snuggled her close.

"Surgery?" Tao wrinkled his brow.

Josi explained. "Yes, Sister Haihua said they'll take her to Ningde for her first operation when she is four months old. Her lip will be repaired there, and she'll return here to recover. There's a mission medical team that comes over from Australia each year, and the sister already contacted them. They've agreed to take Zee as a patient."

"That's great news, but we really need to talk about what we are going to do about going home," Tao said quietly.

"We can't go back." Chai sat up straight. "They think Josi is responsible for Bo's death. Lao Chan is so angry; I don't know what he might do before we can convince him that she's innocent. You know he has the Sandu'ao police force in his pocket. What if they arrest Josi?"

Josi looked stricken, and Chai reached over and patted her hand reassuringly. "Don't worry, Josi. We'll think of something."

"Well, we can't all run away. We don't have any money or anything to get by with." Tao sighed.

"Tao, just admit you don't want to face your father and tell him the truth. He knows Josi couldn't possibly be strong enough to throw Bo in the water. Your father just wants someone to pay for his death. The truth has to come out. You could help us if you wanted to," Chai said angrily.

The three went silent. Only Zee continued to think it was time to laugh and play. Tao looked away and studied the crowd of people huddled around them. Just as he started to speak, Sister Haihua came through the door with another small, bedraggled family. Behind her the woman struggled to carry a toddler while another small boy straggled behind her, clutching the edge of her wet coat. Both of the boys looked traumatized and exhausted.

"Mama!" Tao exclaimed instinctively, and then ducked his head lower.

Chai looked behind her, and when she saw the woman she flattened herself out on the pallet. Josi was caught off guard, and at that moment, Zee decided to display her displeasure at their surroundings. She let out a loud squeal.

Mother turned and looked straight at Tao, then at Josi, then at Chai, and finally at baby Zee. She began walking through the people to get to them, her face unreadable.

"Oh, great. Now we've done it. Tao—your red cap stands out like a beacon. She's going to cause a scene. First about you, Josi—then about the baby. Or maybe the other way around." Chai felt a tiny stab of guilt as she saw the woman's soaked and muddy sandals, the only thing she had to wear since Chai had taken her rain boots. She sat up and tucked her feet underneath her.

Tao stood up, standing as tall as he could, visibly gathering his courage as his mother picked her way through the people stretched out between them.

"Mama. Listen to me. Josi did not cause Bo to drown. I did."

Chai and Josi gasped, shocked that he would deliver the news so abruptly. They waited for Mother to finish crossing the last few feet, both of them nervous about her reaction.

Mother sat Yifeng down on the floor beside her and stood up to face Tao. Then she threw her arms around him and began sobbing.

"I thought you were dead! I thought I had lost two of my sons to those wretched waters. When I came out and found the sampan gone, you just about gave me heart failure. And your stubborn father refused to leave his precious fishing boat. He brought us to the dock and turned around to take it out to deeper waters. So he may be gone before morning, too." She clung to his neck while he peered over her shoulders at the girls, his eyebrows raised in surprise.

Yifeng and Ying spotted Josi and began squealing their delight. Yifeng plopped down in front of her, picking up Zee's hands and holding them to his face. Ying threw his arms around Josi's neck, almost choking her air off in his excitement.

"*Josi!* Where have you been? Did you see the big storm outside?" he yelled in her ear.

"Hey, boys, calm down. People are sleeping. Come here, Ying. Sit in front of me. Tell me about the storm. Were you scared?" Josi hugged them both, obviously glad to see them.

Mother let go of Tao and dropped to her knees, studying Zee as the baby giggled in delight at Yifeng's attempts to play with her.

"And this"—she choked back a sob—"is she my daughter?"

Chai plucked Zee from Josi's lap and held her protectively, even as Zee began to fuss. "Yes, this is Zee. But she is no longer your daughter. For you wanted to be rid of her."

Tears began to roll down Mother's face. They all watched her carefully, not sure what she would do.

"But she is lovely. I asked you to take her somewhere safe, Chai, and you did. *Xie xie.* Thank you so very much." She locked eyes with Chai, and a moment passed between them. Mother held her hands out, silently pleading to hold her child.

Chai hesitated. She could see the love in the woman's eyes for her child that she did not even know, but still a part of her felt Mother didn't deserve compassion. She looked up at Tao for guidance, and he nodded.

"Let her hold her, Chai."

Chai reluctantly handed her over and was at once amazed by how instantly Zee quieted and stared up at her mother as if captivated by her face. Mother hummed to her, rocking her back and forth as Zee settled herself comfortably in her arms and began to look sleepy.

Mother looked up at Tao. "I knew Josi could not have hurt anyone and am glad to know that she's safe. Now tell me, son, what happened to your brother?"

Josi and Chai looked at each other, surprised at Mother's soft tone. Tao sat down and gathered his little brothers in his lap, then he slowly started at the beginning—the very beginning.

As the little boys quickly fell asleep in the safety of his arms, Tao began to tell his mother how much he hated being a fisherman. He told her how he wanted to do something different, and how his brother had bullied him all his life. And as Mother listened intently and continued to rock her baby girl to sleep, Tao told her about the night he had finally stood up to his brother.

As he talked, he was not the only one shedding tears. They all sat crying for him—for the hurt and shame he had lived with all his life, for the dreams he held unfulfilled, and for the sorrow he showed at not saving Bo from drowning. And when he finally rested and hung his head, Mother passed Zee to Josi, and then she scooted closer to Tao and put her arms around him, holding his head close to her chest.

"It's not your fault, Tao. I'm so sorry that it happened, but it is *not* your fault. And things will be different for you, son. I promise—you will get to live the life you want. Things are going to change."

CHAPTER FORTY-SIX

At the church, the parents of the children herded them through the door, and Jun and Ruju were alone again. At least until they stepped through and found themselves surrounded by more than a hundred people from the village—some sleeping and some wide awake. Families gathered in various corners and around the occasional piece of furniture. A peek through the large, elaborate doors into the sanctuary showed every church bench full with even more people, their soggy bags and suitcases scattered around them.

"Whoa, everyone from Sandu'ao is here, it seems." Jun looked around, wondering where he and Ruju could find a place to sit and wait out the storm.

"It looks that way. This place has that reputation of standing strong in the midst of bad times, so the people flock here during storms."

They moved farther into the church and were met by a young woman wearing a black smock. "It's full in here, but there's room in the building in the back, and they may have some pallets left, if you want to try there. Just go around the church and through the courtyard; you'll see it."

Jun looked at Ruju questioningly. He didn't really want to go back outside in the rain and wind, but he knew she was exhausted and wanted to find a place to stretch out and sleep. "It's up to you, Ruju."

She answered by turning and going back through the door they had just entered. He ran to catch up to her, fumbling to get the tattered umbrella open and over her head before she got even wetter.

They quickly came to the other building and ran through the door, Jun struggling to pull it closed behind him as the wind tried to fling it in the opposite direction. In the main hall, they were again met with the possibility they might not find a place to squeeze in among the many people. They stood looking around until a younger version of the nun they had just spoken to in the church approached them.

"*Ni hao.* Please follow me, and I'll find you a spot to rest. I'm sorry, but we're out of blankets." The girl grabbed two rolled-up wooden mats from a small pile next to the door and beckoned for them to follow.

"At least it is quieter here," Jun whispered, looking around at all the sleeping people. The ones who were not sleeping were quietly entertaining themselves, some even playing cards. A few more of the church ladies in black moved around the people, handing out small cups of water and rice balls.

"Yes, and I can finally lie down. My head is pounding."

They were shown to a spot by the far wall, and after handing his bag to Ruju, Jun unrolled the two mats and spread them on the floor. He looked around at the people, and then put his head close to hers.

"You sleep first. I'll watch our things. I'm not tired anyway."

Ruju looked at him doubtfully and struggled out of her rain jacket. "You know they won't let you smoke in here, right, Lao Jun?"

"*Wo zhi dao.* I know." He pulled a large, dry shirt out of his bag and handed it to her.

"Am I supposed to put this on?" she asked.

"No, just cover up with it. Go ahead; lie down." He patted the mat beside his and then pulled a book out of his bag. "I'll read." *At least until the power goes completely out*, he thought as the light flickered once again.

Ruju folded her wet jacket up and put it at the foot of her pallet. Then she lay down and curled up, pulling her legs up close to her chin. Jun helped her spread the shirt over her, and she closed her eyes.

She looks like such a child. Jun opened the book and read a few pages, then realized he had no idea what he had just read. He thought of Chai and hoped she was somewhere safe.

Beside him a mother and her three sons slept. The mother snuggled her smallest boy to her chest, and what appeared to be her oldest son had his arm draped around another little boy. The older boy coughed and reached up and pulled his red cap lower over his eyes.

Jun pulled his phone from his bag and turned it on. He was glad Ruju had reminded him to power it off to save the battery. Holding the phone high above him to find a signal, he looked to see if Wei had tried to call him. She hadn't. He thought of Chai again, and his chest felt tight.

He stood up and paced the three or so empty feet next to Ruju's head. She had quickly fallen into a deep sleep, and the only sound from her was her light snoring.

He paced again, this time stumbling over the pallet of the mother and boys closest to them. The woman stirred and looked up at him, pulling her child closer.

"*Dui bu qi.*" At his apology, she closed her eyes, and he turned and went back to his pallet and sat down. He pulled out his book again, read a page, and shut it. He felt overwhelmed all of a sudden—almost as if he needed to walk off the emotional energy that was bogging him down. He needed to think through what they were going to do tomorrow.

Can I get a bus back to the main town? Will it be possible? Will we be stranded in Sandu'ao a few days? He knew he needed to get Ruju back to her grandmother.

"*Qing wen.* I see you cannot rest. Would you like me to take you to a hallway where you'll have room to walk?" A pretty nun tapped him on the shoulder, startling him out of his thoughts. He looked up into a very strange set of eyes, and then looked away so he wouldn't embarrass her.

Jun looked down at Ruju, then back at the nun.

"She'll be fine. Once I show you to the hall, I'll return and watch over her." She pointed to a chair in the corner, indicating where she'd be.

Jun did feel like he was about to jump out of his skin, and he relished the thought of getting out of the crowded room so he could move about. "*Hao de.*"

He stood and picked up their bags.

"I can also keep those at my chair until you return," she said. "Oh, I'm so sorry, my name is Sister Haihua." She held her hand out to him, and he shook it quickly then dropped it.

"Follow me."

* * *

Jun walked behind the woman wearing the black skirt. They wound through the sleeping forms on the floor until they reached a door on the other side. She opened it and stepped through.

"No one is allowed to camp in this hall—it's where our permanent residents live. But you can walk here, talk on your phone, or read your book. I could tell you were feeling out of sorts in there among all the people. You can spend some time here and come back when you're ready."

"*Xie xie*," Jun said as he walked through the door. "I'll keep my bag, but if you can hold on to the other one, I'll get it in a few minutes." He handed Ruju's bag to the young woman, still trying to avoid staring at the startling color of her eyes.

She put her finger to her lips. "You must be very quiet in here; there are people sleeping behind those doors, and our nursery is right down at the end of the hall." She turned and left him standing there, shutting the door behind her.

Finally able to breathe, he sank to the floor to rest for a moment in the solitude. He looked down the hall at all of the closed doors. He wondered what it was like to live in the little apartments Ruju had told him about. Farther down, he saw another hall separated by a wall of windows.

That must be the nursery she mentioned. He thought about the children who lived there. Ruju had told him about that, too, how there were many unwanted children who lived at the church until families could be found for them. He was puzzled by how some men—and even women, if he was being truthful—could so easily give up their own flesh and blood. *And for what? A simple birth defect, or because they were girls?* It riled him up to think about it, for there he was, searching high and low for his own daughter, while other fathers were throwing theirs away.

Feeling the need to move around—anything to get his mind off the fact that he desperately wanted a cigarette—Jun got up to pace the hall. He passed one room with the door open about a foot and peeked in. The old man inside was sitting up in his bed, fiddling with a hot-water bottle. Jun quietly passed his door, wondering if the man had any family, or if he had been left there alone to live out the rest of his days.

Feeling melancholy, Jun continued pacing the length of the hall until he found himself in front of the glass windows. On the other side were a few rows of cribs and then a few rows of beds. He counted at least thirty babies and children—along with a few young women stretched out in the beds along the back wall. *Those must be the caretakers*, he thought as he moved his focus to the baby nearest the window. He wasn't sure, but he thought it was a girl who lay sleeping with her tiny thumb poked into her mouth. Even under the heavy quilt and strap across her, he could see her knees were tucked under her and her tiny bottom was poked up into the air. It made Jun remember when his girls were infants, and how they'd curl up on his chest and sleep. He'd only wanted to protect them and keep them close—but he had failed, at least with Chai.

He looked around at the rest of the room and thought how much more cheerful it was than the other parts of the building. They had really made an effort to make the living arrangements as pleasing as could be for the orphans. Still, how much consolation could paint, furniture, and a few toys give children who eventually would mature enough to realize they had been abandoned? He frowned, then continued his walk.

On the other side of the windows, he turned down the other hall, and after seeing an old woman on the bed in the first open room, he turned around and began to head back to his original post. He didn't want to get in trouble for going down the women's hall; obviously the nursery was a divider between the two sections.

At the windows again, he paused one more time to look at the nursery. It made him feel a sense of comfort that the children were behind the glass—protected for the moment, one could say. His eyes fell on another baby, and he chuckled at the full head of hair the tyke sported. Tufts of black stuck up all over, making the child look like a tiny man. Jun shook his head and turned to go, just as movement caught his eye.

It came from a bed in the back of the room. Jun squinted and saw a bed with two caretakers sleeping and a baby lying between them. The baby was moving, obviously wanting something. Maybe it was hungry, or wet. Either way, Jun could tell by the quickening of flails and kicks that the baby was about to get someone's full attention. Jun waited another second—at least it was something to take his mind from his own troubles—and he wanted to see if the little one got its way and was able to awaken the sleeping nannies.

Finally the caretaker with her back to Jun sat up and picked up the baby. She threw the cover off of them and climbed out of the bed. Balancing the baby on her lap, she sat down and pulled on her boots, then stood again.

She's probably going to go get a bottle of milk, Jun thought. *I wonder where the kitchen is and if I can find some tea*. Not wanting to get caught looking, he began to walk again—only peeking from the corner of his eye.

Just before he was out of sight, the young woman lifted her face and looked to the window, causing Jun to stop in his tracks.

No. It can't be. His heart began to thump loudly, and he felt dizzy. Putting his hands out, he leaned on the window frame for support and looked closer.

The girl also stopped moving and stared right back. She held the fidgeting baby, and for what was surely only seconds but felt like an eternity, they stared at each other.

Finally the girl began sobbing, putting noise to the tears that ran down Jun's face. "Baba! Baba! Josi—wake up! It's my baba!"

CHAPTER FORTY-SEVEN

Jun let go of Chai and stood back to look at her face again. He shook his head and let out a cry of joy. Pulling her close to him, he playfully rubbed her on the top of the head with his knuckles.

"I can't believe it. I thought I was seeing things. But it's really you."

"Baba, you found me! I can't believe it, either—I thought we had broken our thread!" Chai said, her face wet with tears. She reached up and felt the familiar smoothness of his face.

"Chai, our red thread may have been stretched, but it was never broken. I've been looking for you, girl. I've never stopped searching." He hugged her again—then pulled away and looked down to study her. "Are you okay? Have you been hurt?"

In her father's presence Chai felt relief flood over her and the weight of responsibility she had carried for the last year lifted.

"No, Baba. I'm fine. What about Mama? And Luci? Did they come?" Chai asked, hoping her baba had them tucked away in another room.

"No, Chai. They're waiting to hear if my search was successful. But your mother is going to be so relieved to know you are safe."

Standing beside them, Josi cleared her throat. "Lao Jun, what about *my* parents? Have they looked for me, too?"

Jun pulled away from Chai and turned to Josi. "Oh…well. Josi, you know with all of the children there and your father's job, they couldn't come with me. No one thought I'd really find you girls—I was looking for a woman who was possibly seen with you. I never thought…they didn't think…" He stopped to swallow the lump in his throat. "That I'd really find you."

Josi looked down, and Chai put her arms around her, squeezing her close. She could read her father fairly well and had guessed that Josi's parents must not have been as devoted to the search as hers. It was no secret that she had a closer relationship to her parents than Josi did hers, but she knew her friend's feelings were hurt.

She looked up to see Sister Haihua coming toward them, her face pinched with irritation.

"What is going on here? It is much too noisy; the children are sleeping, girls."

The she noticed Jun, and looked ready to scold him for exploring too far.

"Sister, this is my baba!" Chai clutched her father's arm with one hand and used the other to rub the tears from her face.

"From the fishing village?" Sister Haihua asked, looking from Chai to Jun. "But who did you come in with earlier? Another daughter?"

Before Jun could answer, Chai looked at Josi. "You didn't tell her about us?" Chai thought that Josi showing up looking beaten and claiming a connection with Zee and Chai would have surely led to the story about their kidnapping.

Josi shook her head. "Sort of. I left out some parts until I could figure out how to get you away from there."

Jun stepped closer to Sister Haihua. "Sister, Chai is my daughter, and she's been missing for over a year. My search led me here. Can you tell me how she came to be here?"

Chai thought that Sister Haihua took the news and the question too calmly. She wondered if she knew more than she had let on after all. The woman amazed her with her strange intuitions.

"Baba, I've only just arrived here because of the storm. Sister Haihua has nothing to do with our kidnapping."

"Come on, let's get you all to somewhere you can talk privately. It sounds like quite a story, and I'll make you some tea for your reunion." Taking Zee from Josi, Sister Haihua beckoned them to follow and led them to the kitchen.

They all sat down around the large table. Chai scooted close to her baba; she didn't want to let him out of her sight.

Sister Haihua put a pot on to boil and set out three mugs.

"I'll put Zee back to bed. Josi, you know where everything is. Don't forget to turn off the flame. I'll be back to check on you later and you all can fill me in. I've got to see to the others in the main hall and make sure we've got everyone settled down." She quietly padded out of the kitchen.

Jun shook his head again. "This feels surreal. You would not believe what I've gone through to find you girls. Start talking—how did you end up here? Who took you?"

The water kettle began to whistle and Josi got up to fix the tea.

Chai took a deep breath and started all the way from the beginning with their weakness to go against their better

261

judgment for new dresses. As she described the shed they awoke to and the ropes around their hands, she could feel her father tense up beside her and see his clenched fists on the table. She assured him that except for a few slaps and insults, and the attack on Josi, they were unhurt. She wrapped it up quickly, wanting to know how he had managed to figure out where she was.

"Tell me, Baba. How did you find your way here?"

Jun sighed and then began telling them everything that had happened since the night he returned home to find them missing. He told them about Ruju and her grandmother, the sighting of the woman leading them away, and their trek to Sandu'ao and to the little village.

"I even spoke to a fortune-teller earlier today, and he told me I would find peace where I found refuge." He laughed and threw his arms up, looking around. "This is what he was trying to tell me—he showed me a card with a church on it. He was telling me I'd find you, Chai. He is real—he's not a fake!"

"A fortune-teller? Baba, are you okay?" Chai asked, winking at Josi. She knew that her father had never had patience for that type of thing. He had even told her the story about how he'd dropped the second character of his name when he'd turned eighteen, even though without it *Jun* alone meant *unlucky*. He was determined to lead his generation in the abolishment of old myths and superstitions.

"Okay? I'm wonderful!" He shook his head. "But I thought the old man was a crackpot. My stubbornness almost cost me finding you, Chai. If not for the storm and the hotel being closed, I would have missed you. I can't believe my luck—or whatever it was."

Chai smiled at him and thought how amazing it was to see his familiar face again. She loved every wrinkle and sun spot on it, and she couldn't wait to be home and snuggled beside him reading a book together again.

His face suddenly went blank and he grabbed his bag. "Oh my, I can't believe I forgot. Chai, we have to call your mother! We have to tell her you're okay."

"Mama?" Chai began to cry just thinking about her mother. After so many months of striving to be strong, she suddenly felt younger than her years.

Jun pulled his phone from the bag and turned it on. He waited for a signal, and when he found none, he got up and began holding the phone up, trying to find the best location in the cavernous room.

"What about Luci? Is she okay?"

"Oh, she's fine. She's been very quiet since you left, though. She has refused to play outside since you were taken. But she'll snap back when she hears that I've found you." He held his hand up. "Oh—I have a signal."

With the signal came a series of messages of missed calls. Jun flipped through them, studying the numbers.

"Your mother's been trying to call me. I guess the storm stopped all incoming service." He dialed the phone and put it to his ear. The girls waited quietly.

"Wei?" Jun smiled at the girls, telling them she had answered. He paused, listening at the phone for minutes, the expression on his face turning thunderous.

"Baba? What?" Chai asked, sure there was something wrong. Jun waved her away and walked to the corner of the room.

"When? How do you know? Who told you?" He belted out questions, becoming angrier at each pause.

Chai watched her father, silenced by the look on his face. She had never seen him so angry.

"I will squeeze the life from him with my own bare hands." He snarled into the phone, then walked farther away from the girls and continued in a low voice.

Chai reached across the table and held Josi's hands. They waited for her father to finish his conversation.

Finally Jun hung up the phone and turned to the girls. "Chai, your mother will talk to you in the morning. She is too upset to talk anymore, and the signal was very bad, but she's relieved I've found you."

"Okay, Baba. But what's wrong—tell me. Is it Luci?"

Jun looked at Chai and then Josi, his eyes filling with tears.

"What, Lao Jun? It's about me. What is it?" Josi asked, panicking that something had happened to her mother or father.

"Wei said she has been trying to reach me for over a day. Josi, your mother went to her two days ago after she had a fight with your father."

"A fight? Is she okay?" Josi asked, clutching Chai's sleeve. "Is she okay? Answer me."

Jun nodded his head. His energy looked to have disappeared, leaving behind only a tired old man. "Your mother is fine, dear girl."

Josi sighed and Chai could see the relief on her face. She squeezed her hands again for support. She still felt something terrible was coming.

"Then what, Lao Jun?" she asked.

"I'm sorry to tell you this, but your mother said your father was involved in the kidnapping of you and Chai."

Josi paled under the blue tinges of bruises across her face. She seemed to want to say something but couldn't get the words out.

"But Baba, I don't understand." Chai stood, too upset to stay sitting. She felt sick to her stomach. She had heard of girls and women being trafficked, but she didn't quite understand how it could be done by their own families. *Could Josi's father really be that cruel?*

"I don't see how it can be hidden, and you girls have been through enough that you deserve the truth. Josi, your father took the family out of town that day and set you both off on an adventure he knew would end up with your disappearance." He put his hand on Josi's shoulder. "He sold Chai. He told them exactly where to find her, but you girls threw them off when you came to me first. The woman followed your trail until she found you." He looked down at Josi's foot and then back up at her. "You weren't sold, but they took you, too. You were taken so that Chai would cooperate."

Josi shook her head from side to side. "No. That can't be true."

Chai got up and went around to Josi. She put her arms around her and rocked her back and forth as she cried.

"I'm so sorry, Josi. Your father made contact with a trafficking ring from the city and made the arrangements. He was told you both would be placed with a rich family and treated well—at least that's what he told your mother. He claims he thought it would be an improvement over your current chances of a future. They paid him a bride price and he bought a car and planned to start a new business."

Josi looked at him and shook her head. "No, Lao Jun. This can't be true. Please tell me this isn't true."

Jun held his hands out. "This came from your own mother's mouth. It is true. That's everything. I'm sorry, Josi."

Chai hugged Josi as she sobbed into her shoulder. It was so unfair. Josi had been through so much in her life because of not living up to what her father thought she should be. They had discussed it before; Josi had known she would never be good enough in his eyes. And now he had proved it once and for all. He had shown his daughter that she meant nothing to him.

Josi raised her head and rubbed at the tears running down her face.

"He might have been tired of being a simple farmer, but to me he'll always carry the stench of pigs. I have no father any longer."

* * *

Chai and Jun walked down the hall arm in arm, still nibbling on the deep-fried pumpkin squares they had swiped from the kitchen pastry box. It was almost dawn, but they were both so excited about finding each other that neither could rest. After Chai had comforted Josi for a few minutes, Baba had told the others they'd be right back. He'd grabbed his daughter's arm and then guided her out of the room so they could be alone.

They strolled until they found themselves back in front of the nursery, looking through the window at the content faces of the sleeping children.

Chai pointed to a child curled up in a bed near the corner. "See that tiny girl covered up with the blue quilt? That's Lin. Besides Zee, she's my favorite."

Jun nodded. "Those are some really beautiful children in there, aren't they?"

"Yes, and even without families, the sisters make sure each and every child here feels loved and protected."

"Chai, that is all I've ever wanted for you, too. I'm sorry I let you down. You've been through so much in the last year, and I can't tell you how very proud of you I am for holding it together, as I know your mother is, too." He shook his head from side to side and sighed.

Chai beamed up at him. "Baba, I could not have been strong for myself or for Josi if not for the way you prepared me. All of my life you've taught me that in this world, even though I am only a girl"—she made a face and rolled her eyes—"I still have a right to speak my mind and follow my own path. You've always told me stories of strong women, and you encouraged me that I could be like them. Because of you I know I am capable of accomplishing anything I set my sights on." She thumped herself on her chest, then continued. "I remembered all that you taught me and knew that Josi and I must keep our minds ready and our spirits strong. When the right time came, we were going to run. I was going to get us home. But you found me, Baba, you came. I *told* Josi you'd never stop searching; I just knew you wouldn't give up."

Jun stopped her and turned her to him. He put his hand under her chin and tilted her face up at him.

"Chai, I would say that you are my most prized possession, but that can't be true, as no man can own another. Instead I'll tell you that nothing—and I mean nothing—could have stopped me from searching for you. Surely you know, our house has not been a home without you in it."

Home. The one word that, when she had allowed herself to dwell on it, could put a chink in her carefully constructed invisible armor. It meant so much to her—love, acceptance, and protection. It brought to mind her mother's face, her sister's laughter, and her father's stories. So many things, all wrapped up in one tiny word.

Chai's lip quivered. She didn't want to cry again. All this time she had been the one to dry Josi's tears and stand up for their rights. She didn't want to end her battle with a weak display, even if they were tears of joy.

Her baba smiled down at her and cleared the lump from his throat. "And it's okay to cry, daughter. Sometimes tears are not a show of weakness but rather a display of love and loyalty. It's time for you to relax your warrior stance. Tomorrow, Chai—we begin the journey home."

EPILOGUE

As the storm raged around them, the two families came together and began to try to mend the damage of the last year. Alternating between tears and smiles, Baba introduced Ruju to everyone and told them how with his determination and her assistance, he'd finally found the girls. Ruju proved her cleverness with another suggestion. She challenged Tao's mother that if she was really as sorry as she claimed and wanted to avoid prosecution, she would bring her husband in to talk about making restitution for the grief they had caused.

Keso died down the next morning, and Lao Chan came, though grudgingly. Sister Haihua worked as a mediator to settle things without involving the police—especially since Baba insisted they would be of little help anyway. Before Jun could change his mind, Lao Chan agreed he would sell his fishing boat and give the money to the girls for the trouble he had caused.

By that time most of the people had left the church and nunnery and immediately set to work to put back the pieces of their homes. Luckily, Sandu'ao never took a direct hit from the hurricane, though damage from the edges of the storm was serious enough that many of the mainland families lost everything.

The fishing village was hit hard, but only some boats were lost. Others were saved, and those families were relieved not to have lost their livelihoods.

Chai planned to return home immediately. She longed to see her *mei mei* and even share their bed together again and fight for leg space. Most of all she wanted to wrap her arms around her mother—hug her, smell her, and eat her amazing concoctions of anything that wasn't fish! She was excited to get back to school to begin preparing for a higher learning than her family had originally thought they'd be able to afford. With Sister Haihua's promise to help guide her, she felt like she'd been given a new chance at life and a way to reach her dreams. Even before she left the church with her father, she started making notes for the memoir she planned to write. She wanted the world to know about her and Josi's abduction and the life they were forced into, all in the name of grooming a future daughter-in-law. She felt strongly that their story could help other girls in China who were living the same nightmare they had, as well as families who were dealing with the mystery of lost daughters.

As for Josi, being the compassionate girl she was, she begged Baba not to leave her family without security by turning in her father for his part in their abduction. He told her that Shen would have to find another place to live, but he'd respect her by not prosecuting him. However, Josi refused to return to what she now knew was the despicable man who had arranged their nightmare. Chai was proud of her for standing up and taking control of her future. Josi pleaded with Sister Haihua to let her stay and help care for the babies, telling her that she felt at peace there and never wanted to leave. The sister told her she was welcome to stay, but they'd have to contact her mother and look into a plan for her future. She also agreed that she would hold Josi's share of the restitution money from old Chan until Josi decided how she wanted to use it.

With her usual generosity, Sister Haihua offered an administration position to Ruju. Jun recognized a chance for the girl to live another kind of life and promised to talk the girl's grandmother into a move to Sandu'ao. Jun convinced Ruju that her grandmother might just be ready to trade her hectic city life for the peaceful setting of the nunnery.

Throughout the negotiations, Chai could see her father pulling on every reserve of self-control he could muster to keep himself from beating Lao Chan to a pulp. He finally calmed when Tao's mother broke down and admitted that she had been a stolen child bride, too. It was a sad moment when she admitted to submitting to her husband's decision to buy a bride for Bo to marry—and even worse, for letting him force her to get rid of the children she bore that he did not want.

For her penance, Mother promised to help other stolen girls find their families. She said it was too late for her, but she hoped others in the fishing village would still remember details that could locate their homes. Chai told her when she graduated from university she would lead the charge to help her fulfill her promise. Chai couldn't deny that she felt something for the woman— maybe not love, but a certain sense of pity and affection. After all, Chai told the others, Mother did not get to choose her life, either, and the woman had done her best to keep Lao Chan from abusing them.

Tao's newfound courage surprised everyone. As the day unraveled and plans were laid, he couldn't hide his relief that Josi would remain close—but Chai had known he would feel that way. Things turned out better for him, too. After he explained to his father what had really happened with Bo, the old man stormed out of the building, refusing to believe what they said about his favorite son.

Mother let him go, but she promised Tao that she'd stand up to Lao Chan and get him to agree to let Tao pursue his art. She said she had some leverage to use, and this time, she wouldn't let him take control. She and Tao agreed that if he would stay and help his father fish for the next few years, all the profits after raising enough for a new boat would be saved for his education. She even suggested they look for someone to give Tao art lessons on the mainland.

Together they all decided that Zee would stay in the nursery, being cared for by Josi, until after her surgery, and then she would return home. Tao smiled and said he thought that soon Zee would have their father and every boy in the house wrapped around her tiny fingers. He also declared that as soon as they were old enough, he planned to ask Josi for her hand in marriage. The thought of her leaving forever had terrified Tao; he admitted he was in love with her beautiful, quiet spirit and then said he was ready to show everyone his collection of sketches dedicated to drawings of her face.

"Josi," Tao started as he shifted nervously from foot to foot, "we have *yuanfen*. The connection between us is destiny."

As usual, Josi stood there listening and blushing—unable to say a word—so Chai decided she'd speak for her best friend one last time. She put her hands on her hips and with her eyes shining with unshed tears, asked, "Tao, what took you so long?"

FROM THE AUTHOR

Having lived in China and made friends from several different levels of their society, the subject of child trafficking is not a new one to me. Though this story is fictional, I have read many reports of girls like Chai and Josi who are taken every day and trafficked across China, most never seen or heard from again by their families.

A report from the Chinese Ministry of Public Security said police rescued 8,660 abducted children and 15,458 women in 2011 as nearly 3,200 human trafficking gangs were broken up. [Source: AP, Op Cit]

Statistics reported show that the Chinese government has made attempts to break apart trafficking rings by using strong police force and harsher penalties, but other sources from anti-trafficking organizations in China have reported little to no cooperation from local authorities. In some cases it has been rumored that police have even profited from partnering with traffickers.

There are organizations in and around China working to reunite families with their abducted children. The general lower classes of China already have so much to endure, even without the added heartbreak of their children being stolen. Using

A Thread Unbroken, I want the world to know more about this specific tragedy and how it affects the human spirit.

If you have enjoyed this book, I encourage you to post a short review on Amazon and I appreciate each and every one. Reviews help increase circulation and the more exposure this subject gets, the bigger the chance those with resources to help will become aware of the situation. Thank you for taking time from your life to read *A Thread Unbroken*.

~Kay Bratt

ACKNOWLEDGMENTS

My thanks to…

Terry Goodman, the wizard behind the curtain. Your belief in my ability to spin a tale is a compliment like no other. I'm so glad you picked *Silent Tears* to read so many years ago, and that you decided to take another chance on yet another title. I took to heart your initial review and suggestions to make *A Thread Unbroken* a better story, and once again you were right.

My editor, Charlotte Herscher, your valuable insight and coaching kept me digging deeper to give my characters more depth and emotion. From you I learned more about how to develop a story than I ever have from any writing course, or from the stack of how-to books I've devoured over the years.

To Denise Grover Swank, my critique partner, thank you for your candid comments that kept me cringing, laughing, and striving to write better. Lou Hsu and Lucy Cai, once again you were invaluable as my fact-checkers and go-to panel for questions about China's history, culture, and vernacular.

To my husband and daughter, I can't see how you put up with me when I am having a creative flash and disregarding all my mom duties, but I'm glad you do. You both make my life worth living because you help me to believe in myself.

And lastly, my utmost gratitude goes to my readers. How could I have known what your acceptance and friendship would mean? I cherish every message, e-mail, and letter I've ever received from you. I also thank you for the many online reviews you've written for my books. Your kind words inspire me to write more of my own words.

It is my hope my stories will bring more awareness to the world about the plight of disadvantaged women and children in China.

ABOUT THE AUTHOR

 Kay Bratt is a child advocate and the author of several books, including *Silent Tears: A Journey of Hope in a Chinese Orphanage* and *Chasing China: A Daughter's Quest for Truth*. Kay and her family lived in China for more than four years, where she volunteered at local orphanages. In 2006, she was honored with the Pride of the City award for her humanitarian work in China, which she continued by founding the Mifan Mommy Club, an online organization that provides rice for children in China's orphanages. In addition to coordinating advocacy and awareness projects for the children of China, Kay is also an active volunteer for An Orphan's Wish. Originally from Kansas, Kay currently resides in the rolling hills of Georgia with her husband and daughter.

http://www.kaybratt.com.